To Dee —
Thanks for being
a reader! I
wait to read
your own

♥ Jessica Hawke

PHANTOM

TOUCH

JESSICA HAWKE

Mighty Fine Books, LLC
PO Box 956
Evans, GA 30809

Editing by Kathryn Steves
Cover Design by Steve Novak
Book Design by Jessica Hawke

ISBN: 978-1-944142-04-9

First Edition: November 2013
Second Edition: December 2015

10 9 8 7 6 5 4 3 2

For Mom and Dad, who gave me the strength to start, and for Carmen, who refused to let me quit.

CHAPTER ONE

MOST GIRLS PROBABLY DREAMED about shiny new cars for their seventeenth birthday, but I'd settle for getting back my old life. Ten more days, and I'd be as wonderfully boring as everyone else. Thank God. Since the accident, normal had been a distant memory, but it was so close now I could almost taste it, whatever normal tasted like.

"Maybe like fried chicken, or apple pie, or--" I muttered.

"Hey, Earth to Bridget," Valerie, my older sister, said from across the quiet cemetery, rudely interrupting my reverie. "You planning to do this sometime today?"

Val perched like a preening cockatiel on the edge of a tombstone that read *Newbold: 1915 - 1963*. Rude or not, she had a point, so I snapped back to reality and put my happy anticipation on the back burner. For ten more days, I'd be on a steady unappetizing diet of crazy.

It was a sunny fall day in Parkland, Georgia, cool enough that you knew winter was on its way, but typical Georgia was clinging on to summer as long as it could. We sat in a deep pocket of shade in an overgrown cemetery behind the charred skeleton of the old Creekview Baptist Church. The air was thick with the stink of a Bradford pear tree dripping white petals like snow to the weedy grass beneath.

I sat in front of a flat grave marker veiled in thick green moss. A crinkling, cellophane-wrapped bouquet of grocery store flowers lay in my lap, dripping on my tattered jeans. Mom had tried to throw the jeans away a dozen times, which only made me like them more. They were once Valerie's and I intended to wear them until they disintegrated.

"Here goes," I said as I laid the flowers gently on the moss-carpeted stone. "Anna, are you there? It's Bridget again."

A cool wind raised the fine hairs on my forearms in a tingling rush. I lifted my chin slowly to see the spectral figure of Anna Cole. She had been a beautiful woman before she died, and she was still pretty…at least from this angle. Her brilliant red hair was teased into one of those bouncy sixties styles, embellished by a jeweled green hairpin that matched her dress. But when she turned to face me directly, I remembered exactly how Anna became a ghost. My best friend Emily, who was high priestess of the Selfie Sisterhood, claimed everyone had a good side. I didn't have the heart to tell her that both sides looked the same.

Anna Cole? She definitely had a good side, and with it, a very bad side.

The left side of her face was misshapen and bruised, giving her an oddly asymmetrical look. As her swollen left eye fell on me, I winced--I always did, I *really* couldn't help it--and she turned away in shame. I instantly felt like a huge jerk. She was a ghost, and it wasn't her fault that she looked like a horror movie extra.

Not helping, I thought.

"It's all right," I said. "You don't have to hide, remember?"

Anna didn't speak to me, but I could feel the longing and sadness from her like she was broadcasting on my own exclusive radio frequency. I wasn't psychic or anything, though I'd gotten more perceptive over the last few years. But you didn't have to be psychic to read Anna. It was written all over her, in the downturned eyes, the sad droop to her lips, the slump of her shoulders, bent under the heavy weight of so much despair. It was so intense it made me squirm, unable to meet her eyes for more than a few seconds.

There was also the fact that she was violently and thoroughly dead. After the initial shock, it didn't really bother me much these days. You'd be amazed at what you can get used to over time.

"I found something for you," I said, jamming my hand into my purple backpack. Like my jeans, it was a battered hand-me-down from Valerie. It still had the letters V.R.Y. scrawled on the rough canvas in silver marker.

The backpack held all my stuff for my haunted hobby. Most of the time, I kept it shoved way under my bed. The last thing I needed was to have to explain it to my nosy little brother or, God forbid, my mother. Somehow, I didn't think it would be a relief to Mom that the plastic baggie full of dried herbs was just sage.

While I dug in the bag, Anna flickered and sat next to me. Some ghosts seem to disappear and reappear, but I figured it was that they really moved too fast for my mere mortal eyes to follow.. Watching it too closely made my head spin, like when you cross your eyes too far and make yourself dizzy.

Anna's skirt spread out in a perfect circle, disappearing where it passed through my outstretched leg. It was unsettling to see half of her skirt on one side of my leg and half on the other, with no fabric actually draped over my leg. I felt a chill run up my thigh where she made contact, raising prickling hairs against my jeans. But Anna was on the friendlier end of the ghost spectrum, so it wasn't unpleasant, just a bit chilly. There was a faint pleasant smell around her, like an old dry book with flowers pressed in its pages. This was a marked improvement over many of my spirit encounters, which brought odors no amount of Febreze could fix. Anna hunched over as I spread out a folded sheet of paper on the grave next to the cheap white daisies.

The paper was a photo of a family reunion, about two dozen people in identical turquoise t-shirts. Most had the same shocking red hair as Anna. Hers was muted in death, a dull dried-blood color that almost blended into the torn flesh on her face. It would have been breathtaking when she was alive, if her family was any indication.

"This was a few weeks ago," I said. "I found it on their Facebook group." Anna just stared at me blankly and tilted her head as if to say, *I'm not following you.* "Never mind." If you think trying to explain new technology to old people is hard, try explaining Twitter to a sixty-year-old ghost. "They're so happy."

I pointed to a woman at the front of the group, hoping I remembered all the details. "Katherine misses you, but she has her own family now. Her husband is in the Army. He just came home from Afghanistan and got some award," I explained. "I think they said the Army Commendation Medal? And these are her children, Annabeth, Julianne, and Mary Anne," I said. "All named for you."

Personally, I thought that was a little weird, as had my sister when I told her. But Anna smiled, and making her happy was precisely why I was here. One point for Bridget and her interpersonal ghost skills. I was much better at relating to the dead than the living these days. "And your son Andy," I said. "He hasn't married, but he seems…nice." I mean, as far as I could tell from a good Facebook stalking.

I went on for a few minutes, telling her everything I had learned about her descendants, the living legacy she left behind. According to the papers, Anna died of severe head trauma after her worthless husband beat her to death with a whiskey bottle. His excuse? He thought she was cheating on him, and that was enough reason for him to leave two small children motherless. Anna was a lot better than me, because I would have wanted him dead. And barring that, I would have haunted him until he begged for mercy. Full poltergeist treatment. Instead, he'd served just five years of a life sentence before choking on a lima bean in prison.

But Anna didn't want revenge. She didn't even seem angry about it, and believe me, some spirits are *seriously* pissed off. Anna was just sad and faded, too weak to even speak to me. The best I could do was a game of ghostly charades, which I'd gotten good at over the last two years, and figured out she wanted to know about her children. I got as close to them as I could without being creepy. And the Internet was practically invented for creeping from afar. Hopefully what I'd found was enough for Anna.

When I finished my story, I slid the picture under the flowers and met her mournful eyes. "Are you ready to go on now? You can tell me if you're not. I'll be happy to get more pictures."

"Watch your time, Idget," Valerie whispered. I glanced up to see her pointing to her watch. Mom was hardcore about the sanctity of dinner time, and I'd cut it close too many times recently.

And besides, I really didn't want to go look for more pictures and family stories. I was ready to close this case and hopefully not find another before my birthday. I wanted my work to be done. It was the kind of offer you made to be nice, secretly hoping the other person would say no.

She hesitated, her cloudy eyes drifting down to the picture again. *Come on,* I thought. But she finally nodded, faded hair bouncing slightly. *Phew.*

"You deserve to rest, Anna," I said, feeling a bit guilty at my overwhelming relief. "Your family will always remember you, and you'll see them again one day."

I had no idea if that was true. There's no instruction book on this stuff. Trust me, I tried Amazon. Here and there I found some folklore, but I'd mostly been figuring it out on my own for the last two years. My sister Valerie had insider knowledge and filled in the blanks.

One of the most valuable things I'd realized is that the words were much less important than the feelings behind them. The dead and living had that in common. "It's time to finally rest."

I held my hands out, and she placed hers in mine. I couldn't feel anything but cold, like I had plunged my hands into ice water. But for a moment a spark of connection twanged in my head, like an unexpected but absolutely *brilliant* idea.

Closing my eyes, I began to sing. My voice was a little scratchy, and no one was going to recommend me for American Idol, but it was passable. "My latest sun is sinking fast, my race is nearly run. My strongest trials now are past, my triumph is begun. Oh come, angel band, come and around me stand. Oh bear me away on your snowy wings, to my immortal home."

When the song was finished, a warm wind kicked up, whipping my hair around my face. A whispered *no* rose on the breeze and in the back of my mind. Something was gathering, and the air pressure spiked. What would I do if she refused to go on? It had never happened, but I knew enough to cut the word *never* right out of my vocabulary. There was a long sigh of what had to be relief, and the trees around me whispered their goodbyes in the dying wind.

I opened my eyes. Anna Cole was gone.

"Nice song," Valerie said, her voice distant as she gazed up at the sunny sky without blinking. The sun didn't hurt her eyes like it did mine. Had she seen Anna go? Did she feel whatever had pulled Anna beyond this world? If she did, she didn't say anything, just fiddled with her ragged nails while I rummaged in my backpack.

"Thanks," I said. "Her daughter said she used to sing it when they were little."

"Cute," Valerie said.

"You picked something out yet?"

"Not yet," she replied, her green eyes downcast. "Don't forget the sage."

There was a baggie of herbs in my bag for spiritual cleansing. Based on my highly scientific research, which entailed a lot of Google and Wikipedia, sage was a purifying plant. I set the bundle burning and wafted the smoke around to clean out the lingering sadness and negative energy from Anna's long stay here. Step two was a dash of holy water, smuggled out of the Catholic Church downtown. Hey, I did leave five bucks in the donation box, figuring that probably went a little ways toward forgiveness for blasphemy, or sacrilege, or whatever you would call the sin of stealing holy water.

Once I had blown around enough smoke to make me cough, I extinguished the sage in a damp muddy spot and scuffed out the smoldering remains with my shoe.

"You think that stuff you said to her is true?" Val asked, watching as I slung the strap of my backpack over my shoulder.

"I hope so," I said without meeting her eyes. The warm fuzzies of helping Anna Cole evaporated. With me and Val, there wasn't an elephant in the room--try the whole freaking zoo.

"Me too," Val said. She glanced at her smashed wristwatch and shook her head. Its cracked digital face still read 9:37 p.m, like it had ever since the accident. Even so, she somehow always knew what time it was. "You're gonna be late."

I took out my cell phone to verify the time and groaned. "She's gonna kill me."

"If you're lucky. I'm pretty sure she's not going to buy it if you tell her you were singing old church hymns to a ghost."

"Can't you tell her?" I said, forgetting for one idiotic moment that she couldn't get me out of trouble like she used to.

"Wish I could, Little Bit," Valerie said. "Wish I could." She had once been the master of talking Mom out of being mad, somehow doing it without ever telling a lie.

But everything changed two years ago, when Valerie died.

Chapter Two

EVEN IF I HAD WANTED to get anywhere near the wheel of a car, Mom wouldn't let me get my learner's permit, so I was stuck walking if I wanted to go anywhere without answering a thousand questions. After the accident, we had moved into a house closer to school, so my little brother and I could both walk to school.

And Mom was never going to accept, "If you hired me a limo driver, I'd have been on time," as an excuse. Yes, I tried once. She'd probably add another week of restriction for being a smartass, like the last time I missed dinner time. Then she'd demand to know why Emily hadn't brought me home, which would give her more evidence in her on-going case to prove that Emily was unreliable and a bad influence on me. Even though our house was less than a mile from school, Emily usually drove me home. Walking even a mile in Georgia in August was a miserable experience for anyone who doesn't enjoy marinating in their own sweat.

But on days when I'm working the ghost beat, I walk. Emily didn't know about my hobby. Based on the few nerve-wracking times she'd seen my notes or bookmarks on my laptop, she just thought I was into weird local ghost stories. Like, I-wanted-to-make-out-on-a-fresh-grave into them. And strangely enough, that probably would have freaked out her much less than the truth. Now I made sure to clear my Internet history anytime she used my laptop and kept my notes in a separate notebook from all my school stuff.

So on days like today, it was just me and my two feet. Though she had never lived there, Val had a hard time being in the new house. I thought was being around Mom and our little brother more than the house, but I wasn't about to question her. She usually left me alone before I reached our neighborhood and went wherever it was she went when she wasn't with me. I asked her once about that, and she just shrugged and changed the subject. After being stuck here for almost two years, I figured she was entitled to her secrets. Sure enough, when I passed the bustling Circle K on the right, she waved goodbye and disappeared.

On days like today, when it wasn't ungodly hot, I really didn't mind the walk. For almost a year after the car accident, I had to wear a leg brace to stabilize my knee after all the surgeries to put it back together. The doctor had used the extremely apt phrase Humpty-Dumpty once, which is hilarious now, but was horrifying at the time. Just walking to the bathroom had been an Olympic event back then. Now I was grateful to walk, as cheesy as it sounded. Even with the occasional sore day, I'd gotten off easy compared to my sister.

I glanced at my phone again and quickened my step. Crap. If I caught the crosswalk at Otter Creek Road, I'd make it home with about a minute to spare. I could call Mom and tell her I was on my way, but I could already predict her response. Even so, I called her. Maybe she'd find a shred of mercy in her heart.

"Hey," I said. "I'm running late."

"And?"

"I might be a few minutes late, but I'm on my way."

I mouthed her response perfectly as she said it. "Late's late, Bridget," she said. "No exceptions."

So much for mercy.

I sighed and hung up. Barbara Young–AKA Mom–was a lot of things, but flexible wasn't one of them. She'd been way more lenient with Valerie, but everything had changed when she died. I had once made the mistake of arguing that punctuality had nothing to do with what happened to Valerie. Judging by the ensuing grounding and week of silent treatment, Mom didn't take it well. I wasn't wrong, but I probably could have used a little more tact.

Since hell hadn't frozen over, I hustled a little faster. I was almost to Otter Creek Road, where the little white-lit silhouette was glowing on the crosswalk sign. I could practically hear backlit man cheering, "Go Bridget! Let's see some hustle!"

Clearly I had an active imagination in addition to my more pressing mental issues.

"Come on, come on," I said, sprinting when the sign switched to a blinking orange hand.

The glaring orange hand went steady right as I reached the intersection. Forget the risk – jaywalking wasn't even *really* a crime – I didn't want to be grounded yet again. My foot had just touched down into the crosswalk when a cold hand grabbed my arm. As the cold passed, my arm prickled like I'd slept all night on it.

I knew what came next.

I froze in place, my impending curfew a distant concern. Closing my eyes, I thought about a blank movie screen, tuned out the noise of rush hour and the smoky stink of exhaust. Steeling myself with a deep breath, I opened my eyes, expecting to see the grotesque phantom remains of a vehicular manslaughter.

But I was alone on the sidewalk. My heart thumped sharply in my ears, like someone was flicking my eardrum.

I knew immediately when I saw it.

The poster was on pink paper, so fluorescent you couldn't miss it if you tried. It had been sealed into a plastic sheet protector and duct-taped above the crosswalk button. As I glanced over it, a cool hand against my back pushed me forward.

The poster read "HAVE YOU SEEN ME?" and had a color photo of a pretty brunette taped under the bold name: Natalie Fullmer. She'd been missing for just over three weeks. Her face looked strangely familiar. She had that movie-star wavy hair, the kind I couldn't get with rollers and a whole can of hairspray. At the bottom was a list of phone numbers, emails, and a link for a Facebook group called "Find Natalie SOS."

I took out my phone to check out the Facebook group, but stopped before I opened the app. In gigantic numbers across my phone's lock screen was the time.

"Really?" I complained, like it was the phone's fault. It was already 6:02, and I was officially late. After snapping a picture of the poster, I jabbed the crosswalk button violently.

So much for being on time.

My hopes that Mom might have gotten stuck in traffic were crushed when I ran up to the townhouse to find her silver Civic in the driveway. I sighed and walked up the gently sloping driveway. No point in rushing now.

A Halloween flag still dangled from the flagpole, waving lazily in the breeze. Oops. I was supposed to have changed it to the turkey flag last week and forgot. Mom was probably leaving it up to see how long it took me to figure it out. Life in our house was a never-ending test for which I hadn't studied.

I let myself in and was instantly greeted by a roaring gun battle on the living room TV and the classic rock station blaring from the kitchen radio. The house was filled with the savory aroma of browning beef and garlic.

Maybe she wouldn't notice me slipping in. I darted past the front entrance to the kitchen, heading for the stairs at the back of the house.

"Stop right there, young lady," she said as she emerged from the back door to the kitchen and blocked my path. *Damn.* Mom was still wearing her turquoise scrubs, with her short reddish hair pushed back under a pair of sunglasses. Her face fell when she saw me. "What on God's green earth are you wearing? Haven't I told you to get rid of those jeans?"

"And I told *you* they were comfortable," I said as I looked down at the grass-damp, tattered pants. "They're perfectly broken in."

"They're hideous," she replied as she returned to poke a frying pan of hamburger meat with a wooden spoon. There was a strainer full of spaghetti noodles sitting in the sink with steam billowing up to the ceiling.

"Not mutually exclusive, Mom."

"Cute. Where have you been?"

"Five minutes late," I said, pointing to the clock on the microwave.

"Oh, well in that case," she mused, cocking her head. "Where have you been for five whole minutes?" Mom had really missed her calling. The guys on *Law and Order* have nothing on Barbara Young.

"I got distracted," I said, taking my phone out to show her the picture of the flyer. "I saw this on the way home." If I told Mom what I was really doing, it'd be a fifty-fifty toss-up on whether she'd ground me for being ridiculous or send me back into therapy for being crazy. I wouldn't put it past her to do both just to be thorough.

"Yeah, showing me the picture of the missing teenager is doing wonders for your case," Mom said. "Why didn't Emily bring you home?"

"She left early for a doctor's appointment," I lied. "Totally not her fault."

Mom arched an eyebrow at me, trying to see if I was telling the truth. It was kind of sad, but she seemed to think that I was such a screw-up that she took most of my fibs at face value.

"So am I grounded?"

She glanced at the clock, then back at me. She rolled her eyes and gave me one of those sighs that said, *What did I do to deserve this?*

"No, but I would appreciate it if you showed a little more responsibility considering you're almost seventeen. Your brother is twelve and he manages to be home on time."

"Because he's a dork and has a standing XBox playdate with his equally dorky friends," I said. "Should I get an online boyfriend instead?"

"Shut up!" Colin shouted from the living room, which was currently the site of an epic battle between space marines and aliens, or whatever he was playing today. All I could see over the back of the couch was his light brown hair, spiked up in his wannabe fauxhawk. "My stupid sister," he complained into his headset.

"You shut up!" I yelled back at him. Stupid sister was fast enough to kill the power to the TV before he got untangled from his controller to stop her.

"You don't need to be mean to him," Mom said. "Now go put on some decent clothes. I don't want to see those nasty jeans again."

"You weren't supposed to see them today," I muttered as I brushed past her and clambered up the stairs.

The townhouse was much smaller than our old house, but none of us argued when Mom suggested moving. The old house had felt haunted ever since Valerie died two years ago. Not my kind of haunted, just full of sadness and once-bright memories that had faded to gray. The townhouse was brand new, with decently big bedrooms and private bathrooms for both me and Colin. It felt like a clean slate.

Theoretically.

The stairs were lined with framed pictures in stark black frames; most of them were of me, Mom, and Colin. There were none of Dad–who was just a signature on a check as far as Mom was concerned–and there was only one picture of Valerie, right at the landing where you had to see it every time you went upstairs. It was her senior portrait, all tanned skin and dazzling smile. That beauty queen smile always reminded me why she'd been the Fall Queen, and why she'd always had a constant crowd of admirers drooling in their lunches.

Colin's door was ajar, peeking in on the site of a nuclear blast from his closet. He had a big black and red poster on the door Mom had brought home from work that said CAUTION: BIOHAZARD. And wasn't that the truth. He was a seventh-grader, so he was basically a germ with legs and an unhealthy addiction to video games. He also had the obnoxious habit of getting fantastic grades and being an absolute angel at school, which Mom liked to bring up at every opportunity.

Once I was in my room, I could relax. Mom had let me pick the color and the floors as the house was being built. The dark hardwood floors and walls painted in Vibrant Violet made it entirely mine. The sweet smell of the Buttercream candle jar I'd burned yesterday still filled the air. I slung my backpack off and onto my bed. While I dug out a pair of comfy yoga pants, I started up Skype on my laptop and opened a voice chat with Emily.

"What's up, sexy?" she asked. Loud rock music blared in the background, which she turned down enough that she didn't have to scream into her microphone.

"Hi honey, I'm home," I said, dropping my jeans on the floor. "What are you doing?"

"Dyeing my hair," she said.

"Blue again?"

"Black and pink," she said. Emily changed her hair color more than Colin showered. "Seventeen minutes till I have to rinse."

"Nice," I said as I hopped in place to yank up my pants. My desk rattled as I jumped, knocking over a framed picture of Valerie and me. "Hey, do you know Natalie Fullmer?"

"Name sounds familiar," she said. "Does she go to Fox Lake?"

"Yeah, when she's not missing," I said. I carried my laptop over to my bed and flopped down on the shimmery lavender duvet. "Which she is."

"Oh! You mean *Night*," she said, like I had mispronounced it.

"I do?"

"She goes by Night," Emily said slowly. "She's kinda out there."

Uh, pot, meet kettle. I can't really point fingers, and Emily is no stranger to weird herself. Let's just say that the two of us get our own lunch table every day.

"You know her?"

"I know *of* her. Hachi actually knows her," Emily said. Hachi was a friend of Emily's, really Heather, who was a serious anime fan. "She probably ran away again. Hachi told me over the summer Night took off to follow Blood Kitty on tour. Had her family all freaked out and calling the cops. Then she showed up again two weeks later with a tattoo and a nose piercing."

"Oh," I said. Well that made sense. Logically, at least. But I couldn't shake the weird feeling that it wasn't so simple. Why would I get all creepy-crawly at the poster if this wasn't up my alley? "Yeah, that must be it."

20

"Yeah," Emily said. "I'll ask Hachi, though." She sighed. "Eleven minutes. Hey, did you get good pictures?"

"Huh?"

"At the graveyard," Emily said.

Oh, right. "Yeah, definitely," I lied. My excuse for being at the church that afternoon was a photography project for school. I'd made sure to snap a few on my phone before summoning Anna Cole, in case Emily wanted to see them later. I'm not sure how long my photography excuse was going to hold up, considering I had no photography skills whatsoever. Emily didn't seem to notice. "I was late getting home, though."

"Did Fraulein Young yell at you?" Emily asked.

I laughed as I folded the tattered jeans. They passed the sniff test, although they were close to needing a wash. When Mom wasn't home to intercept them and redirect their course to the garbage, of course. "Not too bad," I said. I leaned over the edge of my bed and pulled out a blue plastic tub full of Valerie's old belongings. When we moved, Mom had trashed or donated most of it while Colin and I were at school. Fortunately, I had already gone through Valerie's stuff and taken what I wanted. It went at the bottom of a packing box marked "Books" and was promptly hidden under the bed when we got to the new house.

The therapist I'd seen--Mom's idea--said that some people coped with grief by cleaning house, because everything was a reminder of what they had lost. Out of sight, out of mind and all that crap. Mom was apparently one of those people, which was fine until she'd tried to make *me* into one of those people.

About six months after Val died, we'd had an epic screaming match. Valerie's red UGA hoodie, the one I helped her pick when just the two of us visited, went missing. When I found it in the outside trashcan, balled up and hidden in an empty cardboard Coke box so I knew she'd deliberately done it, I went straight-up She-Hulk. I'd never been so furious in my life, and the only reason I didn't actually hit my own mother was because I knew how to hurt her even worse.

I'd immediately called my dad and told him I was coming to live with him in Washington, which was the only reason Mom eventually backed down and apologized. Still, she thought I was maintaining an unhealthy attachment to my dead sister.

Well, freakin' *duh*.

Worrying about a sweatshirt seemed pretty stupid when your dead sister was following you around town and keeping tabs on your life, didn't it? I wished I could tell Mom that, but my one and only confession that I thought I was going all Haley Joel had gotten me nothing but months of therapy and mind-numbing medication that was supposed to help me get better.

It didn't.

But that was all going to change soon. Big change was coming, whether I was ready or not.

CHAPTER THREE

O KAY, THE THEME OF HAMLET, GO," Emily said. I was too distracted by her hair to pay attention to her question.

When she said black and pink hair, I assumed she meant a few pink highlights. Oh, no. She had colored the entire front part of her hair pink, and it gradually faded back into black. And not *It's a Girl!* Pink. We're talking full-on neon Sharpie, eighties throwback pink. Between the hair and her matching glittery lip gloss, I was mesmerized by all the neon. It was difficult, if not entirely impossible to concentrate on studying when your friend looked like the lovechild of a highlighter and a light bulb.

"Um," I said, leaning back in the lumpy library chair. There was a definite funk to all the library chairs, like a mix of old gym clothes and feet. "I don't know. Something about his dead father. And something rotten in Denmark? Oh! And Rosencrantz and Guildenstern are dead. I remember that! Is that on there?"

Emily looked down at the study guide and rolled her eyes at me. "You didn't even fill it all in. Although this is some impressive doodling," she said. "How am I supposed to know?"

"You didn't read it?"

"Bridget. If I can live my whole life without reading Shakespeare, I'll die with no regrets," she said. "Why haven't you dropped down to basic yet?"

"Mom won't let me. And they require parental permission. Trust me, I tried. I even tried to sign her name, and they called her just to verify."

I'd been in all advanced classes since middle school, but my grades had tanked when Val died. Mom overlooked it for a while and let me take regular classes sophomore year so I didn't kill my GPA. But now it had been almost two years, and I had to move on. Her words, not mine. After two summers of taking classes to catch up, I had a full load of advanced classes again.

Yeah, *that* was logical.

"My mom is just happy if I'm passing Dummy English," Emily said. "Me read good."

"Yeah, well, me gonna big fail test," I said. "Hit me again."

As Emily quizzed me on the play I hadn't read, not even the Cliff's Notes or the cover of the movie, I pulled out my phone to check the *Find Natalie SOS* group on Facebook. There had been a few posts by people claiming they'd heard from her, but no one seemed to have heard anything in nearly a week. Some people had left pointed comments like "She'll turn up...just like she always does," which sparked a flurry of arguments over the seriousness of the whole thing. No one seemed overly concerned, and the few attempts at organizing search parties had fallen apart.

"Are you even listening to me?" Emily asked.

"Yes."

"Are not," she said, snatching my phone to look at the screen. "Still with the Natalie?"

"Yeah," I said. "Did you ask Hachi about her?"

"Haven't seen her yet today," Emily said. "Now focus, Daniel-san. Okay, Hamlet's dad was..."

"Kenneth Branagh?" I guessed. I remembered someone mentioning his name at some point in the last few weeks. Wow, where had I been? Oh yeah. Up to my ears in dead people drama.

"Screw it," she said. "I love you, but you're gonna fail this one."

"Oh well," I said with a heavy sigh. I had spent a lot more time than usual lately doing research on ghosts and their histories. With my seventeenth birthday looming, I was trying to get in as much good karma as I could before I became Little Miss Normal again. "Guess you can't win them all, huh?"

"Or any of them, apparently. You're gonna flunk for the semester if you're not careful," Emily said as she folded the useless study guide and grabbed my notebook. I watched the motion carefully; the blue spiral notebook held all my notes and clippings about ghosts. But she stuck the paper in without a second glance, then started examining her zebra-striped nails.

"Grades are a form of patriarchal oppression," I told her. I casually slid the blue notebook closer to me and tucked it under my disorganized binder. "And I will not tolerate it."

"Yeah, go tell the Fraulein that. See how far it gets you," Emily said.

"And since when do you care about grades?"

"I don't care about *mine*," she said. "And I only care about yours because when you fail, I have to go to the movies by myself."

"So you're just using me," I joked.

"Guilty as charged."

The dissonant chime of the fifth period bell sounded. Like Pavlov's drooling dogs, my stomach started twisting into knots at the sound. I was going to fail so hard.

"Here goes nothing," I said.

"Good luck."

"You planning to go to class?"

Emily shrugged and took out her compact to check her lipstick. After perusing her lips, she took out a tube of sparkling gloss and carefully reapplied to her bottom lip. "She doesn't care when I'm late."

So completely unfair.

I shook my head and headed out the back door of the library to the Language Arts hall. White cinderblock walls were plastered in neon poster boards reminding us, as if we could forget, about the Fall Court selection and all the spirit days next week. There were themed dress-up days for each day of the week. Cowboy Day, Eighties Day, and Nerd Day led up to Warrior Day on Friday when the Fall Court would be crowned at that evening's football game.

School spirit wasn't my thing, and I had plans to be as far away as possible. Friday was my birthday, which meant I would finally lose this stupid curse. Mom had grudgingly agreed to let me miss school on Friday. Of course, she thought I was simply celebrating my birthday, where I'd really be celebrating being a normal teenager again.

As her gift to me, Emily's mom Kari was taking Emily and me shopping at the Mall of Georgia. Mom didn't really like Kari, but she had stepped up to help us after Val died, when even Dad had ditched us. She'd brought meal after meal for us when Mom was too depressed to get out of bed. She might not have been Responsible Parent of the Year, but Kari was all right by me.

Mrs. McDaniel was standing at the door. "Good afternoon, Ms. Young."

"Good afternoon," I said, ducking my head so she couldn't read the "I Didn't Study" message I felt blazed across my forehead.

There were already half a dozen other students in Mrs. McDaniel's room. The desks had been rearranged from their usual groups into rows for the test, which instantly made me nervous. The straight aisles between the rows were like a one-way street to Failsville, Population: Bridget Young.

A cluster of kids was grouped around Macie Reynolds, who was indisputably the smartest kid in the junior class. She was frantically reading through her flash cards again while her friends asked last minute questions. *Give it up,* I thought irritably. She would get the highest score if she dipped a hamster's feet in ink and let it run across her test.

Another handful of girls milled around Allie Williams, who looked like she always did--picture freaking perfect. They were discussing the impending announcement of the Fall Court, of which Allie would no doubt be a member. She combed her fingers through her already flawless dark hair. I instinctively mimicked her, wincing as my fingers caught a tangle. If I had the best hair day of my life, and Allie walked through a hurricane, she would still have better hair.

Lucky bitch, I thought as I went for a seat. I finally chose a seat close to the window, on the opposite side of the room from Allie. In a final moment of optimism, or maybe desperation, I took out my copy of *Hamlet.* Its spine was still perfectly smooth, without those tell-tale reading creases like callused guitar fingers. I glanced through it, but it was definitely not the kind of thing you skimmed and then faked your way to a D.

I was vainly reading the commentary on the "To be, or not to be…" speech when John Chang slid into the desk in front of me and said, "Sup, Young?"

"Um, studying," I said without looking up entirely. What did it look like I was doing, curing cancer?

"Hey, I'm going to see the new Vin Diesel movie this weekend. You want in?" When I hesitated, he said, "There's a bunch of us. Kristen's coming, and Nick and Justin, and probably Macie and Jaquira. It'll be a group thing, no pressure."

My heart thumped as I pretended to think it over. "Um…oh, gosh, I can't. I just remembered I have to watch my little brother." Truth was, Colin was probably better qualified to babysit me than vice versa, at least in Mom's eyes.

John looked at me for a second like he wanted to give me a hard time, then finally said, "Okay. Well I'll send you an invite on Facebook if something changes, cool?"

"Uh, it probably won't," I said. John winced a little and turned around to talk to another friend. I didn't need pity invites, and I didn't want to spend the whole evening wondering if they were thinking I was a total freak.

Mrs. McDaniel walked into the room and rang her silver hotel bell. As usual, she was dressed in black from head to toe, with huge turquoise jewelry and eye makeup that made Emily jealous. Emily had been trying all year to get me to ask if she got eyelash extensions. Right.

"Please clear your desks except for a pen or pencil," she said as she circulated and checked our desks. "If you have your phone, please turn it off. Unless any of you are planning to be called in for an emergency open heart surgery. Then, by all means, set it to your loudest, most obnoxious setting. However, should your phone ring and you cannot present your current medical license, I will be forced to confiscate said phone and issue you a detention."

Nervous laughter rippled through the room as a few of us pulled out phones. I had two phones--one was mine, and one was Valerie's. I know it's weird. If it was anyone else, I'd be creeped out. I had on her old University of Georgia hoodie for good luck, a silver dragonfly pendant that had been

28

her sixteenth birthday gift from Dad, and I was carrying her old phone. But the phone, at least, was for a good reason.

See, Val's phone was deactivated soon after she died. But no one informed the phone, apparently. Ever since Val's death, her phone would ring every few months, with nothing but static on the other end. Within thirty minutes of the call, I'd encounter a new spirit. It was basically an early warning system for the lingering dead, so I always kept it on me. Unfortunately, it didn't alert me every time a spirit was near. But when it rang, I knew to be ready. Being surprised by a ghost was *not* fun. But for now I switched both phones off and shoved them into my backpack.

A sheet of white paper landed in front of me. "You have the entire class period," Mrs. McDaniel said as she paced, her high heels clicking on the tile floor in a distracting rhythm. "Please read the directions carefully for the essays; pick one or the other. Do not attempt to do both and gnash your teeth in lament when you can't finish them both. I will laugh at your misfortune and point to the directions in a most sarcastic fashion."

We laughed in earnest. Mrs. McDaniel was by far the coolest teacher I'd ever had. I was miserably failing her class, but she didn't hold that against me. She had held me after class a few weeks before to tell me she knew I could do better, and that she knew I wouldn't disappoint her in the end.

I was glad that she had faith in me, because I sure didn't. The test might as well have been in French. Who the hell was Yorick? I sighed and puzzled through it, wracking my brain for snippets of our class discussions. Usually, I picked up a lot by listening. Problem was, I had been listening in class even less than I had been reading at home.

I hadn't planned to be such a slacker. Over the last year, I had developed a bad habit of hiding my phone behind my thick binder. I made sure to periodically highlight my papers and nod thoughtfully while the discussion went on around me. To be fair, I wasn't texting; I was searching old news articles for information on an unsolved hit-and-run from 1979.

By the time I was done with that case, the class had finished Act Two, and I hadn't even bought the book yet. I swore I was going to catch up with a couple of marathon reading sessions. Then Anna Cole appeared to me the day we started Act Four., and before I knew it, we had finished the entire play and I hadn't read a single word.

Enough was enough. I had to start paying attention and studying every day. The next book we read, I'd read ahead, take notes, and ask questions in class. Maybe.

Okay, I thought. *You can do this.* Maybe if I concentrated, I would remember *something*. Ugh. Why couldn't McDaniel give us multiple-choice tests? Then I could have gotten twenty-five percent on dumb luck.

I had just started to remember something about Ophelia when an electronic screech shattered the silence. The ear-splitting blast of music was so loud and distorted it was completely unrecognizable at first. I jumped in surprise and knocked my pencil off my desk. A dozen heads snapped around to the source of the sound. What idiot hadn't turned off their phone? But no one was moving to turn it off, and I felt cold dread twisting in my stomach as the squalling resolved itself into a song I recognized.

From the front pocket of my backpack, Amy Winehouse belted, "Oh won't you come on over, stop making a fool out of me, why don't you come on over, Valerie?"

I looked up to see my sister at the desk in front of me grinning like a fool. She had her head turned carefully so I couldn't see the back. Her fingers twirled a lock of dark hair.

"Ms. Young?" Mrs. McDaniel said.

"I am so sorry," I stammered. My fingers fumbled uselessly as I tried to turn off the blaring phone. I finally pried the battery off, silencing Amy in the middle of a "Valeriiiiie."

"I love that song," Valerie said to me. I ignored her. My problems were big enough without me talking to thin air. This was just *mean*. She knew I had a test.

"The phone," Mrs. McDaniel said. Her hand hovered expectantly over the test, and I didn't even protest as I put the phone and battery in her hand. She didn't look angry, but there was definitely some mild irritation in those arched brows.

"I am so sorry," I said, my cheeks flushing as my classmates stared incredulously. Emily's English class would have been laughing and cheering. Why couldn't we trade?

"Get back to work," Mrs. McDaniel said sharply, and everyone snapped back to their tests like obedient little drones. God, I wanted to sink into the floor and die.

I turned the test over to a blank page and scrawled, *What are you doing here?!*

"Just checking on you," she said. "Sorry about the phone." I heard her voice loud and clear, but no one else paid any attention. She craned her neck, the translucent spill of hair passing through my test and the desk beneath. "You should've studied."

I was busy, I wrote, hoping that I was forming letters in a way that appropriately conveyed my irritation with her. I pondered, then added a frowny face.

"You want some help?" Val asked, unfazed by my frowny face. She moved behind Macie Reynolds in a jerky blur. "Wow, she's already halfway done. The character who represents Hamlet's foil is Laertes. That's number seventeen. Write that down." She reappeared in the desk in front of me. "What else do you need?"

"Stop," I wrote, and then underlined it three times. I turned back to my test. Though my conscience raised a vocal protest, I scribbled *Laertes* in the blank for number seventeen. I stared at it, and then erased it. I was a champion liar but I just couldn't stomach cheating. Besides, I only lied because the truth would earn me an invitation to "talk to a professional."

"It's not cheating," Val said. I raised an eyebrow at her, and she put up her hands in surrender. "Okay, it kind of is. But you're going to fail."

I shook my head and turned my test back over pointedly. I glanced over and saw Allie Williams staring at me like I had fourteen heads. Of course it would be her. I gave her an ugly look that made her snap her gaze back to her test. Allie and I had been best friends once upon a time, back before Val's death. We grew up together, tried out for middle school cheerleading together, and cried together when we both got cut for having no talent beyond being able to walk and hold pompoms at the same time.

But most of my friends--except Emily--had disappeared when I made them uncomfortable with my grief. It had been cool for a while to be friends with poor Bridget, who had this thrilling family drama. I was a social accessory that made them look good for being sympathetic and supportive. But when I didn't bounce back to normal in a couple weeks, they got bored. When I needed them most, my "friends" disappeared. I used to get mad about, but I didn't hold it against them anymore.

I *had* changed. Seeing the dead had a way of changing your priorities in life. I really wasn't the Bridget they used to know. Still, sometimes I wanted to slap them all, one in particular. It really wasn't fair that Allie Williams was Queen Bee around here while I was stuck seeing dead people, among them a prankster sister who got me detention and tried to get me to cheat on tests.

"Fine," Val said with a sigh. "Don't be mad at me, Bridget. I'm just looking out for you."

I glanced up at her, looking around quickly to make sure no one was watching. I whispered, "I know."

"Okay," she said. "Do you want me to leave you alone?"

I looked up at her for a long stretch, the test forgotten. *Yes. No. Never.*

See, the whole haunting thing sucked. But it did have its perks. Two years later, I still hadn't really said goodbye to Val. Even in death, she watched out for me, just like she did when she was alive. She told me how to fix my hair and what clothes matched. She told me what to say to Mom to defuse her when she got door-slamming mad. She even told me exactly what Mom wanted for Christmas each year so I could surprise her and get brownie points. In every way that she could, she had kept on being my big sister, like nothing had changed.

And after my birthday, she would really be gone.

I shook my head at Val, and she nodded solemnly. Instead of trying to feed me answers, she sat quietly and watched me take the test.

Even before I finished my incoherent mess of an essay about Biblical imagery in the play, I knew I had failed. I kept my paper, pretending like I was really concentrating right up until the bell rang. In fact, I was carefully tracing the letters in the first dozen questions with my black pen. While my classmates made a mad rush for the door, I trudged over to Mrs. McDaniel, who already had a yellow detention slip for me.

"I'm so sorry," I said again. "I thought I had turned it off."

"It's okay, kiddo," she said as she looked over my test. "I'm more concerned that you think Ophelia was Hamlet's father."

"Right," I said, looking down at my feet like my shoes were somehow responsible for my humiliating showing on the test.

"Look at me," she said. She wasn't mean, but she was firm. Her face was serious as she asked, "Did you read the play?"

"No ma'am," I admitted.

"Any of it?"

"No ma'am."

I expected her to roll her eyes and shake her head in exasperation before telling me to go on and quit wasting her time, but she didn't. She actually looked concerned as she cocked her head, setting her turquoise earrings jingling. "You've been really distracted these last few weeks. Is there something I can do to help you?"

"Uh…not really," I said. "I've just had a lot on my mind."

"Well, if there's something I can do," she said, her words hanging heavy as she trailed off. When the year started, she had accidentally called me Valerie, who had been a star student in her class the year she died. Apparently, I had looked completely mortified, because she stopped class to apologize. But the whole reason I had looked like that --mouth wide open, tomato red face--was because Valerie happened to be following me around that day, dishing the dirt on the teachers she knew. For a moment, when she called the wrong name, I thought McDaniel had actually *seen* her. Even so, she spent the next two weeks apologizing every time she saw me.

"It's cool," I said again. "I'm going to get it together."

"Tell you what," she said. "I'll let you retake this next Monday. Different exam, of course, and what you get this time is what you get."

"Really?"

"Yes," she said. "But you *have* to get focused. Whatever's on your mind, let's deal with it and get you back on track. And if I can help you, please tell me."

"Thank you," I said. "And I will."

"But you still have detention," she said with a wry smile.

"I know," I said. "Sorry again."

CHAPTER FOUR

F OR SIXTH PERIOD, I had Trigonometry with Allie and Macie. They spent every minute of the group activity eagerly filling in our other classmates on how my phone had gone off, and how McDaniel had swooped down on me like a hawk. This was, of course, a gross exaggeration, but that didn't stop their dramatic reenactment. It made me wish Valerie was a poltergeist. They would stop laughing real quick when she flung a math book at their heads. (Don't think we hadn't tried.)

"Good afternoon, Warriors," the secretary interrupted over the intercom.

"Progress reports on Friday," Mr. Gilbert shouted over the noise of the class packing up. Excellent. Yet another reason for Mom to be disappointed.

The announcements were nothing exciting, but everyone was unusually quiet as the secretary read the daily reminder to move cars out of the main parking lot before band practice. When she finished, there was a series of crackles and bumps as she passed off the microphone.

"Hey guys, this is Taylor Brown, your junior class president," a female voice said. "It's my pleasure to announce this year's Fall Court. As you know, juniors and seniors are nominated for the Fall Court. We had a lot of great folks nominated, but we had to narrow it down to seven."

Now the uncharacteristic silence made sense. As Taylor read the nominees for Fall King, Allie grabbed her new best friend Hannah's hand and squeezed her eyes shut dramatically.

Gag me, I thought. Like there was any question Allie would be nominated. There was always at least one junior girl on the court, and while the junior girl never won, it was almost as good as winning to be the one nominated. That had been Allie's fate since kindergarten just as it had been Valerie's.

"And now for the Fall Queen nominees: Kristen Chang--" Allie shushed a couple of boys in the back of the room. "Madison Dailey, Vanessa James, Sierra Lewis, Katie Rivera, Aisha Townes, and--"

I glanced over to see Allie already grinning. Her eyes cut to me, and I could have sworn that her smile widened.

"Bridget Young," Taylor finished.

Allie's grin melted into a look of shock. Suddenly she realized everyone else was staring at her, and she forced the fakest smile I'd ever seen. "Congratulations, Bridget!" she chirped.

"Wait, what?" I asked, staring up at the speaker like the announcer was there to answer my questions. Surely they meant I needed to come pick something up. But judging by the murmurs and stares, I'd heard perfectly. The guys Allie had shushed were grinning, but everyone else looked surprised.

Join the club.

"All nominees need to report immediately to the front office for their information packets," she finished. "Congratulations to all nominees!"

If it had been one of those mean girl movies, Allie would have shouted "Freak!" or something equally mean as I walked out with a chorus of hysterical laughter behind me. She'd definitely be gossiping about me, but she wasn't going to be that obvious.

"Congratulations, Bridget," Mr. Gilbert said as he opened the door for me.

"Uh, thanks," I said, shuffling out the door. My head was spinning as I walked down the math hall. This had to be a mistake. They had grabbed the wrong *W* file, that was all. Allie and I had been next to each other on class rosters since we were in kindergarten.

"Congratulations," Valerie said as I walked up the empty hallway. I looked over at her, and she was wearing the smile of a cat who had recently dined on the mouse *du jour*.

"You didn't," I said.

"I so did," she replied. "Let's just say the spreadsheet with the votes had a little malfunction."

"Val, what the hell were you thinking? Everyone's going to know."

"No they won't," she replied. "You actually had a few votes."

"Whoa, really?" I said, completely distracted. I was about as unpopular as you could get. I mean, people weren't calling me Idget Bridget and throwing milk cartons at me, but my Friend Request tab on Facebook didn't get a lot of action.

"Yeah," she replied. "A bunch of the boys in your history class think you're cute. They were drawing a picture of you--"

"Gross," I interrupted. "There are things better left unknown."

"This is a good thing, Bridget," she said. "It's going to be fun."

"Yeah, it's going to be really fun when Allie starts up with her shit again," I said. "I can't *wait*."

"Screw her," Val said. "She's a total bitch anyway."

She really was. Right after Val died, I was in and out of the hospital for months. In the car accident, I'd gotten a pretty serious concussion on top of the destruction of my left knee. I used to get migraines so bad I couldn't have any lights on, so I had to stay home a lot. I missed most of the spring of my freshman year, but I went back for a while in January, so I had a chance at making up the work. Then I made the epic mistake of telling Mom I had seen Valerie.

She instantly withdrew me from school and homeschooled me for the rest of the year so I could go to weekly therapy sessions, both emotional and physical, and support groups for grieving teenagers. It wasn't like I got locked up in an institution, and even if I *had*, it wasn't any of Allie's freaking business. As my former BFF, she should have been the one to stave off nasty gossip and set the record straight.

Instead, Allie translated "homeschooling and therapy" to "she's lost her freaking mind." If you could chart popularity on one of those stock market graphs, you'd find a huge spike that coincided with Allie becoming the number one source of gossip related to me and my family.

Mom told me to give her the benefit of the doubt back then, and I had tried. Maybe Allie really *was* so mind-numbingly stupid that she didn't know how people would react to her version of the story. Maybe she was born without the part of the brain that allowed her to behave like a human being.

But even if that was the case—and it wasn't—it hadn't been her story to tell. Since then, I hadn't had much to say to Allie. At least not after I punched her in the nose and gave her a black eye right before the Spring Fling freshman year. That might have had something to do with the rapid deterioration of our friendship and my ever-shrinking social circle, but I was no expert.

"So now I have to walk across that stupid football field and have everyone laugh at me," I said. "Thanks for that, Val. I'm ecstatic."

"They won't laugh," she said. "If you quit hiding from everyone, you'd have a ton of friends. You're not as much as a freak as you think you are."

I stopped in front of a water fountain and looked at her dead on. "First, I don't hide."

"You do so. You avoid everyone but Emily."

Whatever. "Second, I'm walking down the hallway talking to my dead sister, who just rigged the Fall Court nominations in my favor. Freak doesn't begin to describe it."

"Okay, that's fair enough," she said, raising her translucent hands in surrender. "But you'd be surprised."

Detention was mind-numbingly boring, which I guessed was kind of the point. It was in Mrs. Purdue's classroom on the science hall. The apple-cinnamon air freshener couldn't quite cover that special science classroom blend of formaldehyde and rotten eggs from the gas lines. The room was full, and I was surprised that Emily wasn't here for once. I was always waiting on her to get out of detention, usually for dress code violations.

While I waited for the hour to be over, I thumbed through the info packet I'd picked up at the office. Printed in a cutesy font on orange paper, there was a whole list of rules about campaigning, guidelines for propriety on dresses, and fundraising information, including sample letters for local business. Part of the Fall Court was soliciting donations for the school. What a crap deal—I had to buy a fancy dress *and* raise money to give to the school? The fun factor just kept coming.

Valerie read the packet over my shoulder. My right arm prickled with goosebumps from her proximity, but I was mostly used to that. That was part of the reason I wore her old UGA hoodie all the time. "I went to all the local restaurants. Everyone goes to the big box stores, but the little guy is where it's at. Try Giavino's," she said. "They'll give you at least a hundred bucks."

"Ms. Young, put the papers away," Mrs. Purdue snapped as she looked up from her grading. "This is not your personal study hall."

I sighed and closed the packet, then leaned over to slide it into my backpack. As I did, a flash of bright pink caught my eye. Sticking out of a black messenger bag across the aisle, I saw the top halves of bold black letters printed on pink paper. The owner of the messenger bag was staring blankly out the window, so I grabbed the pink paper and slid it up a little. It said "HAVE YOU SEEN ME?" It was the same as the poster I'd seen the day before. My heart thumped as I tried to inch it up a little further.

The faded boat shoes next to the bag shuffled, and someone cleared their throat. Following a pair of artfully-ripped jeans up slowly, I saw the bag's owner bent over looking at me. He didn't look amused. I snatched my hand away like a hairy spider had run across it and sat up fast enough to make my head spin.

Flyer Boy looked vaguely familiar and more than vaguely attractive. He had thick dark hair and pretty lashes framing brown eyes. A plain gray t-shirt hugged sporty muscles, and he had a nice tan. A faded line around his elbows said he must have been a football player.

After checking him out, I became keenly aware of my appearance. Minimal was the nice word for my daily look, although Emily preferred *lazy* and *plain*. Those were the kindest of her descriptions. Ponytail, blue jeans and a plain colored t-shirt were my usual uniform, and the only time I wore anything except a coat of mascara was when Emily cornered me to try out some makeup thing she found online. I didn't usually care about my appearance, but I suddenly felt ugly next to Flyer Boy.

"That's Michael Fullmer," Valerie said appreciatively. "Cute, right?" I nodded a little, and she smiled. "You should have seen him when he was a freshman. Chubby, glasses, bad skin. He had a crush on me back then. He's definitely dateable now."

41

She continued to talk about the eligible bachelors of detention, but I wasn't really listening. I was still stuck on Michael, who was obviously Natalie Fullmer's brother. I wanted to ask about her, but I didn't want to overstep my bounds. I also didn't want to get into trouble for talking in detention, which would earn me the door prize of two more days of detention.

Detention passed at a snail's pace, but Mrs. Purdue finally dismissed us at 3:47, two torturous minutes late. The silence shattered in an explosive burst of conversation as everyone finally got a chance to talk. Michael grabbed his bag and shoved past a cluster of girls lingering by the door. One of them called "Congratulations, Michael!" after him, but he ignored her. Right—he'd been nominated for the Fall Court too.

"Follow him," Val said. "Unless of course, you'd rather avoid him."

"You're on," I retorted.

With my backpack bouncing, I dashed out of the room after him. I yanked the elastic out of my hair and ran my fingers through it quickly, hoping I didn't have that annoying ponytail crease around my head. Val grinned and called, "Saucy girl."

"Shut up," I hissed as I ran after him. "Hey, Michael?"

"Thanks," he said without turning around. Instead of heading to the commons area and out the main doors, he hurried down to the exit halfway down the science hall, which led to the senior parking lot.

"Huh?" I caught up to him and grabbed his arm. He whirled and glared at me. I might have been intimidated, except I'd seen enough nasty, bloody ghosts that a cute guy trying to look mean didn't have much of an effect on me.

"What do you want?" he snapped.

"I was going to ask you about Natalie."

His face softened for a moment as he stared at me. Then his eyes went hard again, like a bank vault slamming shut. "What about her?"

"I saw your flyer yesterday," I said. "She's missing, huh?"

"Congratulations, you can read," he said.

"Look, you don't have to be so rude," I said. His cuteness? Rapidly disappearing.

"Don't waste your time, okay? I know how the rest of this conversation goes," he snapped. "She probably ran away just like this summer, because she's a total screw-up."

"Whoa, defensive much?" I asked, wrinkling my nose.

"Get him," Valerie said, raising her spectral hands like brandished claws. "Rowr."

"What?" he snapped.

"I didn't say anything like that. I did—" I stopped myself, correcting myself for using the past tense. As far as we knew, she was still alive. "I don't know her at all. I was just curious when I saw the posters."

"Oh," he said, frowning suddenly. "Well." He stared at me, his brow creasing, and I realized he didn't know what to say. It made me a little angry—on his behalf, this time—that he was surprised because someone *wasn't* badmouthing his sister.

"If you want some help, I'm pretty good at research," I said.

"It's not a school project."

"No, but there's a lot of public records you can get into pretty easily. You never know what you might find," I said.

I was always searching newspapers and public police records for information on my different ghost cases. I was also good at faking voices and sticking my nose where it didn't belong, which also came in handy for ghost research. I wasn't sure how much I could find on Natalie, but I could try.

"Really?" he asked, looking interested for the first time. "Why do you want to help me?"

I shrugged and glanced at Valerie. "I know what it's like to lose a sister."

CHAPTER FIVE

AFTER TRADING PHONE NUMBERS with Michael and getting a stack of neon pink posters, I called Emily to pick me up from school. In exchange for help on her math homework, she agreed to drive me around to put up posters. After a stop at Sonic for a snack and a refresher on factoring quadratics, we headed out to Mount Sharon, the ritzier suburb west of Fox Lake. Our next stop was a strip mall, which had all the same restaurants and stores as we did in Fox Lake. But here, the buildings were stacked stone with matching green and white signs. Even the McDonalds looked like an upscale store except for the neon yellow arches that gave it away.

Emily held a poster for me while I tore off strips of packing tape. "So what the hell is this Fall Court business?" Emily asked. "Did you secretly campaign or something?"

I cursed and tried to untangle myself from a piece of tape like a Chinese finger trap. "You caught me. I stuffed the ballot boxes, because my life's dream is to parade across a football field in a slutty dress."

Emily snorted a laugh. "So are you going to do it?"

"You know how there's always that one person where no one claps except like, the psycho band moms and the teachers? That's going to be me."

"I would clap for you," she said. "But I think you should make a statement and drop out. It's just a big ego fest, and the same people get told yet again how great they are."

"I know," I said. I tore off another piece of tape and plastered the poster to the window. "But–"

"I know, you still care what people think," Emily interrupted. "At least rebel a little. Let me do your hair and makeup. I found this hair style that would rock on you. Your hair is probably thick enough for it." She put down the posters and started messing with my hair, pulling a handful up in a ponytail. "Oh yeah."

I'd probably come out looking like a punk rock star, but who really cared? It wasn't like I would get a single vote anyway. Might as well have fun with it. "Sure."

"Awesome," she replied as she smoothed my hair back down. She pulled out her phone and checked the time. "Okay, let's finish these last couple places, and then I gotta head home."

"What's the rush?" I asked as we strolled down the strip to the next shop, a little nail salon with its door open. The overpowering scent of the chemicals hit us like a wall, and I winced. Emily held up one of the posters and pointed to it. An older woman looked up from filing her client's nails and nodded.

"Faceless Dark is playing at Warehouse Eleven tonight. Me and Hachi are going early for the VIP pre-show," Emily said as she positioned the poster in the corner of the salon's window.

"Oh," I said as I taped it down. Faceless Dark was an indie band we both liked. Warehouse Eleven was a club downtown that catered to the high school crowd. I had only been once, and Mom had pitched a fit when she found out where we had gone. I wasn't such a fan that it would break my heart to miss them, but it bothered me that Emily had invited Hachi and not me. "I didn't know that."

"Sorry," she said. "I didn't ask you because I knew your mom wouldn't even consider letting you go out on a school night."

"It's okay," I said, forcing a smile. "What are you wearing?"

Emily was always good for an epic-length conversation about her clothes. By the time she finished describing how she was going to do her eyeshadow, we had finished putting up posters and were back in the car. Then she regaled me with the many difficult decisions on her outfit, and I tuned her out. I loved her dearly, but I just couldn't match her enthusiasm for fashion. After six years of being friends, I was good at nodding at the right times without actually listening to her.

"Thanks for the ride," I said as we pulled up in front of my house.

"Anytime," she said as I got out. "I'll text you later. Hey, BB?"

BB was short for Brooklyn Bridge, which was an old elementary school nickname I used to hate until Emily decided it was actually cool. "Yeah?"

"You're not mad, right? About the concert, I mean."

"No, it's cool," I lied. "Have fun."

"Okay," she said, looking relieved. "I'll text you later."

"Cool." I waved goodbye as she peeled out of our neighborhood. I wasn't mad, but I was a little hurt. She was right; Mom wouldn't have let me go out on a school night. But it still would have been nice to be invited. Either way, it wasn't worth drama with Emily, who couldn't stand to have anyone upset with her.

The driveway was empty, so it would just be me and Colin for a while. I let myself in and headed to the living room, where he was already camped out playing video games. A crumpled bag of Doritos lay next to him. "Did you do your homework?"

"Did *you?*" He didn't bother to look up from his game. "Sorry, sister aggro."

"I'm serious," I said. "What is aggro?"

"It means you're getting on my nerves. And yes, I finished it at school."

"You left the front door unlocked," I said. "You're lucky I came home first."

"Thanks, Mom," he said. "Cover me!"

There was a house-shaking explosion that would have had Mom screaming at Colin to turn down the TV. I took that as my cue to leave. I ran upstairs for my laptop, grabbed a snack of peanut butter crackers and a soda from the kitchen, then headed out to the back patio to start doing some research on Natalie.

Fall leaves were starting to build up in the wicker patio chairs, so I had to brush off a pile to sit on the scratchy blue cushion. I caught the smell of burning leaves on the breeze. Even with winter approaching, it still felt good out here in the sun. Like my sister, I'd always loved being outside. I propped my feet up on an empty wooden planter and turned on the laptop.

Honestly, I wasn't sure I'd find anything. Everyone I'd ever found had been dead for years, and their affairs were long a matter of public record. Natalie had been missing for only a few weeks, so she probably hadn't left the kind of paper trail my usual targets did. But I honestly wanted to help, and not just because Michael was cute.

My laptop's login screen had just loaded, glowing blue and patiently waiting for my password, when I felt the telltale cold breeze of a spirit near me. It wasn't the weather; my outstretched legs were warm in the afternoon sun, even as a chill ran down my spine. I frowned at the computer screen, resisting the urge to look up until I had prepared myself.

I took a deep breath and looked up. Standing in the middle of the leaf-carpeted backyard was a blinding pillar of light. "Evening," it said in a playful masculine voice.

Stepping out of a filmy halo of white light was a spirit named Kale. He was handsome, verging on pretty, with glowing blue eyes and soft dark hair

48

that I always wanted to touch. His fitted white shirt and loose linen pants made him look like he'd just finished a fashion shoot on a beach somewhere.

Kale wasn't like any spirit I had ever seen. There were no signs of his death, and he communicated perfectly clearly to me. He also smelled like fresh-cut grass and a hint of citrus instead of rotting meat, which was a definite plus. I asked him once if he was an angel. He just laughed. Kale called himself a Guardian, and when I asked him "What's a Guardian?" I always got the same response: "*I am.*" But he'd never done anything but help me, so I figured he was entitled to his secrets.

"Howdy," I said, setting the laptop aside.

"Birthday's close," Kale said. He didn't flicker like most spirits. Instead he walked in a graceful gliding gait toward me. I caught a whiff of his grassy smell, that green, living scent on a cool breeze. Neat trick.

"Next Friday," I said as I watched him sit in the other patio chair. My birthday was two days after the anniversary of Valerie's death, ensuring I'd never forget that terrible day.

Kale was a lot better at appearing real than most spirits. But there was no crackling sound of wicker straining under his weight, nor whispering shuffle of leaves under his bare feet.

"Are you getting excited?"

"You have no idea." Neither of us was talking about turning seventeen.

Kale laughed, a melodious sound that echoed like chimes. "I think I do."

"Is it really going to work?"

"It really is," Kale replied. "Did you find the candles?"

"I found them online," I replied. "They should be here sometime this weekend."

A while back, Kale told me there was a way to get rid of what he called *my gift*. I thought it was a curse, but he didn't like me calling it that. It had been after a particularly ugly case, sending off a little girl who had drowned in the bathtub while her mother shot up in the other room. I'd never forget her, lost little Mia. I could still see her perfectly, every little brown curl plastered to pale white cheeks as she mouthed over and over, "Help please?"

I'd shown Mia the newspapers, where her big sister went into foster care with a seemingly kind family. But what did that mean to a dead little kid, or me for that matter? It wasn't going to make life easier for the people who were left, so what was the point of any of this? Tragedies were written in ink, and there was no erasing the stains. No matter how much good I did, these people were dead and gone forever.

Kale had found me crying in my room, one of the few times I had openly wept since Val died. I begged him to take it away, and he said there was a way if I earned it. Needless to say, he had my full attention. There was something mystical about birthdays, he said. I just had to hold out until my seventeenth birthday.

All things considered, I had a lot to atone for, but I'd brought peace to a lot of unhappy spirits over the last few years. My karma meter had to be pretty full. Now seventeen was on the horizon, and I couldn't wait to be normal again. It had only recently occurred to me that no gift meant no Kale. I'd miss him, but I could live with it.

"Kale?"

"Yes?"

"Can you find missing people?"

"Alive?"

"Preferably."

50

"Hard to say," he replied. "It's not really my area."

"What exactly *is* your area?" I asked as I entered my password and waited for the laptop to finish starting up.

"Watching out for you," he said.

"Dude, seriously, will you at least tell me before we do this witchy thing on Thursday?"

He shrugged and laughed again, the way he always did when I pried into exactly what he was. "Why do you ask—about the missing people, I mean?"

I told him about Natalie, and he nodded as he listened. "I just have a weird feeling about her."

"Do you have a picture?" he asked. I nodded and showed him her Facebook picture. "Natalie, huh? I'll put my ear to the wire, but no promises."

"So are you going to tell me what I have to do yet?" I asked, changing back to the subject of my birthday.

Every few months, Kale told me another piece of the ritual I had to complete to get rid of the curse. He called it "closing the door." He could call it whatever he wanted as long as it worked. With the candles, herbs, and crystals he was having me order off the Internet, it was starting to sound a little too toil-and-trouble for my tastes. It might have sounded stupid, but after a couple years of being at the beck and call of ghosts, you'll do just about anything to get back to normal.

"Thursday," he said. "I promise."

"Isn't that cutting it a little close?"

"Don't you trust me?" Kale asked, looking at me with those bottomless blue eyes. They were brilliant turquoise, like those cruise-ship commercial shots of the Caribbean. But there was something dark shifting in their depths. Those eyes reminded me that there was something unseen and maybe even dangerous behind the beautiful surface.

I wanted to respond, *as a matter of fact, I don't trust you*, but I kept the thought to myself. Whatever he was, Kale had given me good advice over the last few years. When he could be bothered to show up, that was. And right now, he was my only hope at a normal life.

"Sure I do," I said.

"Who are you talking to, weirdo?" Colin asked from behind me. I felt the cool breeze of Kale disappearing, and I turned to glare at my brother.

"Emily," I said, digging my phone out of the pocket of my hoodie to show him.

"In your pocket?" He had his cell phone pressed against the shoulder of his Angry Birds t-shirt.

"Speakerphone, moron. Welcome to the twenty-first century."

"Whatever," he said. The sun reflected off his black-rimmed glasses as he shifted impatiently. "Mom called and wants to know if you'd rather have pizza or subs for dinner. She said she has to stay late for shots but she'll be home by seven."

"Subs," I said. "I want the Golf Club with-"

"No mustard, I know."

Without another word, he walked back into the house, talking to Mom as he went. Colin and I didn't get along very well, but I don't know how much of that was Valerie's death and how much was being nearly five years apart. He seemed angrier than when he was younger, but we didn't talk about it. What did a twelve-year-old boy talk to his sixteen year old sister about, anyway? That was a pretty good rule of thumb in the Young household. *Whatever's bothering you, for God's sake, don't talk about it.*

I sighed and looked over at Kale's now-empty seat. There was no telling when he'd show up again. All I had was Kale's word that he was going to show up next Thursday night.

Now, to be fair, I was glad to do something good for these spirits, and not just in that "I'm saying it so I don't sound like a bad person" sort of way. When I first started seeing them after Valerie's accident, I freaked out about thirty-seven times on a *good* day. I eventually figured out that I only saw the wrongful dead, people who died before they were supposed to, usually at someone else's hands. So it's not like I saw the ghost of everyone who had ever died. That would have definitely put me on the VIP list in the psych ward.

But I was so tired. I never slept well, because I was always waking up from nightmares that were in the "based on true events" genre. I couldn't concentrate in school. With all the research to appease the ghosts clamoring for my attention, I barely had any time to study or do homework. And I was tired of feeling like a freak because I didn't have anything to talk about except some weird local crime story I looked up. Being a teenager was hard enough without all of that. Surely I'd earned some peace by now.

My excitement was mixed with dread at finally saying goodbye to my sister, but I was steeling myself for that. On Wednesday, the anniversary of her death, I would say goodbye to Valerie for good, sending her on like I had Anna Cole. I wasn't exactly sure what happened, but it seemed to cut the ties binding a spirit to the world of the living. All the spirits I'd sent on, I had never seen again, even when I went back to their remains or the place they died. And when that was done, I would take my life back.

I just hoped I remembered how to be normal.

CHAPTER SIX

A S I SAT IN MRS. BRASCO'S CLASSROOM after school with the rest of the Fall Court, all I could think of was that old song from Sesame Street. "One of these things is not like the other, one of these things just doesn't belong." Even though I'd taken the time to actually do something to my hair and put on a little makeup that morning, I was still the ugly duckling.

There were two junior girls on the court this year. Besides me, there was the endlessly talented Kristen Chang. She wasn't the prettiest girl in the room, but she was super smart, a brilliant painter, and piano virtuoso. She was also on the math team, the debate club...you get the picture. If there was an award for most yearbook appearances, she'd win it.

The senior girls were all gorgeous, ranging from the cheerleading captain to the state cross-country champion. As amazing as my sister was, she would have fit right in with these girls. Me? With mediocre looks, less-than-mediocre grades, and virtually no involvement with school, I was the black sheep. No, I was the goat that was busy chewing on an old Coke can while the rest of the sheep tried to figure out what dumbass shepherd let me in.

"All donations should be collected and turned in to the main office no later than next Wednesday," Mrs. Brasco said. "While they have no bearing on votes, do keep in mind that every dollar donated goes directly to the school. And of course, the candidate bringing in the most donations will have their name added to the "Royal Philanthropist" plaque in the trophy case."

Woo-freaking-hoo, I thought as I watched her light up with excitement. I was more interested in Michael Fullmer. Sticking out from under his homecoming packet was a thin stack of pink flyers, and under that, his fingers were slowly typing a message on his phone without disturbing the papers.

"Ms. Young?"

"What?" I asked, startled. "I'm sorry, I missed that."

Mrs. Brasco sighed. "I asked if you'd brainstormed any ideas for where to fundraise. We're trying to avoid double-dipping."

I scrambled for what Val had told me. "I was going to try some of the restaurants in the Plaza. Like Giavino's and maybe the Vanilla Dipper."

"Excellent thinking," Mrs. Brasco said, a smile replacing the irritated look on her face. I gave her my brightest smile, and slumped back in my seat as she made a note on her clipboard and went on to Kristen Chang, who had a neatly typed list of ideas in a pink folder. Seriously?

When the meeting was finally over, I stayed back to wait for Michael. "Any news?" I asked as we walked out to the parking lot.

The drumline was already warming up on the asphalt as the last few stragglers moved cars to make way for marching band practice. Their cadence reverberated in a disorienting echo, and it was deafening as we walked past the snare drums.

He stared at me curiously. "You seriously want to help me?"

"Why wouldn't I?"

"I just got nominated for Fall Court. Girls who never spoke to me before are suddenly paying attention to me."

"You certainly think highly of yourself," I said.

"Maybe so, but that still doesn't explain why someone who doesn't know me or my sister is going out of their way to help us."

We stopped at a little white Toyota that was splattered with pollen and mud. A quick peek through the window revealed a clean car, except for the blanket of bright pink flyers across the backseat. I smiled despite his skeptical expression and said, "I care because that's what people should do."

"Oh," he said as he slumped into the driver's seat. He looked embarrassed as a plastic soda bottle fell out, and quickly leaned over to grab it. As he talked, he toyed with the cap and didn't look at me. "Her Facebook has been updated saying she's okay, and she apparently texted her best friend Makayla. But she won't return *my* calls or texts. Mom said she's on her own this time. She said she's not letting her back in the house even if she does come back."

"But if her Facebook is updated—"

"It just doesn't feel right, okay?" he interrupted, glaring at me. "She wouldn't ignore me."

"Okay," I said, but I was starting to think this wasn't my type of thing after all. I had suspected that something bad had happened to Natalie. But if she was updating her Facebook, then Michael just needed help getting out of denial. And that was definitely not a task I wanted to take on. I went for practical instead. "Have you gone to the police?"

"I called this morning and they told me Mom reported that Natalie had been in contact, so it's no longer a police matter," he said. "Even though *she* hasn't actually heard a word from Nat."

I sighed. My mom would have been contacting Facebook and the FBI and freaking CNN until she found me and dragged me home. "That sucks. Well, what can I do?"

"Nothing, I guess," he said, shaking his head as he threw the soda bottle into the backseat. We stood in tense silence for a while, and the only thing that saved me from awkward conversation was one of the band officers running over to wave him off. A long train of band kids was snaking out of the band room and walking our way. Michael had to move his car before the notoriously feisty band director gave him detention for holding up practice. He shook himself from a daze and said, "Hey, you want a ride home? Least I can do, right?"

"I've got some stuff to do," I lied. "But thanks anyway."

"Yeah, you too," he said. "Hey, Bridget, I really do appreciate that you offered to help. It just seems screwed up that a stranger wants to help more than our own mother does."

That it did. "Anytime."

Once he had driven away, I noticed a glint of silver against the yellow lines of the parking lot and stooped to pick it up. It was a slender silver cuff bracelet, engraved with the initials "N.A.F." - Natalie something Fullmer. I jogged after Michael, waving it at him, but he was already at the exit and turning onto the main road outside the school.

I hustled out of the way of the incoming color guard and onto the sidewalk outside the fenced-in lot. My feet found their way to the beat as the band warmed up, and I was accidentally marching along before I realized it. I examined the silver bracelet as I walked. It was thin and polished to a mirror shine, with the initials engraved in a pretty, looping script.

"That's pretty," Valerie said from behind me. I yelped and whirled to glare at her. She was wearing the pretty black cowl neck sweater from her seventeenth birthday.

"Can you not sneak up on me?"

"It kind of comes with the territory," Val said. "What are you thinking so hard about?"

"Natalie. I don't know anymore," I said, walking slowly out onto the sidewalk along Otter Creek Road. I slipped the bracelet onto my wrist to keep it safe, then dug in my backpack for an old Bluetooth headset. Mom had trashed it after it fizzled out, but I'd recovered it from the trash when I uncharacteristically offered to take the bag out to the curb. This was the only way I could walk around talking to myself without people thinking I was nuts. I wedged the earpiece into my ear as I turned back to Valerie. "I thought she might be dead, honestly, but Michael said her Facebook was updated and that she texted her friend."

"Interesting," Valerie said. "So you think she really might be a runaway."

"It seems like it," I said. "I mean, she had to be alive to update her Facebook, so that's pretty much case closed."

"Right," Val said. She shrugged. "Oh well. So what's your campaign strategy?"

"Campaign?"

"For Fall Queen," she said. "Duh."

"Val, that's not my thing," I said. "You know that."

"It should be," she said. "It would've been if all this hadn't happened."

"Exactly," I said. "And that's why it's stupid. It's not me. Not anymore."

"It's *normal*," she protested as she walked into the street. I teetered on the curb as a FedEx truck whizzed through my sister's insubstantial body. *Some* of us still had to worry about getting hit by cars. As I crossed to join her, she said, "You deserve normal."

I shrugged. I knew I *wanted* normal, but I wasn't sure I deserved it. Valerie wasn't entirely wrong, though. She'd paved the way for me to be popular and successful like she had been in school. I'd exploded onto the social scene my freshman year, and had been surrounded by smart, popular friends—mostly hers. If she hadn't been killed, I probably would've been on the Fall Court on my own merits.

"Ugh," she said. I felt a sensation like cold water running down my back. I squealed and shimmied in place, and instinctively reached back to touch my hair, but it was dry. Val had long figured out she couldn't touch me, but she had the phantom ice water trick down pat. "Stop that."

"What?"

"Feeling sorry for yourself," she said. "And all that guilt crap. It wasn't your fault. You got like this last fall."

"I can't help it," I said. With my birthday looming, I also had the anniversary of Valerie's death on the brain. How could I *not* be gloomy about it?

"How many times do I have to tell you? I'm a big girl, and I chose to drive the way I did," she said. "It wasn't your fault. End of story."

But that wasn't the end of the story. Val didn't even know how that story ended, because she was dead wrong about it being my fault.

As I lay in bed reading that night, I discovered that *Hamlet* was actually a halfway entertaining play. Who knew it was actually a ghost story? I could relate to old Hamlet more than most. I had a Spark Notes page pulled up on my laptop, and I was currently reading the synopsis of Act I, making sure I had deciphered all the *thees, thous,* and *thines* correctly. I even had the Kenneth Branagh version of the movie playing quietly on my TV. Call it overly optimistic, but maybe I'd absorb something from the background noise.

"What are you watching?" Colin asked as he stuck his head in my door.

"Shakespeare," I said. "Go away."

"Sounds boring," he replied, wrinkling his nose. He had just gotten out of the shower, so his usual Mohawk was wet and plastered against his head, making him look like a little kid again.

"It's the most exciting thing I've ever done," I said. "Please go away so I can continue."

He ignored me. "So I know your grades kinda suck, but I was wondering if you could look at my math homework."

"Despite how nicely you asked, no," I said. God, he was annoying. He had been so cute before he learned to talk.

"It's seventh grade math, Idget. It should be easy even for you," he said. Considering how much I hated that nickname, he really needed to do some work on his persuasive skills.

"Do it yourself," I said. "I'm reading."

"No you're not," he said. He pointed to the closed copy of the play lying at the foot of my bed. "You don't even have the book open."

Brat. "I'm absorbing through osmosis." Silence from Colin. I sighed. "Will you go away if I help you?"

"Yes."

"Come on," I said. He hurried into my room, holding out his marbled composition book like a peace offering. There was a mechanical pencil stuck halfway through, and I opened to the page with his homework and glanced over the problems. The page was dingy gray from repeated erasing and rewriting. The only thing Colin wasn't perfect at was math. He worked hard enough at it to keep a B, but it had always kept him from being the perfect A student. "Okay, look, dummy. Two negatives don't make a positive when you add and subtract."

"But my teacher said they do."

"I'm sure she didn't say that."

"Yes she did," he said. "She said two negatives always make a positive–"

"When you multiply or divide," I interrupted. "Look, check this out. If you laugh, I will delete all your characters while you sleep, I swear to God."

"Don't you dare."

"Watch me," I said. I sang a song to the tune of *Row, Row, Row Your Boat*, "Same signs, add and keep, different signs subtract. Take the sign of the bigger number, then you'll be exact."

He looked at me like I had sung him a Chinese lullaby.

"Look," I said, pointing to one of the problems. "Same signs. Add and keep the sign. Five negatives plus eight negatives is thirteen negatives." I pointed to another. "Different signs, subtract. Take the sign from the bigger number."

"Oh!" he exclaimed. He blushed furiously as he hummed half of the song. "So this is...negative seven."

"Yep."

"Thanks, Bridget."

"You're welcome. Now I need to resume my awesome night of Shakespeare, so get out." I tipped my head toward the door.

But I didn't pick *Hamlet* back up. Instead, I rolled onto my back and stared up at the plastic stars stuck to the popcorn ceiling. In the low light, they made a little neon green constellation that formed a smiley face. My eyes were getting heavy, but I had enough good sense left to realize what was about to happen. I had a bad habit of falling asleep when I read, so I reached for my phone and set the alarm for thirty minutes later. *Hamlet* could wait a little while.

A sharp creak woke me from my nap. My eyes were prickly dry as I slowly opened them to a dark room with only the faint glow of the DVD pause screen. There was none of the usual noise of people being awake in the house: no showers, no XBox, no dishwasher running downstairs.

"Damn," I said, though it came out something like, "Urm."

Without getting up, I grabbed my phone and saw the battery had died before the alarm went off. Awesome. I squinted over at the alarm clock, where red numbers glared "12:23." Super awesome.

My stomach let out a protesting growl as I sat up. I hadn't eaten since my PB&J lunch at school, and I was starving. Mom was supposed to bring home dinner. Surely Colin wouldn't have risked life and skinny limb by eating my sub. As I let out a jaw-cracking yawn, I jammed my feet into a pair of fuzzy pink slippers and headed for the door.

Two glowing white eyes blinked open in the darkness. Adrenaline flooded my veins as my throat closed up. I wanted to scream, but all I could produce was a thin whistling noise. I scrambled back into my dresser hard enough to knock it into the wall and topple a line of framed pictures. Flinging myself across my bed, I flailed for the lamp, fingers fumbling at the switch.

I immediately regretted *that* decision.

Looming over me was a mutilated ghost, so filthy with grime and blood that I couldn't even guess its gender. Its face was bruised and cut in long, deliberate gashes. I heard no sound, but its lips were moving silently. I couldn't help what I did next.

I screamed like a little girl, or at least I tried to. Before I knew it was happening, ice filled my throat and a corpse-cold hand clamped over my mouth. The ghost pinned me on my bed, bathing me in its rotten-meat stench. Another cold hand clawed at my stomach, its ragged nails scratching at my skin. Oh God, it was *touching* me. I squirmed like a whole nest of spiders had crawled into my pants.

Blood roared in my ears as I tried to fight it off. The ghost was all over me, but my hands passed through it uselessly. Nothing like this had ever happened to me before. Ghosts weren't supposed to be able to touch me at all. Even Valerie couldn't do more than make me uncomfortably cold.

What the hell was I supposed to do now?

My ghost supplies were in the backpack under my bed. That was my only shot at getting this ghost off me. Bracing my feet on the wall, I shoved myself backward and slid off the bed, comforter, ghost, and all. With my head pounding, I strained to reach the backpack under my bed. Spots pulsed in my vision as my fingers finally brushed the strap.

Holy shit, I thought as I jammed my hand into the bag. My fingers found smooth plastic, and I yanked out the sports bottle of holy water. Water sprayed in an arc and splattered onto the ghostly invader. It released me, and I sucked in a breath of air that immediately made me cough.

"What the hell?" I hissed. The spirit reached for me again, mouth open in a soundless scream of fury. "Oh hell no." I gave it another liberal squirt as I shoved my hand into the backpack again. My hand found a scratchy bundle of sticks, a bagged clove of garlic, and finally the big canister of iodized salt.

White granules flew in an arc as I yanked the salt out of my bag and made a messy circle around the bed. Dancing and squirming in place, I must've looked like a squealing girl after seeing a rat run across the floor. As soon as the circle closed, there was a pressurized feeling in my ears. The ghost pounded its bloodied hands against the invisible barrier then threw its hands up in frustration and turned to my desk. The spirit blurred, and then there was a thunderous crash as it swept everything off my desk into a pile. There was an aftershock as books flew off their shelves, and my TV switched on in a deafening burst of static.

"Oh no you didn't," I said in a hissing whisper. "I freaking see you! You don't have to do all this to get my attention."

If Mom heard that racket, she would run up here and demand to know what was going on. And with a line of salt that could have been a trap for the world's biggest slug, the covers entirely off my bed, and water sprayed all over the room, I was going to have no Mom-approved answer.

This wasn't the first spirit who tried to get my attention by having a temper tantrum. But it was the first who'd ever been violent with me, and I certainly didn't like it.

"I didn't want to have to do this," I said. Kale had taught me a few things the first time I saw him, when I thought I was really going nuts. He showed me basic protections like the salt circle for times like this. When he told me it was possible a spirit could get aggressive, I thought they might just be annoying and make the shower go cold. I wasn't expecting the full Poltergeist imitation. "In the name of the Father, the Son, and the Holy Spirit, I command you to leave this house."

The ghost froze, its bruised jaw dropping in shock. Then its milky eyes flared, and it disappeared. I waited, breathing shallow and fast as I waited for it to reappear. It could be a trick. I counted, and at twenty, I figured it was gone. The ghost couldn't have been as surprised as I was that it had worked. I wasn't exactly Joan of Arc with the faith. Before I could say anything else, I heard the creak of stairs.

"Crap," I hissed. I shook out my comforter like a bullfighter's cape and tossed it over the pile of junk on my floor as Mom knocked.

"Bridget, are you all right?" Mom said. "I thought I heard something fall."

"Uhhh…" Salt stuck to my feet, turning to a sludgy mess as I stepped back into a puddle of spilled holy water. "Something scared me. A spider. Big one. I knocked over my table killing it."

"Are you sure?"

"I'm sure. Thanks Mom," I said, opening the door enough to peek out. I gave her a manic grin and a thumbs up. "I'm good."

"Okay," she said hesitantly, giving me a suspicious look. "Try to keep it down, Colin's sleeping."

Of course. Precious needed his beauty sleep. "Gotcha. Night."

"Sleep tight."

Doubtful, Mom.

I had no intention of going back to sleep after my rude—understatement of the year—awakening. Instead, I dumped the rest of the salt on the floor, making a four-inch thick circle around the bed as I muttered, "Oh my God, oh my God." When I hit the wall, I turned around and started doubling over the line. The can lasted until halfway around my bed.

Every light in my room was on, but every corner swelled with shadows. The breeze was an ominous voice whispering, waiting for me to close my eyes before it struck. Screw that.

I leapt into bed and yanked the blankets up over my head. The "I can't see you, so you can't see me" strategy had worked fine for monster protection when I was five, and it was strangely comforting now. A moment later, I snaked my hand out to grab the plastic bottle of holy water from the nightstand and curled up with it like a teddy bear.

"Kale?" I said, my voice high and shaky. "Kale, if you're anywhere nearby, you better get your little Guardian ass here right now, so help me God, or whoever your boss is." I kept calling him quietly, his name blurring into a mumbling prayer as my heart raced. Maybe it was all a really bad dream, and I was going to wake up any second now to my alarm. Yeah. Right.

Another creak shattered the silence. I thrust the bottle out and brandished it as I threw the blanket off. "Get the hell out of—"

65

"For God's sake, what?"

Kale materialized at the end of my bed. He was dressed in his usual white clothes, feet bare and dark hair messy. He also looked mad, which somehow made everything worse. This was *not* my fault. The temperature in my room dropped as he paced back and forth.

I immediately burst into tears and clapped my hands over my face. "There was a ghost."

"Kind of old news, Bridget."

"Not this one," I blurted into my cupped hands. Oh yeah, I was doing a full-on ugly cry now. Through snot-filled sobs, I described what had happened. Finally, he sighed and the cold in the room lifted.

"All right, kiddo, you're fine," he said. "You banished it, huh?"

"Yeah," I said, scrubbing at my eyes with my sleeve. It left crescent streaks of mascara but I couldn't even manage weak irritation at the stains. "It was so..."

The right word eluded me. Scary didn't seem right, almost insulting and disrespectful in its small scale. Whatever happened to that ghost was in a whole different universe from scary. Its mangled face was burned into my vision, as clear as drowned Mia's.

"It must have been a new death," Kale mused as he paced my room, carefully avoiding the salt line. As he walked, I noticed he didn't quite touch the floor. His luminous bare feet floated a few inches above the ground. "They're usually confused."

"Why would it try to hurt me, though?"

"It probably didn't mean to," Kale said.

I could still feel its cold hands around my neck. If it hadn't meant to hurt me, that was one hell of an accident. I told Kale as much, but he was obnoxiously casual considering I'd almost just joined the Ghost Club.

"Most ghosts carry over an imprint of their final moments. If it died violently, it's not going to be peaceful in death. Sounds like it was trying to communicate with you, but it couldn't, so it tried to throttle you into understanding. I know it doesn't make you feel any better, but it probably didn't set out to hurt you."

"I don't know."

"It'll be all right," he said. "Do you want me to stay and keep an eye on you?"

"You don't have places to be?"

"Guardian, remember?" he said with a sweet smile. "Kind of my job."

For one stupid, irrational moment, I looked at that smile and wondered what his lips tasted like. Wow, fear could do crazy things to your brain. My brain cells were currently marinated in a high-octane cocktail of adrenaline, exhaustion, and sheer terror. Any lustful thoughts were not at all my fault. Seriously.

Kale smirked at me, and I was instantly mortified at the idea he had read my thoughts. But if he had, he wasn't saying anything. Instead he held out one hand, and my *Hamlet* book drifted out of the pile of junk the ghost had knocked off my desk. The pages fluttered as the book floated over Kale's open palm. "Ah, *Hamlet.*"

"You know *Hamlet?*"

"I saw it a long time ago. At the Globe, in fact. To be, or not to be," he began, reading the famed monologue as he paced back and forth. "Whether tis nobler in the mind to suffer the slings and arrows of outrageous fortune..."

I settled back into my bed, tucking my covers tight under my chin as I let his voice wash over me like a soothing song. As lullabies went, it was pretty weird, but beggars–and I was a pro beggar at that point–can't be choosers. Before long, I drifted off to a fitful sleep.

CHAPTER SEVEN

WHEN I WOKE to a screeching alarm in the morning, I sat up to see the aftermath of an indoor tornado. My laptop was buried under paperbacks with bent covers, all sprinkled with a grainy flurry of salt. The water-spotted comforter was crooked, and throw pillows stood around the bed like cushioned tombstones. Crushed sage leaves lay in puzzle piece fragments around the rug.

Not a dream, then.

I felt strangely self-conscious as I got out of bed. Sleep had come quickly, but I'd gone to sleep with Kale watching over me. God, I hoped I hadn't snored or farted or something. He was a ghost and by most rational definitions non-existent, but he *was* undeniably hot. And was I setting back the feminist movement by feeling so comforted by the presence of a male entity best described as "yummy?"

"Screw it," I muttered. If it was wrong, then forget being right.

I scooped up an armful of books and tossed them onto my bed. With a sigh, I dropped to my knees and swept the salt into a big, dingy pile in the middle of the room. I shook out my shaggy violet rug and carefully arranged it over the pile. Except for the conspicuously empty bookshelf over my desk, the room looked almost normal.

My morning routine was a streamlined fifteen minute process. I could do it half asleep, and did just that most days. However, halfway through the makeup stage–wash face, cover up obnoxious zit on my forehead–I remembered that I was supposed to be photographed that afternoon for the Fall Court bulletin board. My eyes were ringed in puffy crescents of shadow. My nose and cheeks were blotchy and red from crying. If Merriam-Webster needed a picture for the word *haggard*, my reflection today was it.

With a hint of optimism, I dug out an old curling iron to attempt a salvage operation on my hair. Just as the orange light began to blink, I heard the low rumble of Emily's car in the driveway, followed by a shrill honk. I yanked the plug out of the wall and grabbed a ponytail elastic instead. So much for Operation Decent Hair. Maybe Emily could do something with it before picture time.

I was halfway down the stairs when she honked again. "Chill," I muttered. She was awfully impatient considering she was ten minutes late. I grabbed a granola bar out of the cabinet and sprinted out the front door. I yanked the car door open and said, "Hey, I need you to—"

"I called you like a hundred times last night," she interrupted. "Where were you?"

"My phone died," I said. And also, I was busy starring in an indie horror movie. But that was normal teenager stuff. I mean, getting choked halfway to blackout by a vengeful spirit was nothing compared to a zit on picture day, right? "What happened?"

"So Kari decided all of a sudden to be parent of the freaking year last night and wouldn't let me go to the concert," she said. I frantically buckled up as she peeled out of the driveway. Her tires screeched as she threw the car back into drive. I lurched forward as she stomped the gas. "I'm literally dressed and about to walk out the door when she stops me."

"Bus—" I warned, gripping the door handle as she swerved around the school bus slowing ahead.

"I know!" she snapped. "Anyway, I seriously spent like three hours getting ready. Hachi was on her way, and Kari walks in my room. And she

70

was all, 'Emily, you need to get these grades up,' and I was all, 'you couldn't think to tell me this before the night of the freaking concert?'"

"That sucks," I said. Except the part where my night involved an angry ghost that destroyed my room. But I was completely and unsarcastically sympathetic. *Really.*

"It completely blows," Emily said. "I was going to just meet Hachi there, but Kari took my freaking keys!"

"Dude, that sucks," I said, bracing my feet on an imaginary brake pedal as she screeched to a halt at the end of a long line of cars in the left turn lane.

"I know, right! So of course Alistair hung around and did a Q&A with all the VIP bracelet people." She held up her skinny wrist to show me the blue rubber bracelet. "Which I spent fifty-two dollars on, and do you think Kari's going to refund me? Hell no. I could have been talking and flirting with freaking Alistair Montblanc, and I had to sit at the kitchen table writing a paper. By *hand!*"

"That super sucks," I said, though I honestly couldn't have cared less.

"I swear, I'm going to take off and live with Aunt Stacey," Emily said as she accelerated through a yellow arrow turning red. It left her car hanging halfway in the intersection and prompted a chorus of honks until she scooted up within inches of the red pickup truck in front of us. "Chill out, assholes!"

Must not argue, I told myself. It was best to let Hurricane Emily run its course and blow over. As for the running away threat, I wasn't concerned. That was the very definition of an idle threat. Emily threatened to run away to her Aunt Stacey's at least four times a year. She'd actually done it once last year, right after getting her car. After her mom had the nerve to take her keys for breaking her eleven o'clock curfew for the fifth time, Emily skipped school and drove nine hours straight to Orlando. The engine hadn't even gotten cool when Stacey handed her a peanut butter sandwich and twenty bucks for gas, locked the front door, and made her turn around and go home. "Your mom is—"

"Don't even," Emily said, raising her finger to point at me.

"Being a total cow," I finished.

"Seriously!" Emily said. "Ugh."

She complained all the way to the next traffic light. By then, I felt I had been the supportive best friend long enough. "Hey, I have to get my picture taken at lunch. Can you do my makeup so I don't look like crap next to the rest of the girls?"

"Hell yeah," Emily said. "I don't have all my stuff, but I should have plenty to make you hot. I mean, not that you're—"

"I know," I said with a laugh.

"Yeah, we can do a smoky eye and some nice glossy lips. And I can tease your hair, and...crap."

"Crap? In my hair?"

"Gross, Bridget," she said, but she smiled, her outrage with Kari suddenly forgotten. "No, crap, because I'm supposed to go check in with the counselor at the beginning of lunch."

"That time of the month?"

Since she ran away last year, she had to go talk to a counselor a couple times a month to check up on what she was up to. That was part of the deal with Kari, or she could say goodbye to her car. So Emily told them whatever they wanted to hear just to get out as quickly as possible. After six months of Mom-mandated therapy and group talk and support groups and every kind of talk-it-out thing there was, I'd learned a thing or two about that.

"Even less fun than the other one," she said. "But I'll meet you in the bathroom by the art room as soon as I'm out."

"Sounds good," I said. "See you then."

We parted when we got in the building. Emily had Spanish first period, and I had US History on the opposite end of the school. The crowd of kids around me annoyed me with their conversations about boyfriends and the tests they hadn't studied for. It was all so normal. *I bet none of them got woken up by a ghost*, I thought. Even so, I couldn't muster much of my usual self-pity for being a freak. All I could think about was the huge unanswered question: *what the hell was going on?*

The shrill warning bell jarred me from a daze, and I sprinted down the hall to class. I might as well have stayed home that morning for all I learned in my first three classes. But to be fair, even Girl Genius Macie Reynolds and her bionic Bic couldn't have kept up with taking notes in US History after last night.

Most of the ghosts I encountered weren't nearly that *fresh*, for lack of a less disgusting word. No, this was something new altogether, and I didn't like new when it came to this. It made me that much happier to be getting rid of this curse next week.

Lunch couldn't arrive soon enough. As soon as the fourth period bell rang, I trudged toward the bathroom in the art hall. I had a text from Emily saying, *See u @ lunch!* She would be in the office for at least ten minutes, long enough to convince the counselor she wasn't a flight risk.

The bathroom was empty, but it reeked of cotton-candy body spray that didn't quite mask the scent of fresh cigarette smoke. The middle sink was still running as I leaned over to examine my face in the mirror. Well, a beauty fairy hadn't visited while I wasn't looking. I still looked exhausted. Haunted, even.

I used to be kind of pretty. No one would call me gorgeous, but with a little effort I looked okay. I had the Young family hair: thick, stick straight and glossy brown like Valerie's, like our dad's and his mother's before it turned white. But since Val's accident, I lost interest in dressing up and looking cute for school. What was the point? I didn't have the energy or the interest to primp every day. Besides, who was I trying to impress?

Up close to the mirror, the bags under my eyes looked like thick smudges of dirt. My overgrown eyebrows needed some serious TLC, and I had the beginnings of a zit on my chin. Awesome.

"Ugh," I said, dabbing at the dark circles like I could rub them away. Just because I didn't care about dressing up didn't mean I wanted to have my picture posted in the main office looking like a mug shot from the Jail Report. I started combing my fingers through my hair while I waited for Emily. I needed all the help I could get.

The mirror fogged, turning me into a featureless shadow as I paused, fingers halfway through a big hank of hair at the back of my head. While I rarely made the mistakes of doomed horror movie characters, I slipped up this time. Come on, I was only human, and a teenager at that. It was practically my destiny to make stupid mistakes.

I looked up at the unfogged corner of the mirror, and saw a gory specter peeking over my shoulder. My legs went rubbery and loose as I whirled to see the bloody apparition coming for me. I didn't waste time screaming and bolted toward the door. The ghost disappeared, and a freezing wind buffeted me, powerful enough to blow a stall door open with a metallic *clang*. A big brown trash can flew from the corner into my path, spilling out a mound of scratchy brown paper towels. My foot slipped on the trash, and I went down hard.

74

"Kale?" I said in a weak voice. The ghost stood in the doorway, its cloudy eyes pulsing slowly like there was a light flickering behind them. I scrambled to my feet and backed away, but it matched me step for step. Cold kissed the back of my neck as I reversed into the cinderblock wall. My heart pounded so fast that I felt light-headed. I didn't have anything from my ghost kit here—no salt, no holy water, no nothing. But the ghost didn't know that.

"I'll banish you again," I bluffed. "I mean it. I have the power of God on my side."

The ghost looked surprised for a moment, but advanced again when I didn't yank a cross from my pocket.

"Get back!" I told it. "I'm warning you."

Unless I wanted to rush the ghost and risk getting strangled to death, I had no way out. The best option I could see was screaming bloody murder. At this point, I didn't care how crazy I looked as long as I got the hell out of there. But the ghost stopped a few feet away, its milky gaze fixed on my dropped backpack. It pointed at the backpack, then at me, then back at the backpack.

"You want something in there?" I asked. It nodded, matted hair swinging like tattered curtains around its face. "Okay," I said. "But if I help you, you gotta stop with the sneaking up and scaring the hell outta me." The ghost nodded again, looking as apologetic as it could with its bruise-darkened face and milky dead eyes. It looked so forlorn that I almost felt guilty for scolding it. *Almost*, I said. Evil Casper here had a good scolding coming after last night. "I mean it. I'll banish you if you do it again."

Once the ghost backed away, I knelt by my book bag and started taking things out. Math notebook, minimally used copy of *Hamlet*, bright pink flyers, colored pencils. A cold sensation poured over me like water, and I stopped with the pencils in my hand. "This?" The ghost shook its head and pointed to the flyers.

Sue me, I was tired. A ghost might have a perfectly good reason for wanting some Crayolas. Everyone likes coloring.

"You want this?" I asked as I held up the pink flyers. The ghost nodded slowly, pointing to the picture of Natalie. It took me another five seconds to put it together, which had nothing to do with me being slow and everything to do with me not wanting to accept what was right in front of me. "Oh God...no."

Please, no.

I heard the click of high heels outside the door. My heart thumped as I scrambled to scoop up my belongings. Whoever it was, I didn't want to have to explain why I was sitting on a dingy bathroom floor talking to thin air. With my stuff piled in my arms, I dashed into the handicapped stall and pulled my feet up onto the toilet seat. I swore under my breath as my eyes fell on the pack of colored pencils just outside the stall door. The purple one had slipped partway out of the package, pointing toward the stall like a neon sign saying "Crazy chick in here!"

The door squeaked, and there was a rustle of paper towels. "Bridget?" Emily asked. "Are you in here?" There was another rustle. "Gross."

The ghost–Natalie–was inches away from my face. I closed my eyes, but her face was seared into my memory. I would never forget it as long as I lived. Most ghosts wear their death. It usually starts subtle, then becomes more pronounced over time. Subtle was long gone for Natalie. Her face was a mottled topographical map done in blacks and purples, with sharp rivers of red where something–*someone*, I realized with horror–had sliced into her. Her formerly bright blue eyes were clouded over, completely white in their misshapen sockets. She prodded me with spectral hands. I had to bite my lip to keep from saying something.

"Such a flake," Emily complained.

Hey, *she* was one to talk.

An icy tingle radiated from her phantom touch as Natalie got a handful of boob. The after-effects were entirely because of her freezing hands. Not that I'd ever tell anyone that I had just gone to second base with a ghost. What the hell was she doing?

I mouthed "Stop!" and blushed. Her hands worked down to my jeans pockets. I squeezed my eyes tight and clenched my jaws. *Don't make a sound.* Over the quiet rush of water in the sink, I heard the wet smack of a lip gloss tube being opened.

Finally, the door squeaked twice in quick succession. I bent over to look for feet under the beige metal partition. Satisfied that we were alone again, I stood to look at Natalie. "What's with the grabby hands? You could at least buy me dinner first."

Natalie didn't seem to appreciate my weak humor. She held up her hand and made a circle around her wrist with the other. She pointed to me, made the wrist gesture again, then pointed to herself. As understanding dawned on me, I reached into my backpack and dug out the engraved silver bracelet I'd picked up from Michael's car. Suddenly last night made sense.

"Is this what you wanted last night?"

She nodded. She got very close to me again, and for a brief moment I caught that sickly scent of decay. I tried not to recoil as she traced a square area across my stomach. Her bracelet had been in the pocket of my sweatshirt, which was where she'd been clawing at me last night.

I held out the bracelet. For a single triumphant moment, she grasped it in dirty, trembling fingers. The glinting silver rose an inch off my hand. But it fell a second later, tinkling to the ground. Her face fell as she looked at her incorporeal hand, and we both watched silently as the bracelet rolled onto a crumpled brown paper towel. Her head hung down, hair concealing her face as she stared at her bracelet. I finally knelt and picked it up, not meeting her eyes. "I can hold it for you. Is that okay?"

Without looking up, she slowly nodded.

"I'll make sure Michael gets it back, okay?"

Another nod.

"So you're Natalie," I said finally. My last chance at denial flitted away like a butterfly when she nodded again.

For a while, I didn't know what to say. She'd been barely older than me when she died. Now we had to talk about her in the past tense. And I knew from experience that nothing hurt quite like that first "was" when you were used to saying "is." Worse still, she wasn't some ghost whose family had moved on years ago, a black-and-white photo in a newspaper obituary. She was someone's sister, someone's daughter who had been here just weeks earlier. The fact that I saw her was the death notice for what remained of Michael's naive hope. This would shatter him, and he'd never put himself back together just right. I knew that all too well.

I put my face in my hands, and desperately wished for it to go away. If I could've forgotten everything I had seen, I would have. I was freaking sixteen years old. I didn't want to see what kind of horrible things could happen to me. Most people had the luxury of being horrified from a safe distance. They would only see something like this on TV, and then forget about it as soon as they changed the channel. Everyone knew that bad things happened, but they happened *out there* to *other people*. This was staring me down, seeping down into my bones. This darkness was part of me, so I couldn't look away and pretend everything was fun and Fall Courts.

An icy finger poked my shoulder, and I looked up to see Natalie tapping me in a strangely normal gesture. As I looked up at her mangled face, I felt the trickle of tears on my cheeks, blazing hot against my ghost-chilled skin. She pointed to the toilet paper roll. I laughed despite myself. She was the dead one, after all. What the hell did I have to cry about? I tore off a strip of the flimsy paper and scrubbed my nose with it.

"Let's talk."

She nodded and managed to keep her hands to herself while I jammed all my stuff back into my backpack. After checking that the coast was clear, I headed down the art hall and out a side door to a rarely used picnic area. Between the weather and the smell from the kilns, no one ever ate out here. It was the perfect place for a conversation with a ghost.

Natalie paced in front of me, her dirty feet a few inches above the ground. The more I looked at her—though it was hard—the more I could see her pretty features through the mask of death. I had to look at her. *Someone* had to remember her this way so she wasn't alone and forgotten in her awful last moments. Her beautiful hair had been cut messy and short, and her blue eyes were clouded to fish-belly white, but now I could see the girl that had smiled off of Michael's flyers.

God, what was I going to tell Michael?

"Natalie, I really don't know what to do, or even what you want," I said, turning the silver bracelet over in my fingers and idly tracing the engraving. "What happened?"

She ran both hands through her matted hair, her eyes flashing like strobes for a moment. My skin prickled with goosebumps as the temperature around me plunged. She didn't speak, but in the back of my mind I sensed a wail of fear, like a distant sound that blended into the background noise if you weren't really listening for it. The rotten-corpse smell sharpened as she grew visibly agitated.

"It's okay," I said quickly. "Look, I'm sure you know this now, but you realize you're dead." She didn't speak, but her arched eyebrows and pursed lips said *no shit.* "Sorry. And I can't bring you back. You understand that, right?" She nodded. "But I'll do what I can to help you, okay?"

Before next week, that was. I hoped for both of our sakes I could help her make things right by then. After next Thursday, Natalie was on her own. I didn't mention that to her, but honestly, what else could I do?

"Do you know where your–" I broke off, not wanting to use the word. "Where *you* are?"

She frowned and pointed to the ground, then around in a broad arc, like she was saying *I'm right here, dumbass.* "No, where your body is?" Her shoulders slumped, and I imagined her sighing as she shook her head.

"Did someone do this to you?" I asked. It had to be that. Even an atrocious car accident–and I'd seen the aftermath of some of those up close and personal–wouldn't have been so precise and surgical.

Her eyes narrowed down to white slits as she nodded again. Her torn, bloodied fingernails drew my eye as she drew her finger slowly across her throat. Those were the hands of someone who had fought for her life.

"Do you know who?" I asked. She nodded quickly, then frowned and shook her head. "Which one?" She shrugged. I hated Ghost Charades. "Is it someone you know?" She shook her head–*no.* "Did you see his face?" She nodded, her eyes going distant again for a moment. I didn't want to think about what he had done that made her glaze over with fear that way. "What do you want me to do? Do you want me to tell Michael?"

80

That was when the tears started, glittering against her grimy skin without washing the dirt away. It was a thousand times worse than when she was choking the life out of me.

Ghosts were always sad. Even Val, who didn't hide it nearly as well as she thought. And they could never really get over it. After all, if they'd been at peace when they died, they wouldn't be stuck here.

Natalie should have understood that she was dead, and that no amount of crying would change what had happened. I got it, but it was easy for me to accept when I was the one still breathing. But Natalie was frozen forever in her terrible final moments and all the fears that crowded her mind as she took her last breath. And hers were obviously centered on her baby brother, who was unreachable across a gap only someone like me could bridge.

So watching Natalie cry almost broke my heart. She'd had an awful death, and she *still* couldn't rest. Her anguish was like a physical force as her clouded eyes spilled over. She covered her face with bloodied hands. My throat pinched tight, and I had to look away to keep from crying. It didn't help when I had the awful thought–did Valerie cry when she saw me? I hoped she didn't, because I had enough angst and guilt over the whole thing for the both of us.

The fifth period bell rang, and I let out a heavy sigh. *Thank God.* "I have to get to class, but what do you think about telling him? If you want me to, I will."

She shook her head slowly. "Don't tell Michael?" She nodded. "Then what do you want?"

She narrowed her eyes and pointed at me. She made a gun with her fingers. Then with a slow, but deliberate motion, she fired it.

CHAPTER EIGHT

MY AFTERNOON CLASSES weren't any more productive than the morning. Despite my best intentions to pay attention after my miserable showing on the *Hamlet* test, I was still reeling from learning what had happened to Natalie. When I got my progress report, I barely managed vague dismay at the two F's in English and Biology. Mom was going to flip out, but I right now I had Natalie and her ghostly gun on my mind.

I got called out of math class fifteen minutes early to have my picture taken. Since encountering Natalie, I'd forgotten all about the pictures. On a positive note, I was going to give the photographer some real practice on his Photoshop skills.

When I emerged from Mrs. Brasco's room on the vocational hall, Emily was waiting outside with her phone in hand. Her fuchsia lips were pursed, and her expression was a few shades shy of a glare. I couldn't blame her one bit. "Where the hell were you?"

"I'm sorry, I got called up to the office," I said.

"For the whole lunch period?" she asked incredulously. The hall stretched on forever as we walked farther apart than normal. Her arms were folded tightly across her chest, like she was holding back what she really wanted to say.

For a second, I felt a bitter note of resentment. *Say something. I dare you,* I thought. Instead of snapping at her, I said, "Yeah, something about my grades falling. I'm sorry I didn't text you." I glanced at her to see if she was buying the story.

She rolled her eyes. "Whatever. Kari says I have to come straight home and do my homework today, or she's taking my credit card. She called all my teachers to find out what I haven't turned in, so now I have to do it all."

"Gross," I said. Unlike Emily, I had figured out that I could skate by if I at least turned something in, even if it was crap.

"Seriously," she snapped.

Normally I'd get the full recap of her day; Emily and I didn't have any classes together this year, so she had to make sure I got caught up on all the excitement for the day. Her silence spoke loud and clear. She'd have to get over it, because I wasn't about to tell her I skipped my makeover to talk to Natalie.

My mind thoughts kept circling back to her. Trying to get her face out of my mind only made it worse. Everything, including my own angst over Valerie, seemed so stupid in comparison to the fact that Natalie had been murdered and expected me to do something about it.

The problem was that I didn't know where her body was and I had no idea where to start. Did I tell Michael? Even more importantly, did I tell the police?

Like an answer to a psychic 911 call, my phone vibrated against my hip and started playing music. I didn't recognize the gentle bass rhythm at first, but I knew it had to be Valerie's phone. I shook my head when I recognized the song. By the time Sting sang his first, "Every step you take, I'll be watching you," my sister had completely materialized on the other side of Emily. Valerie passed completely through a boy tugging his hoodie down over his chest. He shivered violently and looked back warily, then scurried away from us.

Val waggled her fingers in greeting as I dug out the phone from the side pocket of my backpack. Her phone was an older Blackberry, a Christmas gift from our absentee dad, and it was still covered in the pink rhinestones she'd painstakingly covered it with.

"You're still carrying that?" Emily asked, watching with thinly veiled exasperation as I pried off the back to remove the battery. It was the only thing that would stop the phantom music once Val got it going. She claimed she didn't know why the music started when she showed up sometimes, but I had a feeling it was one of the few forms of entertainment she had.

"What can I say? I'm sentimental," I said as I turned it off and put it away again. Sentimental was putting it lightly. "Hey, I think I'm going to walk home today."

"Look, I'm not mad at you, BB," Emily said, although I knew her well enough to know she was. She just didn't *like* being mad at me, and she'd lie through her teeth to avoid conflict.

"I know," I said. "I need the walk to clear my head. Mom's going to go ballistic over this progress report."

"Join the club," she said. "I'll guess I'll talk to you later if she doesn't bitch-slap you back to the Stone Age."

Whenever either of us got into trouble—okay, when I got into trouble, because Colin didn't blink wrong if Mom was around—she took the works. Computer, TV, phone, everything. In Colin's terms: the Cave Man treatment.

"Sounds good," I said. "See you later."

"Later," she said flatly.

When Emily kept walking straight into the student lot, I turned down the sidewalk that led out to the road. A constant wind from the passing cars whipped my hair around my face. As I twisted my hair into a bun, I turned to look at Valerie. I didn't bother giving her a hard time about her entrance music. "Have you seen what's going on?"

"With the ghost?"

"The ghost is Natalie Fullmer," I said. I filled her in on what I'd learned that afternoon, and her pale, luminous face went even whiter.

"What are you going to do?"

"I have no idea," I said. "Hey, could you try talking to her?"

"No," Valerie said. "I couldn't even get close to you while she was around. When you were outside with her earlier, I tried and ran smack into a wall."

"Weird," I said. It was more than weird; it was yet another way that Natalie was freaking me out. If she could block Valerie, did that mean her presence was a no-Kale zone too? Not cool.

"Yeah," Valerie said. "Never seen that before."

"Seems to be a lot of that going around."

As we approached the Otter Creek Road intersection, I paused with my finger on the crosswalk button. The bright pink flyer was still taped to the silver light pole. The plastic sheet protector was streaked with water from a midday rain, which looked like tears running down Natalie's cheeks. I saw her cloudy eyes and bruised face superimposed over the beautiful smile and clear eyes.

"Cross," Valerie said quietly.

The walking man on the crosswalk sign flashed, but I shook my head. I didn't want to go home and brood about this, so I turned right instead.

"Where are you going?"

"I have an idea."

A ten minute walk took me a half mile out of the way to the municipal center behind the grocery store. Val left me halfway there, claiming she was going to go look around at some of Natalie's friends' houses. I was dripping with sweat by the time I got there and desperate for some time in the air conditioning.

The complex was home to a bunch of government offices, including the DMV. I remembered going with Valerie to get her driver's license, and making faces at her while she got her picture taken. Of course, she still looked stunning. The police department was in front of the complex. Fox Lake was a boring little suburb, so they didn't do too much business over here. Natalie's murder would certainly change that.

The police station looked more like a dentist's office from the outside; it was a plain brick building with glass doors. The office was quiet, nothing like TV. There were no noisy phones, pissed-off criminals, or cops shouting orders. I wondered what it said about me that I was disappointed at that. However, it was cold enough to double as a walk-in freezer, which made it my new favorite place after my long walk.

A young cop in a sharp-pressed blue uniform was lost in thought as he stared at a wall of pictures under a plaque that said, *Some Gave All.* He looked barely older than me, with a head of curly hair and smooth, dark cheeks marked only by dimples. He didn't look up as I entered. Apparently there really was nothing to do here, if the cops were hanging out in the lobby.

A wood-paneled counter took up a good part of the lobby. A pretty middle-aged woman sat behind a pair of computer monitors, nodding her head to the beat of the country station playing quietly. She smiled as I walked up. Her engraved gold name tag read *Donna - 10 Years of Service.*

"How can I help you?"

86

"Hi," I said. "I, um, was wondering about a missing person." Her eyebrows lifted slightly as she gave me that look that said ...*and?* I took a deep breath. It was troubling that I was getting so quick at lying. "My friend, Natalie Fullmer, is missing."

"Fullmer," Donna said. "Fullmer, Fullmer," she murmured. She tipped her head as she placed the name. Her acrylic nails clacked on the keyboard as she typed in a search. Her expression changed as she obviously found what she was looking for, but she didn't give me an encouraging look. Instead, she frowned and shook her head. "The Fullmer case has already been closed."

Michael had told me as much, but I still wanted to poke around. "Oh, really?"

"The girl made contact with her mother. She's not a missing person anymore," Donna said. "Besides, Natalie's eighteen. She's got a right to go where she pleases."

I wondered exactly how Natalie's mother was going to react when she found out the daughter she'd washed her hands of was the victim of a vicious killer. I couldn't help but wonder if they could have saved her if only someone had taken the disappearance seriously. There wasn't anything Mom could've done to save Val, and she'd barely made it.

Well, it was too late for Natalie now. But maybe I could help bring her some peace. I took a deep breath and spread my hands out on the counter. I asked, "What if I knew something bad had happened to her?"

"If you know something, you're required by law to report it," Donna said, her tone suddenly sharp. My heart thumped as I took a quick step back. I must have looked upset, because she immediately softened. "Honey, what do you know?"

I sighed. What *did* I know? Rather, what did I know that they would believe? I certainly couldn't tell them I'd seen Natalie's ghost, so I knew she was dead. Well, I could, but down that road lay a very concerned phone call to my mother, followed by Round Two of therapy. "I just have a really bad feeling," I said. "I mean, the Facebook thing doesn't mean she's alive. It just means someone got her phone. Anyone could have done that, right?"

Donna sighed, and it was the same sound of exasperation my mom made every time she looked at my report cards lately. "Sweetie, I can't file a report because you have a bad feeling. If you know something, you need to tell me."

But there was really nothing to tell. I just shook my head slowly. "I guess I don't have anything then."

"All right," Donna said. "If you do hear something, be sure to let us know." She went back to her work, and I could hear the other half of her message loud and clear. *If not, go away.*

But I didn't leave. Instead I left Valerie peeping over Donna's shoulder while I walked over to the wall of plaques. The young cop was still lost in thought as he gazed up at the pictures, so I carefully sidestepped him. A dark stain on the back of his otherwise clean uniform shirt caught my eye. My cheeks flushed as he turned slowly and caught me staring. But instead of commenting, he dramatically puffed out his cheeks and tweaked his ears like a cartoon monkey while he jumped up and down.

I just gaped at him. What the hell? "Uh," I said as I watched a grown man doing a gorilla imitation. What kind of police station was this?

"Did you need something else?" Donna asked. Her nails tapped an accelerating staccato beat of annoyance. She didn't even seem to notice the police officer.

Son of a…two in one day? Really? The universe was just screwing with me now.

"No ma'am," I said. The cop stopped his dance and stared back at me. He pointed at me, then to himself, and back again. I flashed a quick thumbs up, hoping Donna didn't notice, and he broke into a grin. "I'll just be going."

"No rush," she lied.

When I looked back at the cop, I noticed another dark stain over the left side of his chest. It was small compared to the other one, but up close, I could tell it was blood. Something had gone right through poor…Officer Salazar, I read on the glinting name tag over the bloodstain.

Salazar gestured emphatically, and Donna's radio erupted in a burst of static. She picked it up and tapped it, then turned the volume down. The cop gestured again, reaching out like he wanted to grab my arm. The radio screeched loud enough to make me wince. Donna muttered under her breath, then hit the button and said, "Pete, when are you going to look at this damned radio? It's still doing that static thing I told you about last week."

I did *not* have the time to play charades with yet another ghost. *Sorry buddy, I'm all booked.* I turned on my heel and headed out the door. I froze when Salazar appeared suddenly in my path, shaking his head rapidly. He pointed back over my shoulder. I rolled my eyes. He clasped his hands in a praying gesture.

Please.

Even if he hadn't been dead, I couldn't have resisted the puppy dog eyes. I nodded, and his face broke into one of those full-face smiles that went all the way up to his eyes. He pointed again over my shoulder. My eyes followed his gesture to the next to Donna's desk.

89

After getting directions to the restroom, I hurried down the hall. Salazar did that flickering ghost run and reappeared way ahead of me. He whirled in place and gestured wildly to follow. Halfway down the hall, I glanced back at Donna, who was smacking the radio against her palm. She was completely oblivious to me, which was exactly what I wanted. I paused in front of the restroom door, which stood ajar with a hint of apple cinnamon wafting out.

But Salazar kept moving. Two doors past the bathroom was a closed door. The sign next to the door labeled it the "Lounge." Someone had posted a handwritten sign on red paper that said, *STOP! NO WORKING ALLOWED PAST THIS DOOR!* Salazar pointed to me and held one finger up. It was good that human gestures were pretty universal.

Wait.

I stood outside while he passed through the door. A moment later, he returned with a broad smile and made a "come here" gesture. I pushed the door open carefully and froze in place as it let out a loud creak. Salazar gestured again, and I tiptoed in.

The lounge was small and packed with old, comfy-looking couches. Mounted on one wall was a TV playing ESPN Classic. Another restroom door was opposite the entrance, and it was closed with light streaming out from the crack along the bottom.

Salazar stopped at a plastic-topped table next to the Coke machine and gestured broadly. *Ta-da!* A police radio stood there, abandoned next to a ring of keys. He nodded as I reached for it, and I hesitated with my fingers brushing the smooth plastic. What the heck was I doing? It was dumb enough to be wandering around the sheriff's office. I had to be triple stupid to steal a cop's radio from the lounge while he was peeing.

The toilet flushed with noise like a jet engine. Well, the verdict was in, and I was triple stupid. I snatched the radio and jammed it under my hoodie. The bathroom door swung open. A short, stocky cop emerged. He gave me a suspicious look, the crow's feet around his eyes crinkling up as he regarded me. "What are you doing back here?"

What I did next gave girls everywhere a bad name. But I had discovered a good policy when nosing around where I didn't belong. When in doubt...play dumb.

"Oh, gosh," I stammered, backing up toward the door. Without meaning to, my voice had gone up an octave. "I was looking for the bathroom, and I guess I took the wrong door."

"Yeah, it was the one you had to pass to get in here. That one that said restroom on it," he said, arching one bushy eyebrow. "This one's for personnel only. Sorry."

"Oh yeah, I totally understand," I said. "I'm so sorry!"

I banged my shoulder against the door jamb as I scrambled backwards. The pilfered radio was like a lead weight in the pocket of my hoodie as I hurried down the hall and out the doors of the police station. Valerie stayed behind, enrapt by something she saw on Donna's screen. With my thieving hands as red as they could get, I didn't stick around to find out what. Salazar was close on my heels as I speed-walked, and I didn't stop until I got out of sight of the station.

Just down the looping access road from the police station was a community park with a shiny new playground. The sky was gray and overcast, and no one was risking their playdate being rained out. The abandoned swings swayed lazily, rust-speckled chains whining in the faint wind. I found a green metal picnic table next to the jungle gym and sat down. Salazar watched eagerly as I took out the stolen radio. We both stared at it like we were waiting for a lottery announcement.

Nothing happened.

He frowned and made a twisting gesture with his thumb and finger. He tried to show me where, but his hands passed through the radio. He looked forlorn as he tried to touch the radio. He finally settled for pointing in the general direction. After he gestured to the knob on top, I clicked it one notch to the right. His lips moved, but the only sound was the creaking swings. Salazar was pacing two feet off the ground by the fifth channel and stirring up an icy breeze. Great, another unhappy ghost. Hopefully he couldn't shoot me with the phantom gun on his belt.

"—testing, testing, please let this work," said a soft tenor voice. His voice was staticky, coming through the radio. It was a little weird, but his lips moved right with the sound coming from the radio. It was quite a statement about my life that this was not even *close* to the weirdest thing I had seen all day.

"Holy crap," I said.

"You can hear me!" he exclaimed, then let out a manic giggle.

"Loud and clear," I said.

"Oh thank God," he said. "I've been trying to get someone's attention forever, and no one can see me or hear me."

"Yeah, that tends to happen," I said, watching him grin at no one in particular.

"But you can," he said. "I mean, obviously you can. I'm sorry, I'm just excited. It's been really lonely."

I had to smile. He was actually kind of cute, in a baby-faced sort of way. Then again, he was also dead, which knocked the smile right off my face. "What's your name?"

"Luis Salazar," he said, extending his hand. He gave a wry grin as he looked down at his translucent hand, and I just smiled at him as he retracted it. "Most people call me Sal."

Over the next half hour, I learned quite a few things. Most of them came back to this: Luis Salazar loved to talk, and he had a lot of conversation to catch up on. He had died nine months ago, the victim of a traffic stop turned ugly when his speeder turned out to be a drug runner. Sal hadn't hung around for revenge; his girlfriend and her daughter were caught up in a lawsuit over his life insurance. The intricate details went over my head, but it came down to the fact that he wanted to make sure they would be okay without him. Same old story, different characters.

"So, Officer—"

"Sal," he interrupted. "Call me Sal."

"Okay, Sal," I said. "No offense, but you seem to be pretty at peace with your death."

"Pretty much," he said. "Just lonely."

"Well, I'll be glad to come and talk to you once in a while," I said. I didn't mention that my offer was only good for another week. "But right now, I really need some help."

"The girl," he said. "Natalie?"

"You heard," I said.

"I heard," he agreed. "Unfortunately, Donna's right. Especially if her mother closed the case. If she's eighteen, she's legally allowed to leave. And if she made contact, she's not missing. This is a family matter now, not a police one."

"I didn't tell Donna the whole story," I said. "I've had contact with Natalie too, and I don't mean she texted me. She's dead."

Sal's face fell, and if he wasn't already a ghost, he would have gone pale. "I take it she didn't die of natural causes."

"Someone killed her," I said. "And bad. Really bad. But I don't know where she is, or who did it. And without that—"

"The police can't do anything," he said. "No body, no evidence, no case."

"And Natalie's not going to rest until something happens," I said. "Any tips?"

He pondered for a moment, pacing in circles around the park bench. "If you could find where her body was, the police could probably get enough evidence to start looking for someone."

If only it was that easy. I couldn't even talk to Natalie. And she had already confirmed she didn't know where her body was. I told Sal as much, and he pondered for a moment. "If she could describe him, you might be able to get somewhere. Or her location. Start there. It's better than nothing."

CHAPTER NINE

I MADE IT HOME a few minutes before six and found Kale waiting for me. He was perched on the edge of my desk, watching me with those eerie blue eyes as I gasped in surprise. It occurred to me that my life had taken a bad turn somewhere when I had ghosts waiting in my bedroom, even if they were cute.

"Do you ever knock?" I joked as I slung my backpack onto my bed. My room was still trashed from Natalie's midnight visit. When I kicked off my shoes, I felt the grainy scratch of salt on my bare feet. "You could have cleaned up a little."

"Not in the job description," he said.

"You know, for once, I'm not going to touch that one," I said as I flopped backwards onto my bed. "Guess what I found out today."

"Natalie Fullmer is dead?"

"Thunder-stealer."

"Sorry," he said. I filled him in on what I had learned at the police station, and my encounter with Sal. "You know, you could–" He stopped mid-sentence, and his handsome face wrinkled into a grimace. I had never seen Kale look confused. For a moment, it looked like he was going to throw up, if a ghost could do such a thing. "What the..."

And then he was gone, flickering out like someone had flipped a switch. A shiver ran down my neck. Suddenly Natalie appeared where Kale had been sitting only moments before, mimicking him down to the way her legs were crossed. That answered my question about her effect on Kale. Awesome. Maybe it was just psychological, but Natalie's face seemed cleaner now, and I could make out her features more clearly than before.

"I haven't found anything yet," I told her. The sight of her made my stomach start turning flips. I immediately looked around the room for my can of salt. Crap, it was empty. Note to self–stockpile salt ASAP. "But I went to the police station and met another spirit who said I should–"

I stopped, my unfinished sentence sparking an idea. Natalie looked at me quizzically.

"I have an idea," I said. She shrugged and watched as I took the police radio out of my backpack. I sat cross-legged on the bed and laid the radio in front of me. After switching it on, I gestured to her and said, "Okay. Talk."

Her mouth moved, forming silent words. The gashes in her cheeks flexed and opened like mouths, and I had to look away to keep my lunch from making a return appearance. The radio was set to Sal's channel, but there was no sound. No universal frequency for the dead, then. I gestured for her to keep talking and started flipping through channels again. I had gone through all them twice when I finally realized it wasn't working.

"Well, damn," I said. Natalie just sighed, her shoulders slumping as I turned off the radio. "Let me think."

The radio may not have worked, but I was convinced I was on to something. Valerie and Salazar had both communicated with me through electronics. Val's phone trick was more for her amusement, but it had once been the only way we could talk. Right after she died, I had to access Valerie's contacts for Mom and got my first voicemail from beyond the grave. When I woke up–fainting is a perfectly legitimate response to getting a phone call from a dead person–I actually spoke to Valerie for the first time since she died. Once I accepted what was happening, I could speak to her directly. My theory was that my brain had to find the right frequency just like Sal's radio.

In any case, most spirits needs were easy enough to handle without direct communication. And I had never spent enough time with another ghost to speak directly like I did with Valerie. But this wasn't like any other case, so it was worth trying to find some conduit for Natalie to communicate with me.

I looked around the room for anything I could use. Just inside the pocket of my backpack, I had my cell phone and Valerie's, which I laid out on the bed. I powered them both on and gestured to Natalie.

"Just keep talking," I said as I walked around the room, scooping up the other electronics in the room. By the time I was finished, I had tried my laptop, an alarm clock, the Bluetooth, and the TV. As late as it was, a trip to Best Buy was out of the question.

Well, it had been a good idea, even if it was a total failure. I felt defeated, but Natalie just looked pissed. Her slumped shoulders were thrown back, milky eyes narrowed to glowing slits as she stared at me. Not like she was doing anything to help. Ghost logic was not the best.

"Wait," I said, putting my hands up to ward her off. "Just be patient." She scowled and started pacing rapidly across my room with a cold breeze in her wake.

Shit, I thought as I hurried into the hall and opened the linen closet. The top half of the closet was filled with neatly folded towels and sheet sets in giant plastic bags. The bottom half was crammed with boxes from the old house. Just on one shelf, there was a white banker's box labeled "Christmas," a Crock Pot still in the original box, and a cordless phone set. The last caught my eye, and I grabbed it.

"Try this," I said to Natalie as I walked back into the bedroom. I untangled the power cord and plugged in one of the charging cradles. A few seconds later, the phone chirped, and I pressed the green button to turn it on. Natalie bent over and shouted at it.

Still nothing.

I returned the cordless phone to the closet and scanned the other boxes. There had to be something else I could try. Then I saw it: black messenger bag with V.R.Y. embroidered in pink.

Of course.

I put away the phones and pulled out the computer bag. When I returned to my room, I unzipped the bag and took out Valerie's laptop. The sleek red computer had barely been touched, as it had been a late gift from Dad for Valerie's birthday just a month before she died. I plugged in the power adapter and started the laptop.

Instead of the usual black loading screen for Windows, a flash of white burst from the screen. I jumped a little. As the light faded, a pretty brown-haired girl appeared on the screen. The red light on the webcam blinked a steady beat. "Can you hear me now? For the love of Christ, can you hear me now? It's like that stupid commercial, Jesus—oh shit. You can hear me, can't you?"

"Yes," I said, nodding at the computer as I settled into my desk chair. Finally, a break.

I looked over my shoulder and saw Natalie gesturing eagerly. I didn't know where to look; her ghost stood behind me, looking as freshly and gruesomely dead as ever. But her image, which was alive and well by all appearances, spoke to me from the laptop. Despite her clean and healthy appearance, it was completely disturbing.

"Oh, thank God," she said. She had a surprisingly high-pitched voice, almost like a little girl's. For some reason, I'd imagined her with a raspy smoker's alto.

"Oh my God," I whispered.

"Oh my God," she echoed.

"Oh my–what the hell, are we in a time loop? Natalie, what do you want from me?" I sank into my computer chair and hugged my knees.

"You have to find him," she said. "You have to find him before he hurts someone else."

"Who?"

"Who do you *think*, dumbass?"

"Hey! I mean who *did* it, dumbass," I replied.

Her lips played up in a smile for just a second, then she remembered what we were talking about. Her face slowly crumbled, eyes widening and jaw shaking.

"I don't know," she moaned. The temperature plunged as the screen flickered. I held up my hands defensively. If she freaked out, she might destroy the computer and then we'd be back where we started.

"Calm down," I said. "Tell me what happened."

"I don't know," she said. "I was downtown at Warehouse Eleven, and I stepped outside to smoke. Then someone hit me from behind, and I woke up in a dark place." She shuddered, and the screen flickered again. "I was blindfolded and tied up. I–" she broke off, and covered her face on the screen. Her wavy brown hair spilled over her pale hands. There were quiet sniffs through the speakers.

"You don't have to tell me," I said quickly. Morbid curiosity stops at a point. I really *didn't* want to know what had happened to Natalie. This wasn't TV, where you secretly wanted to know all the sordid details. Those were actors with fake blood and CGI. Natalie was a real person who died a real, completely horrible death. The only thing I would get out of her telling me the whole story was exceptionally vivid and detailed nightmares. Part of me could still believe that there weren't people out there who were capable of the brutality carried out on Natalie, "What can you tell me that's going to help me find him?"

"It was a man," she said, wiping her face as she raised her head and shook her hair back in a sassy, confident motion. Her shoulders came up again, like she was steeling herself against the fear. "Not very tall, kind of scrawny. He covered his face. But the night he—he killed me, he took off his mask. His hair was brown, kinda buzz-cut, and he had these deep scars on his face, like really bad acne."

"Okay, that's good," I said as I scrawled down her description on the back of a failed Spanish quiz still lying on my desk. "Anything else?"

"He was strong," she said. "Much stronger than he looked."

"What about the place where you were taken?"

She shook her head. "Most of the time my eyes were covered. I got the blindfold off once, but there wasn't much to see. There was a bright fluorescent light, and some empty metal shelves. It smelled weird, really strong but not bad. The wall I could see was all grimy and dirty, except this one light square right in the middle."

I kept writing, and I looked up to her when she finally stopped, staring off in the distance. "Okay, here's what I'll do. I'll make an anonymous report to the cops, and then—"

"No cops!" she said, and it was punctuated by a squeal of feedback from the computer speakers.

"But Natalie—"

"*You* have to do something about it."

"What am I supposed to do?"

"I don't know, but you have to."

"Natalie, I hate to break it you, but you're already dead," I said. "Nothing I do is going to change that."

A cold hand closed around my throat. Frozen lips brushed my ear. As my guts turned to ice, I remembered I was actually talking to a dead girl, not some random friend on video chat. Computer-Natalie leaned forward in the webcam, pointing her very alive finger at me while her dead hands sent a shudder across my skin. "I know that, Bridget. I'm dead, not stupid. But listen up. I wasn't his first, and I won't be his last."

"What?" I asked, squirming in her cold grasp. She wasn't squeezing to choke, but just to make a point. There was no version of this contact that I would have liked, as it reminded me that Natalie could do a lot more than make some noise to get her point across.

"He's already picking out another girl," she said. "Before he killed me, he said I wouldn't be alone for long. He was already looking for his next victim." She shook her head and released her cold grip on me. "He's evil, Bridget."

The word sent a twist of fear through me. Goosebumps prickled up my neck and tingled my scalp. "But what am I supposed to do about it?"

"Find him," Natalie said. "He'll kill again on the full moon unless someone stops him. You have to."

I frowned and opened the web browser on Valerie's computer out of habit. Of course, it wasn't set up to connect to our house network, and I couldn't remember the password since I hadn't used it except for the first time I entered it when we moved in. I grabbed my phone instead and searched for the full moon date.

My stomach dropped. The next full moon began next Thursday, the day before my birthday. The day my life was supposed to go back to normal.

CHAPTER TEN

I COULDN'T EXACTLY SAY I woke up Saturday morning ready for action. Waking up required falling asleep in the first place, and I'd spent all night debating a single question:

What do I do?

After a sleepless night of chasing my thoughts in circles, there were several things I knew. I had to call the police. I was sixteen, and I had no business trying to find a murderer alone. And I had to move fast. If Natalie was right, he was going to kill again by next week. Not only that, my ability to speak to her was going to be gone by then. If I was going to do anything, I had to do it *now*.

"Not *if*," I said to myself. I *had* to do something, because if I didn't, no one else would. How could they, when no one even believed she was missing?

First step: getting out of pajamas. I rolled out of bed and headed for the shower. I even put on a touch of makeup and pulled my hair up into a ponytail. See that, world? I meant business. After I dressed in a comfy pair of jeans and a t-shirt, I tiptoed past Colin's door and down the stairs. Mom was a late sleeper on Saturdays, so I could probably get out of the house to "study" long before she got up.

I stopped in the kitchen long enough to make some breakfast. My cinnamon raisin bagel was halfway through toasting when I heard the squeaky door open from the master bedroom just past the kitchen. "Crap," I muttered as Mom padded on slippered feet into the kitchen.

"You're up early," she said as she scrubbed at her still half-closed eyes.

"So are you," I said, faking a smile.

"When were you going to tell me what happened the other day?" she asked me as she popped a coffee pod into the coffee maker..

When you're a teenager, certain phrases from your mother make you freeze. She had just uttered one, and I frantically thought back. She hadn't seen my progress report, so that wasn't it. Most of the events of my last few days would have made her hair go gray. I wasn't grounded yet, so I had to assume she didn't know about any of the big ones.

The coffee burbled as I stood there staring. Finally I shrugged. When it doubt, playing it dumb was best. "What do you mean?"

She held up the orange homecoming packet. "You got nominated for Fall Court," she said, a broad smile spreading across her face. She sounded surprised. Thanks a lot, Mom. "Congratulations!"

"Oh yeah," I said. "Must have been a mistake. Bridget's easy to mess up, rhymes with–"

"Don't say that, Bridget," she said as she pulled down a coffee cup. I wanted to tell her *no, seriously, it's a practical joke by your dead daughter.* Somehow, I didn't think she would find it funny. "I thought we could go shopping for a dress today."

"Oh, that's okay–"

"I already scoped out some online that would look so pretty on you," she continued. "I also called Melinda and she's going to do your hair."

"Emily's doing my makeup and hair," I interrupted. Mom started to argue but I cut her off. "Mom, I promised her. You know she'll do a good job."

"Fine," Mom said. "But I still want to find you a dress today. If we head out early, we can beat the crowds."

"Actually, I have stuff to do."

She looked disappointed. "What stuff?"

"School stuff," I lied. "I kinda bombed a test this week, but my teacher said I could retake it, so I was going to study all weekend."

"Well," Mom said, looking torn. Considering how much she harped on me about my grades, she should have been ecstatic that I was trying to be studious. But she loved silly stuff like the Fall Court, and loved shopping even more. She used to always take Val, who could rival her for shopping endurance. "Why don't we go out first thing this morning, and then you can spend the rest of the day working?"

I wanted to talk to Sal, but that would have to wait. Mom had a point. I *did* need a dress for the Fall Court. I knew we still had some of Valerie's old formal dresses, but even if I could fit into one of them, I couldn't have stood the sight of it.

"Let me just take care of something, and then we can go," I said finally.

Mom smiled at me, which was such a rare sight that I felt like I had done something right for her for once. That alone was worth the shopping trip.

"I'll just get cleaned up real quick," she said. "Be done in fifteen minutes!"

Once I heard her shower running, I walked out to the porch and looked up the number for the sheriff's department. They didn't have an anonymous line listed, so I started to dial the main line. Halfway through the first ring, a thought struck me. What if they traced my call and thought it was a joke? That had to be falsifying evidence or hindering an investigation, or one of those minor crimes the cops were always threatening to charge unhelpful witnesses with on TV.

I needed Salazar.

I dashed through the living room and upstairs to my room, where I dug the radio out of my backpack and switched it on. I switched it back to Sal's frequency, then felt stupid as I pressed the Talk button and said, "Sal?"

There was no response. So it wasn't my personal ghost phone. Too bad. I called a little louder and nearly jumped out my skin when I heard someone say, "Bridget?"

But it was just Colin at the door. "What do you want?" I demanded.

"Why are *you* up so early?"

"Me and Mom are going shopping," I said. "Again I say, what do you want?"

"Mom and I," he said, with the snotty air of a grammar teacher. What a little dork. "Bring me a cinnamon roll."

"Please?"

"It's not like you're buying it."

"Neither is she unless you ask nicely. Ooh, I've got some power here, and Colin, let me tell you, it feels great."

He rolled his eyes. "Please, annoying and obnoxious older sister, get me a cinnamon roll from the mall."

"Nope, although you have a great vocabulary," I said, brushing past him. "And if you go in my room while we're gone, I'll lock you in the attic."

"Like I want to go in your stupid room," he said. "Loser."

"Geek," I shouted over my shoulder as I thundered down the stairs.

"Bridget, be nice," Mom said absently. She was standing at the bottom of the stairs putting in her earrings. I bit down on a *he started it* and just followed her out the front door.

To put it mildly, Mom and I had had issues since Valerie died. I'd done a lot of reading about grief in the last few years. There were as many ways of coping with grief as there were people, it seemed. Sadly, there didn't seem to be an "I See Dead People" model for coping, so as far as I could tell, I was alone on that one.

Anyway, some families got closer together in the wake of tragedy, while others were driven apart. One guess which kind we were. These days, Mom and I only talked when she wanted to criticize me. That wasn't to say things were quiet between us. Between my grades and my friends, or lack thereof, I gave her plenty to talk about. She didn't directly compare me to Val–wouldn't even say her name–but after every admonishment, I heard it. *Why aren't you more like your sister?*

So this had the potential to either be a very awkward or a very nice morning out. I knew she had to be thinking about taking Valerie shopping for her own Fall Court dress two years ago, because I certainly was. I just hoped it didn't get weird. We made small talk about the Court and the competition on the way to the mall, and I told her about my–okay, Valerie's–ideas for sponsors.

"Give me a couple forms," she said. "My office will donate. I can probably get some of the reps to do something, too. We have a bunch coming in next Tuesday." She worked as a nurse at an oncology center. They were always getting pharmaceutical reps with tons of swag. I hadn't bought a pen in like five years.

"Really?"

She looked at me like she was surprised. "Of course. Just remind me to make some copies and I'll take them in on Monday."

"That would be awesome."

"Have you told your father yet?"

"No," I said. "I haven't talked to him since last week."

Mom and Dad were on the verge of getting divorced and had been for over a year. They hadn't said as much, but they were already separated. Dad did subcontract work as an engineer that took him all over the country. He made a lot of money, but he was away from home for six months at a time. It had been that way for years, but he used to stay involved by calling every night and coming home once a month if not more.

But since Val died, he'd been distant, and he was obviously relieved when he left from one of his infrequent visits. Neither Colin or I overlooked the fact that he stayed in the Holiday Inn, since "there wasn't room in the new house." Not even in Mom's room, apparently. Now Dad worked in Washington State, pretty much as far as you could get from Georgia. He'd been home about a month ago, which meant I wouldn't see him again until Christmas at the earliest, if not April.

Mom nodded, her face stony. "Well, make sure you tell him," she said, though it was clear from her tone that she didn't give a damn if I told him.

"I will," I said. There was an uncomfortable pause. I didn't know how to talk to her anymore, so I just turned to look out the window. I couldn't tell her about Natalie, and any talk of school would turn to my disappointing grades. Awkward silence was better than yet another lecture.

The mall was just opening as we arrived, so the parking lots were still nice and empty. Small crowds meant we could get in and out quickly, and I could get to Sal faster. I intended to buy the first thing that looked decent and got the Mom seal of approval, so we could get on home. Once inside the mall, we headed straight for Macy's. After dodging a perfume salesgirl with a sample bottle, we took the escalator up to the dress section.

"Mom, it looks like a sequin store threw up in here," I said as I took in the blinding rainbow display.

She ignored me and headed straight for a bright blue dress. "Oh, look at this. Your sister–" She stopped mid-sentence and gave me an apprehensive look. "Sorry."

"Mom, it's really okay if you say her name around me," I said. We had to chase the elephant out of the room eventually. "She would have liked that one."

"I know," she said, dropping the fabric and yanking her hand away like it had scalded her. She paused at a pink dress, one of Valerie's other favorites, then walked past it like she hadn't seen it. Her next choice was a green one held on by a precarious array of thin straps that looked like a ribcage. I wrinkled my nose. Beyond the bizarre structure, Valerie and I both hated green. Not that I expected Mom to know that about me. "What color do you like?"

"Purple," I said. Wasn't that the kind of thing your mom was supposed to know about you? The dresses were sorted by color, with a rack of purples near the dressing rooms. "Whoa," I said, pulling out a dress that was cut all the way down to...*all* the way down. It looked like something one of the ballsier celebs would wear to the Oscars.

"Oh my," Mom said, covering her mouth as she laughed. "Wardrobe malfunction incoming."

"Seriously," I said as I put it back. "Okay, let's do this. Size eight."

Operation Dress Blitz commenced.

Without even looking at them, we just grabbed all the eights we could find, and had a heaping armful within a few minutes. Surely something had to fit. Mom carried them while I found a saleswoman to unlock a dressing room.

"Show me before you take them off," she said through the door.

"Okay," I said. There was something weird about trying on the super-formal dresses with my hair in a messy ponytail, but we'd get the idea. As I tugged my t-shirt off, a cold chill ran down my back. I yelped at the sight of Valerie's reflection in the mirror.

"You okay?" Mom asked.

"What the hell?" I mouthed to Valerie as I folded my arms across my bare chest.

"I wanted to help you pick a dress," she said. "Cold?"

"Bridget?" Mom asked.

I just rolled my eyes. "I'm fine, Mom. Pinched myself with a zipper."

"Purples, good choice for you. Try that one," Valerie said as she pointed to one that I hated. It looked like a beaded curtain with armholes. I pulled on the heavy, beaded gown and instantly hated it. It was cold and scratchy and incredibly heavy. Who liked this sort of thing?

"Do I have to show them all to you?"

"Yes," Mom said.

I walked out with my head down and said, "It sucks."

Mom tried for diplomatic, frowning and starting to speak several times before stopping. Finally she just nodded. "Okay, that one sucks. Next."

I went back in the dressing room and shimmied out of the dress. Valerie rolled her eyes. "You should eat more," Valerie said. "It would look better if you had more meat on your bones." Valerie had never been skinny in her life. She had that bombshell figure that had guys drooling after her all the time. I had never been a big eater, and with all the walking I did now, I was pretty lean. Upside, I had a nice flat stomach. Downside, I looked like a fourteen-year-old boy unless I wore a padded bra.

"Whatever," I said quietly.

I kept trying on dresses and showing Mom, but none of them appealed to me. Even the ones that fit looked silly, like Halloween costumes. I didn't belong on the Court, and I didn't belong in these big princess dresses. I made it halfway through the stack before admitting defeat. I rapped on the door and asked, "Can I just wear jeans?"

"No," Mom and Valerie said at the same time. Part of me wished Mom could see Valerie. It would have meant the world for her to know that Val was her accomplice in tormenting me with satin and sequins.

"I'll get fancy jeans," I said. "And sequined shoes. Ruby slippers, even."

"Bridget," Mom said in a warning tone. "Keep trying."

"What about that one?" Val said, pointing to one sticking out from the bottom. It was strapless and fitted tight, with a band of sparkles around the waist. I managed to zip it up with some shimmying and twisting, then stood back to check the mirror. Okay, I had to admit I liked this one.

"Take out the ponytail," Val suggested.

I did, and I had to stop for a minute. I barely recognized myself. The dress was slit up high, and it made my legs look good. With the sparkly band, it looked like I had some hips, too. If Emily curled my hair and put some makeup on for me, I'd look pretty nice. When I stepped out of the dressing room, it was obvious Mom agreed. "You look just like...so pretty," she said finally, wiping at her eyes surreptitiously. *Close one, Mom.*

"Oh, come on," I said. "I don't look pretty enough for you to cry."

"You do," she said. "I wish your sister was here to see you."

I expected a smart remark from Valerie, but she didn't come out of the dressing room. It was hard to get my sister to shut up sometimes, but she was noticeably silent about Mom. They had been close when she was still alive, and Mom's response to her death had basically been to pretend she had never existed.

"The leg is a little high," Mom finally said.

I stuck my leg out at her. "You think so? I don't think you can see my buttcrack yet."

She laughed and scrubbed at her eyes with her sleeve. "Not quite. I could get Donna from church to stitch it a little further down."

I nodded. "I like it." It was more important to me that Val liked it, and it seemed to make Mom happy.

"Let's get it."

Chapter Eleven

OUR "SHORT" SHOPPING TRIP stretched into an all-day extravaganza when Mom decided I needed matching shoes and accessories. I had never realized there were so many shades of purple, but I learned quickly that violet and orchid were *not* the same. After half an hour, I quit protesting and just let her pick things out. Then Mom sat me in a chair at Sephora and had one of the girls do my makeup, stacking up a pile of products in a basket in my lap. Several hundred dollars later, we finally headed home.

"Thanks for all the stuff," I said when we got home.

"You're welcome," she said. "I wish we did this more often."

"Yeah," I lied.

But I was exhausted. Valerie had followed us around offering her opinion on everything. Even with practice, it was really hard to not react to someone speaking to you. I had to spend all morning pretending to be totally focused on Mom while Val yammered in my ear.

"You know if you ever need me, you can talk to me," she said. "I know that this hasn't been easy for you either."

What was I supposed to tell her? As a matter of fact, I see dead people and now I've got to find a psycho killer before my birthday? Oh, and Val says hi! Instead, I gave her a tight smile and said, "I know. Thanks, Mom."

My arms were aching from carrying all the bags when we walked into the house. It was blaring with the gunfire and explosive soundtrack of Colin's latest game. He was still in his pajamas.

"Turn that down!" Mom bellowed as we walked in.

"Where's my cinnamon roll?"

"You might find out if you follow your dear mother's directions and then ask politely," Mom replied. Colin paused and immediately turned down the volume. He was an obedient little puppy, I had to give him that.

"Did you get me a cinnamon roll? Please?"

"Yes," she said, putting the folded paper bag on the counter as he ran into the kitchen.

"Thanks, Mom," he said, looping his arm around her waist for a quick hug. He tore the bag open and seized the cinnamon roll. It was like watching a velociraptor eat a bunny. Gross.

I ran upstairs and grabbed the purple backpack with my ghost stuff in it. Mom didn't know the difference, so I looked like the studious daughter as I walked back downstairs to the kitchen, where she was thawing out a package of hamburger meat.

"All right, Mom, I'm heading to the library to read," I said. "It'll help me avoid distractions."

"Sounds good," she said. "Be home by six."

I was barely out of the house when Valerie rejoined me. "Where are you going?"

"To talk to Sal," I replied.

Instead of walking to the library, I walked to the park by the sheriff's office. The park was crowded with families enjoying the sunny afternoon. Frisbees sailed overhead, and I narrowly dodged an oncoming soccer ball as I crossed a big grassy area. At the corner of the park was a single picnic table placed dubiously close to an overflowing trashcan. It wasn't exactly a popular spot, so it was perfect for me. I sat down on the sun-warmed metal bench and took out the police radio.

"Sal?" I said.

"At your service," he said. I heard his voice from the radio but didn't see him. A second later, he materialized across from me at the bench. He took off his cap and gave me a crooked smile. "Afternoon."

"This is my sister Valerie," I said. "She's also, uh...life-challenged."

"It's a pleasure," Sal said. He grinned and tipped his hat to her. He was, by far, the most chipper ghost I'd ever met.

"Nice to meet you," Valerie said. She settled onto the bench next to me, but her butt passed through the metal so the seat was nearly at her waist.

"Sal, I figured out how to talk to Natalie," I said. He sobered as I relayed what I had learned from Natalie the night before. "I tried to find an anonymous tip line, but–"

"They just set it up recently, so it's not online yet," he interrupted. "Right now you'd have to walk into the station to get it."

"Doesn't that kind of defeat the purpose of an anonymous tip line?" Val asked.

"706-555-9832," Sal recited. "Not when you have friends in high places."

I took out my notebook with my notes from Natalie's story. "One more time," I said. I scribbled down the number as Sal repeated it, then dialed the tip line. As I waited through the rings, I watched a group of high school kids playing soccer on the other side of the park. They were a hundred yards away, but it might as well have been a whole universe.

The recording picked up mid-ring. A pleasant female voice said, "Thank you for calling the Byron County Anonymous Crime Stoppers Line. Your name and number will not be recorded. Please only report in good faith. You may leave your information after the tone."

The machine beeped, and I took a deep breath. "Um, I have information about a missing girl. Natalie Fullmer was taken from

Warehouse Eleven several weeks ago. She was killed by a man, probably in his thirties, between five six and five ten, short brown hair, with deep acne scars. I think he's going to kill again soon." I hesitated. "Please take this seriously. It's not a joke."

When I hung up, I looked at Sal. He nodded encouragingly and said, "They check it every few days."

"Every few days? Shouldn't someone be checking it all the time?"

"Bridget, it's Byron County, not New York City," Sal said. "Since they set it up a month ago, exactly three people have called, and two of them were trying to get to the parking citation department." The fact that he knew told me he'd spent a whole lot of time lingering at the police station.

"Fine," I said. "When someone gets around to checking it, will they actually do anything about it?"

"I hope so," he said. "I'll keep an ear out for you."

"What else can I do?" I asked. "I can't just sit around for two days and hope they take it seriously."

"What about going to the club?" Valerie asked. "Maybe someone there saw something."

"You shouldn't contaminate the scene," Sal said automatically.

"Sal, it's been weeks," I said. "And it's a club. The scene was contaminated like thirty seconds later."

"That's all the way downtown," Valerie interrupted. "No car."

"Emily," I said and dug out my phone.

Emily answered after a single ring. "What's up?"

"You up for doing a few errands today?"

"Can't," she said. "I'm totally grounded until I finish this history project."

I heard her mom shout, "Which is going to be in January if you don't quit answering the damn phone!"

"Thank you, mother," she snapped. "Anyway, sorry. Maybe Monday."

We chatted for another few minutes before Kari yelled at her again to get off the phone. As I tried to think of a Plan B, I lamented my abysmal social life. I didn't have many friends, which Valerie helpfully pointed out as I thumbed through my contact list. Thanks, Sis. Well, there was Michael Fullmer. If anyone should drop everything to help me, it was him, but it wasn't like I could tell him that. I hesitated, then called him.

"Hello?" he said. My stomach fluttered when he answered.

"Hey Michael, it's Bridget Young." I traced the thick metal diamonds of the picnic table. *Don't say something stupid,* I thought.

"I can read, Bridget," he said, but his tone was mild, not biting. "What's up?"

"Listen, this is probably really weird, but I can't stop thinking about Natalie. Where was the last place you know she was?" I asked, even though I already knew the answer.

"Warehouse Eleven."

"Have you been down there yet?"

"Of course."

"Would you be willing to go again? I was thinking another set of eyes might help," I said. "I understand if you don't, but–"

"No, I'm game. I'm not doing anything anyway."

"Cool," I said. "I'm hanging out at the park. Can you pick me up please?"

"Give me ten minutes."

By the time I got off the phone, Salazar had disappeared, leaving me and Val alone. While we waited for Michael to arrive, Valerie walked right

116

through the picnic table and started pacing, her brow furrowed. "What's wrong?" I finally asked.

"I'm not going to get to see you in the Court on Friday," she said. She stopped at the edge of the picnic area and watched as a soccer ball soared in a speckled arc across a brilliant sky. "I'll be...wherever it is they go after the sending."

"Oh," I said. The ball thumped to the ground. There was a nasty, twisting feeling in my belly as I said, "I could tell Kale I won't do the ritual."

"Bridget, don't even say that," she said. She turned and shot me an incredulous look. I had to concentrate hard to not let out a sigh of relief. "You have to. It just sucks."

"I know," I said. She sat on the edge of the table again, looking over my head at the sky. Her body was translucent in the afternoon sun, like a painting on a window. Was it just me, or was she less substantial than usual, like she was fading away? When I looked right at her, I could see the deep wound at the base of her skull that had ultimately killed her. It was usually well-hidden, but today I saw the mottled bruising like splotchy paint around her neck. That was new, and like I said, I didn't like new.

"I guess we all have to say goodbye sometime," she said. I had always thought it would be a relief to pass on, so it hadn't occurred to me that she might be sad about it too. Afraid, even. I knew what was coming for me, but her fate was a mystery.

"Are you scared?" I asked.

She shrugged and said, "A little. Sometimes I think maybe there's nothing after this. Maybe I'll just turn to dust and be gone forever. But you know, maybe that's okay. There are worse things."

No. I had to believe there was more than that, that she would get a chance to be happy somewhere after this. It would be so cosmically unfair if she only got those cruelly short seventeen years and then disappeared into oblivion. There *had* to be something else.

"I hope not," I said. "It seems like most of the spirits are pretty peaceful when they go on." She nodded, but didn't respond.

The selfish part of me wanted to keep her around. If I couldn't have Valerie alive, I wanted her spirit around to give me advice and tell me how to do things like lift my boobs in a dress or text a guy I liked without looking desperate. Assuming I ever quit being a recluse long enough to meet one. I wanted her to help me write my college essays and pick a major and all that.

But I had to say goodbye, or else be stuck seeing the dead forever. In a way, I was jealous of Mom. She'd dealt with the worst of Val's death. She'd gritted her teeth, yanked out that splinter, and took the pain of it. Now she was healing, although she had the scars to show for it. But me? I had yet to truly grieve for Valerie, and I knew it was coming, like a storm on the horizon. I'd been prodding that splinter, watching it fester and swell, knowing it was going to hurt that much more when I finally dug it out.

"Are you moping?" Val asked.

I folded my arms and laid my head down. "Yeah," I said, my voice muffled against my sleeve.

"Me too," she said as she mimicked the position and looked over at me. We sighed in unison. Some days, life just sucked and there was nothing you could do about it.

A shrill car horn signaled Michael's arrival ten minutes later. I stashed the radio in my backpack and jogged to the parking lot. Valerie stayed in the park staring up into the sunny sky. She claimed it was so I could focus, but she wasn't fooling me.

As I climbed into the car, I saw the toll Natalie's disappearance was taking on her brother. On a good day, Michael was a grade-A hottie. But today, his warm brown eyes were ringed in shadow. His dark blue polo was wrinkled, and he needed a shave. Honestly, I couldn't decide which was worse; not knowing what happened to Natalie or knowing *exactly* what happened.

"This probably seems really weird," I said as I settled into the car and buckled my seatbelt. It felt like a really morbid date. But hey, it was the closest I had gotten since I was in ninth grade. Michael gave me an appreciative look, which stirred the butterflies in my stomach. I hadn't gotten checked out by a guy in a long time. Good on me for not washing off my mall makeover.

"It's better than sitting around the house wondering about her," he said. "I still can't believe my mom is just giving up on her. Even with the Facebook thing. All someone would have to do is post from her phone."

Thank God I wasn't the only who had thought of that. "Yeah," I said. "But hopefully that's not what's going on. I mean—"

"It's okay," he said. "I just wish I knew. The not knowing is driving me crazy."

Natalie's battered face flashed in front of me as he spoke, and I thought, *I'm not sure you want to know.*   "I understand."

For a second, I saw the faintest flare of irritation flash across Michael's face. I wasn't psychic, but I knew exactly what he was thinking. It was what I thought every time someone said they understood how I felt about Val.

No, you don't. You don't have the first clue, he was thinking. But this time, I actually did. Maybe even better than he did.

The engine roared as he stomped the gas and merged onto the interstate. I felt clammy as the lines blurred ahead of us. , I sat back with my eyes closed. Michael said, "You okay?"

"Yeah," I said, sweaty fingers curling around the door handle. The door vibrated under my tight grasp, sending a sickening vibration up my arm.

"Wait, this isn't—"

"Yeah."

"Oh, shit," he said. "I'm so sorry. I should have gone on the bypass or something."

"Don't be. It's just a road."

I opened my eyes long enough to see mile marker 192 pass by in a blur. Just ahead, between markers 194 and 195, was the gently curving section of interstate where Valerie's car had flipped. She hadn't been texting or anything, and she wasn't even driving that fast. But ten miles over the limit was enough when she hit the standing water that hydroplaned the car. She lost control, turned the wheel the wrong way to correct, and it was all over. But it wasn't her fault. We'd have never been on the road if it wasn't for me.

Even though the road had long been washed clean, I could still see the glittering spray of broken glass and twisted metal. The guardrail was still dented; I guess it wasn't important enough to budget for that kind of repair. A few yards past the bowed-out section was a memorial, a simple wooden cross with the initials V.R.Y. engraved on it. Mom hadn't put it there, and she always wanted to know where it came from, saying she didn't want to see it every time she drove on the interstate.

I never told her, but I'd put it there myself a few months after the accident. Val's former boyfriend drove me around to have it made and then took me to the site of the accident. It wasn't right for anyone to forget her, least of all me. It was when I brought the cross out here that I had actually seen Valerie for the first time since she died. Now *that* had been a day to remember. Her boyfriend had no idea how right he was when he told me I looked like I'd seen a ghost.

"Your sister was cool," he said, keeping his eyes glued straight ahead. "I really liked her."

"Surprise, so did I," I said to my reflection. The girl in the window looked tired and forlorn.

"Sorry, how stupid did that sound?"

"It's okay," I said, turning away from the window and forcing a smile to my face. I hadn't meant to snap at him. "You really don't have to walk on eggshells."

"Okay," he said. "How did you make it through?"

I shrugged. I hoped it looked more casual than I really felt. "Didn't have much choice," I said. What was I supposed to say? *Well, actually, I see her pretty much every day.* "It was really hard at first, but it eventually got easier. It never really goes away, though. It still hurts every single day when I wake up and remember that she's gone." In fact, I'd started to sink deeper into that same sadness, realizing she was about to *really* be gone. Not that I could tell Michael, or anyone else for that matter.

"I just keep holding out hope Nat's going to come home," he said, shaking his head slowly. "But it gets harder every day to hold out hope, not easier. I can't quit thinking about it. Every time she ran away before, she'd eventually call me to tell me she was fine, no matter what. Why hasn't she called me yet?"

I took a deep breath, feeling sick as I lied to him. Was it cruelty or kindness to string him along like this? "I'm sure she will. You'll get in touch with her."

"I hope so," he said, setting his jaw. "So have you gotten any sponsors yet?"

"Haven't even started yet. You?"

He snorted in derision. "This whole thing is such a joke."

"I know right?" I said. "But my mom is all into it. She dragged me shopping for dresses this morning."

He smiled, though the sweet expression didn't make it to his brow, which was still etched with his unspoken fears. "I'm going to my dad's tomorrow to borrow a suit from him."

"Your parents are—"

"Never married," he said quickly. "I live with my mom."

"What does your dad think about the whole situation with Natalie?"

"Oh. Well…" he said, looking embarrassed. "He's not Natalie's father. Her dad's never been in the picture. They only met once when she was little."

"Oh," I said. My family drama seemed much less dramatic in comparison.

"It's okay," he said. "My dad is pretty cool. I hang out with him a lot, actually. He's always said that both of us could come live with him, but he doesn't have any legal claim to Natalie. I can't leave her alone with Mom, so I stay."

"That borders on saintly," I said. "Where's your halo?"

He didn't laugh, and my cheeks flushed. "She's my sister," he said. "You do what you have to." He nodded toward an upcoming green sign and said, "I think it's this exit."

"Yeah," I said. He took the turn a little fast for my tastes, but I clamped down on the door handle and stayed as calm as I could. The exit took us onto Silverlake Parkway, a winding highway that connected the suburbs to the downtown area.

"I kinda wonder if that's why she left," Michael said. "She and Mom got in a fight a couple days before she disappeared."

"Maybe so," I said. Ugh, was there a place in hell for people who lie with good intentions? Like, no pitchforks and burning but an eternity of accordion music and waiting in line?

Warehouse Eleven was actually a couple miles outside of downtown on the southbound side of Silverlake. Michael eased to a stop at a red light. Off to the left was a huge red patch of clay that had been bulldozed to make way for a new Costco. On the right side was a building that had once been a warehouse, hence its very uncreative renaming. By night, the whole place would be glowing with the UV paint that turned its walls into a glowing dreamscape of constellations. By day, it was unimpressive, with its dingy red brick and dull gray siding. The parking lot was empty except for a single red car parked in a handicapped spot by the front doors.

Gravel crunched under the tires as Michael turned into the parking lot. We got out and started wandering around the building. After a few minutes of inspecting the ground, the sky, even the strip of neglected weeds between the parking lot and highway, we paused and looked at each other sheepishly. "So, what exactly are we looking for?" he asked. We both laughed nervously. We were like little kids playing cops and robbers.

Well, maybe Michael didn't know what to look for, but I did. I was hoping for Natalie to appear, hopefully with some warning this time, and point me in the right direction. A business card, maybe, or a bit of graffiti that said "For all your murderous needs, call 555-555-5555!" That would certainly make life easier.

"Anything, I guess," I said as I kicked a pebble.

The club was one of the few places in town that allowed people under eighteen, which meant they couldn't serve alcohol. But the straggly brown grass was still littered with the rusty flecks of bottle caps and crunched brown glass. The walls surrounding the chained and padlocked front doors were plastered with rain-soaked posters for bands with names like Jello Massacre and Alberto's Lament. Broken orange plastic bracelets and crushed cigarette butts littered the sidewalks.

"They need to fire their cleaning lady," Michael said. His voice in the silence made me jump, and I let out a titter of nervous laughter that embarrassed me with its silliness. He gave me a look that was equal parts amused and incredulous. The half-smile brought out a dimple I hadn't seen before. My cheeks went hot as I heard my annoyingly high laugh echoing in my head.

"I'm going to go around back," I said, keeping my eyes down as I hurried down the sidewalk. I wasn't so silly that I was trying to turn everything into a chance to go out with Michael. But he was cute, and even if I wasn't at all interested in him, it was an undeniable law of the universe that girls do not want to look stupid in front of attractive boys. Or girls, if that's the way your cookie crumbled.

"Focus," I muttered as I walked around the corner of the club to the back entrance. A few feet from the door was a dumpster that reeked of trash and vomit—awesome—with mounds of cigarette butts around it. Most of the back wall was dominated by an elevated wooden deck. The latticed area beneath was surrounded by clear plastic cups. I bent down to inspect the debris, but found nothing unusual. On the opposite end of the building was a red painted door with a white plastic sign that said, *Employees Only*.

My foot crunched into a pile of glass. I looked down to see a bright pink streak next to my mud-streaked sneaker. I bent down to find the streak was

124

a feather. It was soaked with a dubious liquid that probably wasn't all water, but I picked it up anyway and brushed off the grit and flakes of cigarette ash. The feather was attached to an earring hook, nestled among strands of thin silver chain and pink beads. I didn't know Natalie's taste, but something told me it was hers.

I heard the grinding sound of a shoe on gravel and whirled to see Michael coming around the back of the building. I froze with the earring in my hand.

What did I do?

Seeing the earring would just make him think that something awful had happened to Natalie. I mean, something awful *had* happened to her, but right now he still had the option of thinking she was really off in Florida chasing down Jello Massacre or getting a new tattoo. This would shatter his dream. I jammed her earring into my pocket as I turned to greet him. Though it was literally as light as a feather, I could feel it weighing me down like a huge lead weight. "Nothing here unless you want to go dumpster-diving."

There was a crashing noise as the employee door flew open. A skinny guy walked out with a black garbage bag slung over his shoulder. His flannel shirt flapped open over a stained undershirt as he hurled the trash into the dumpster. Glass clinked as it landed in the metal container, and I got a fresh whiff of dumpster aroma. He was brushing his hands off on the paint-streaked overshirt when he noticed Michael and me. His eyes narrowed and he asked, "What are you doing back here?"

But I couldn't speak. My mouth was a desert, my throat a parched river as I stared at him.

He stood a few inches taller than me, and his cheeks were pocked with dark purple scars like a splatter of tiny bruises. His eyes were watery brown.

There was something predatory about the way he sized me up. Did he look like a killer? My suddenly shaky bladder seemed to think so.

"Sorry, we were just looking for her ID," Michael said as he came up next to me.

My mind screamed *Get out, run away!* but I was frozen in place. This had to be the guy. He could have been dumping her remains in that trash bag, for all I knew. The world narrowed down to the man's face as I committed every line and pore to memory.

"Come on, I got a bunch in my lost and found," the guy said as he gestured over his shoulder toward the club. "You wanna check?"

Michael looked at me and shrugged. "Let's go see," he said. The man walked into the building without looking back, but I didn't budge. "Bridget, come on. Maybe we can ask him about Natalie."

"Michael, no," I hissed. He gave me an incredulous look. Couldn't he see how creepy this guy was?

"Just go with it. It'll be fine," he said.

At that moment, I reached the point where horror movie fanatics would have screamed at me for being an idiot. Hmm, was it smarter to walk into the isolated warehouse with a suspected murderer, or to run the other way and immediately call the police? Maybe we could check with MENSA for a second opinion.

But it was different in the midst of the situation. What if he *wasn't* the killer? How crazy would I look? There was also something weirdly prideful about it, sort of like most people would go look outside if they heard a noise. Something bad couldn't happen to me, could it?

Natalie probably thought so too, a cold, logical part of me thought. I sighed and followed Michael into the club. At least I knew in advance that this guy was probably an axe murderer. Surely the fact that I should have known better would be comforting when he attempted to kill us both.

The club's interior was small and plain without all the flashing strobes. All the tables had been pushed against the walls. There was a pile of dirt and paper scraps in the middle of the floor. Instead of pounding club music or screaming rock, a country station twanged out of the speakers. A wide push broom leaned against one high-top table.

While the owner—Chuck Manson Junior, I decided—retrieved a box from his office, Michael took out his phone. That gave me two ideas. The first was to have my phone ready to call 911 if Manson made a move. The second was to take his picture for the police. I dug out my phone and pretended to check my text messages. Surprise, there were none. I opened the camera app.

Manson was looking down at the stack of IDs in his hands as he returned, so I only had a shot of his slightly balding crown. I held up my phone and frowned. "Dude, the reception sucks here," I said as I held up the phone and poised my finger over the touchscreen to take the picture.

"What's your name, sweetheart?" Manson asked. Beer-bottle brown eyes filled my screen as he looked up. I fumbled the phone and dropped it on the floor.

"Allie Johnson," I said as I stooped to pick up my phone. It had taken a blurry picture of a table on its way down. "What's yours?"

He looked at me like I'd been eating paint chips. "Carl," he said sharply. Killer Carl, sounded about right.

"Hey, while we're here," Michael said. "Our friend is missing."

"You tried a lost and found?" Carl asked without looking up. Michael gasped sharply, and Carl looked up with a sneering expression on his weasel face. "What? What the hell would I know about some missing chick?"

Son of a bitch. Who said anything about a chick? I gave up on the idea of taking Carl's picture and primed my phone to call 911. If it wasn't for Michael, I'd already be halfway out the door.

"She used to come to this shithole all the time," Michael said sharply.

"You know what, no Johnsons," Carl said, stopping his search halfway through the stack. He pointed at Michael with the inch-thick stack of plastic. "You can let yourself out of my shithole."

"No," Michael said, taking a step closer to Carl.

"Let's go," I said quietly.

"Look at this. You know her?" Michael asked, shoving his phone at Carl.

The older man's face lost its hard cast, shifting into an expression of confusion. Carl obviously recognized the picture, but the look on his face could have been guilt, lust, or maybe just indigestion. Honestly, I didn't care at that point. Adrenaline was drowning my brain and translating all of my logical thoughts into *Holy shit get away!*

"Is that Night?" he asked. "Got black hair and them weird contacts now."

"Natalie," Michael said irritably. "And yes."

"Haven't seen her in a few weeks," Carl said. *Because you killed her and put her in your dumpster,* I wanted to scream.

"But you know her," Michael said.

"What the hell is this, CSI?"

"How did you know her?" Michael asked.

"Cause I saw her in here hanging all over a different guy every other day," Carl said with a sneer on his face. "And if he was lucky, she'd go home with him instead of screwing some other guy in the parking lot."

Michael's fists clenched, and I put one hand on his arm. His muscles were locked and trembling slightly. He could have smashed Carl's face into the table without breaking a sweat, and the only thing that made me want to stop him was my unwavering conviction that this was a cold-blooded killer. "Now if you're done playing 5-0, get the hell out."

"I just want to ask—"

"Michael, let's go," I said, squeezing his clenched forearm tight enough to draw blood if I'd had any fingernails.

"Yeah, you better go," Carl said.

Finally, Michael relaxed, and he turned toward the door with a grunt. My knees shook as we walked briskly out the back door.

It was him. It *had* to be. Carl fit Natalie's description. He knew her well enough to recognize her picture and make comments about her boyfriend habits, and he had the demeanor of a criminal in my expert opinion. I wanted to scream, throw up, piss my pants, and pass out all at once. Instead, I broke into a run for Michael's car, heart thumping as I skidded in a patch of loose gravel.

"What the hell, Bridget?"

"What the hell, *Bridget?* What the hell, *Michael!*" I hissed. "That guy was creepy as shit and you were begging for a fight."

"He deserved it," he spat back. "I could handle him."

"And if he decided to stab us to death and throw us in the dumpster, how would you handle that?"

He just stopped with his keys halfway to the door. His mouth worked for a minute as he tried to think of what to say to his obviously crazy companion. Finally, he said, "Bridget, you don't think..."

Oh crap.

"No, of course not," I said quickly. Damn, that was close. Thank goodness he didn't seem to have picked up on Creepy Carl's "chick" slip. "But I do think it's generally a stupid idea to antagonize someone who that could play Low-Life Thug Number 3 in any action movie ever made."

He just laughed a little and unlocked the door. "You're really weird."

I slid into the seat and buckled up before I responded. "Michael, you honestly have no idea how right you are."

CHAPTER TWELVE

I F OUR LIVES WERE LIMITED to a certain number of heartbeats, then I probably used up an entire year's worth on the fifteen-minute drive back to Fox Lake. I spent most of the drive trying to figure out what to do next. Michael was talking to himself about who he could still call about Natalie, and I gave him half-hearted responses as I sorted through what had just happened.

I didn't even notice when we drove past Val's memorial. It wasn't until we passed the Cracker Barrel just off the interstate that I felt safe again, like I wasn't going to turn around and see Carl in the back seat.

"Are you okay?" Michael asked as he came to a stop in the left-turn lane, waiting for a green arrow onto Otter Creek Road.

"That guy just freaked me out," I said. "Sorry I got so weird on you."

"It's okay," he said, giving me a weird look. Was it pity or something else? "Do you think he knew something about Natalie?"

"Green light," I said. The car behind us honked and Michael stomped the gas. "I don't know. He just seriously creeped me out."

"Yeah, there was definitely something creepy about him. You're down here, right?"

"Yeah, but you can stop here," I said, pointing to the Kwik-Stop convenience store up the street from my house. It was a popular hangout for Fox Lake students, and even on a Saturday, there were a dozen kids gathered around a couple of pickup trucks parked along the side of the building. I didn't have aspirations of joining their social circle, but the walk home would give me time to clear my head. "My mom thinks I've been studying at the library all day."

"Oh," he said. "You want me to take you back over there?"

"No, no," I said quickly. "This is fine. She doesn't care as long as I'm home by six."

"Okay," he said. "Well, thanks for going with me. It sucks that we didn't find anything."

"Yeah," I said absently as he parked by the coin-operated air pump. And there was the awkward silence.

One of the boys sitting on his tailgate waved to Michael, who raised a hand in response. He turned to me, his face serious. "Hey, Bridget, can I ask you something?"

My heart plummeted. Did he know? How was I going to respond? *I'm sorry, your sister is dead and yes, that creepy guy killed her* was the only thing I could think of. "Okay."

"Will you be my partner for Fall Court?"

"Huh?" I couldn't have been more surprised if he'd said, *Bridget, I'm a woman.*

"The guys are supposed to designate someone to escort for the group pictures and the big processional thing on Friday night," he said. "The other guys are going to fight over Aisha Townes so they can touch her boobs. No offense."

"So I'm a last resort?" I said, hoping it sounded confidently self-deprecating instead of completely pathetic.

"No," Michael said quickly. "But I wanted to ask you before anyone else did."

My heart woke up and knocked hard on my chest. My voice shook as I said, "I don't think there's going to be a waiting list." Despite everything, I liked the idea of Michael–in a dashing suit, no less–on my arm. "But sure. That sounds nice."

"Cool," he said, his face breaking into the first smile I'd seen since we met. A glimpse of straight white teeth, a crinkle around his warm eyes; the smile was a good look on him. "What color is your dress?"

"Purple," I said. "Excuse me. Royal violet, according to my mom."

"Then I'll dress to match," he said, still smiling. "Thanks again. For everything."

Then, he completely surprised me. This made twice in as many minutes. I usually hated surprises, but Michael was two for two. He leaned over and hugged me, an awkward motion between the combination of seatbelts and a center console, but it worked somehow. His scruffy cheek was scratchy against mine, and I hoped he couldn't feel the thumping of my heart. I inhaled his warm scent of clean laundry. God, it was nice.

He looked a little embarrassed as he pulled away, and he said, "All right, I'll quit being all sappy now. See you soon."

"It's okay," I said. My mouth was disconnected from my brain. "You too. Later. I mean, bye."

My head spun as I got out of the car. I should have been excited. Michael wanted *me* for his Fall Court partner. Not one of the hot senior girls. Me! I was entitled to a girly squeal of delight. But the fact of the matter was, we were only hanging out because of Natalie, like a couple meeting on the Titanic. It was only a matter of time until it all unraveled.

The nervous flutter in my stomach was dread, not a new crush, as I watched him drive away. I walked into the Kwik-Stop and perused the sodas like there was some hidden advice or lesson in Zen wisdom to be found there. No profound life lesson in *quench your thirst*, so I grabbed a root beer and paid the cashier without speaking.

I walked out of the Kwik-Stop and into the cold apparition of my sister.

"That sounds nice?" Val asked. I jumped a little, splattering the foaming soda on my shirt. "Sorry."

What else was I supposed to say to him?" I slurped the overflowing fizz and coughed. If Michael had seen me struggling with basic life skills like drinking a beverage, he probably would have reconsidered his proposition.

"Something that makes you sound a little more appreciative of his complete hottie status," Val said. "You sounded like he was offering to cook you homemade brussel sprouts."

"I *am* appreciative," I said. "But it just seems weird when I know his sister's dead."

"Yeah, I guess," she said. She frowned. "Did you find anything?"

"I'd say so," I said, pulling the feather earring out of my pocket. I told her about Carl and his reaction to Natalie's picture. "It was him, Val. It had to be."

"Then you need to call the police," she said. "Trust your instincts."

"I *know* I should," I said. "But what am I supposed to say? This creepy guy might have killed a girl, but there's no body, so good luck on that case. I'm pretty sure there's no crime if there's no body. They'll just think I'm prank calling or crazy, neither of which gets us anywhere." I didn't realize how heated my tone had gotten until Val recoiled like I had slapped her.

"Well, you don't have to be snippy with me," Val said as she walked out ahead of me toward the neighborhood. "Newsflash, I didn't kill her.""I know, and I'm sorry," I said as I scrambled to catch up with her. "I just have no idea what to do from here."

"Well, you do need to call the police," she said again. "Once you tell them, it's up to them to deal with it. And you should tell Michael. He deserves to know."

"At least I can call an anonymous phone line for the police," I said. "How exactly do I tell Michael that I've seen his dead sister's ghost and that I've known all along that she was dead?"

She had no answer, and for once, we were on the same page. I didn't want to fight with Valerie, especially when we were in our final days together. So instead, I told her about Emily, about school, about everything that didn't fit in the bubble of *Serious Stuff*. It seemed to soothe her, and she seemed to be in a good mood again by the time she left me at the entrance to our neighborhood. Thank God.

Dinner was ready by the time I got home. Natalie was also ready, and she paced in the living room as we ate. It wasn't her fault, but her presence pretty much obliterated my appetite. She kept pointing to her wrist as if to say *hurry up*, but I shook my head slightly at her. She held up her hands in a questioning gesture, and I nodded. Colin caught me looking over his shoulder at the empty living room.

"Uh…what are you doing?"

"I had a really good idea," I said. "For a project."

It was a fairly incriminating statement on my typical behavior when Mom didn't even notice anything amiss as I sat quietly through the rest of dinner. After helping clear the table, I mumbled an excuse about finishing my project and ran upstairs. When I got to my room, Natalie was already waiting by the desk pointing at the laptop.

"Hold on," I said, pulling out the laptop and powering it on. The webcam software opened automatically, going full screen as the light next to the camera lit up. "So you can choke me, but you can't get the computer out?"

"No, I just really felt like waiting for you to finish family time. What the hell do you think?" Natalie said.

"I think you have no idea how polite conversation works," I replied.

"Well I think I get a pass for being dead," she said. I still had the double-vision sensation of watching Dead-Natalie off to one side while Alive-Natalie talked to me via webcam. "So?"

"Well, I went down to Warehouse Eleven with Michael."

"You went with Michael? How is he?"

"He's obviously hurting," I said. Her face went somber. "I want to tell him, but—"

"He needs hope."

"That and I don't want to look batshit crazy. Someone's updating your Facebook and texting your friends so it looks like you're alive. People think you just ran away again."

She gave me a sneering smile and said bitterly, "Girl who cried wolf, huh?"

"Michael says your mom isn't pursuing the missing persons case," I said, hoping it wouldn't upset her.

Too late.

The temperature plunged. I had never noticed it as much with other ghosts, but Natalie's emotions were like a volatile snowstorm. Whenever she got excited or angry, there was an icy breeze that went straight to my guts. Not to mention that ghostly B.O. "My mom is a total bitch," she said. "She's probably relieved I'm gone."

"I'm sure she's not—"

"You don't know her," Natalie said sharply. It got even colder. I shivered and hugged myself for warmth. Add that to the list of topics not to bring up with Natalie.

"Chill," I said. "Okay, bad choice of words."

"Sorry," Natalie said. Both Natalies closed their eyes. It took a minute or two, but the cold eased. Warmth crept back into my fingers and toes. If Natalie was going to be a regular house guest, then I was going to have to drag a space heater into my room. "Anyway, what did you find with Michael?"

"I found this. I didn't show him," I said, pulling the sodden feather earring out of my pocket. I didn't even have to ask. The way Natalie's l went wide was enough to tell me it was hers. "But that's not the biggest thing. There was this guy Carl. He was the owner or the bartender or something. Looked just like you described, and he knew who you were. Was it him?"

"Carl..." Natalie said absently. Maybe he had some dramatic alter-ego too, like Midnight or something. "I don't know a Carl. Do you have a picture of him?"

"I was too busy getting the crap scared out of me," I said. "He was way creepy."

"It's called the Internet, Bridget," Natalie said.

Oh. Well there she went with the obvious solution. I started my laptop and ran a search for "owner Warehouse Eleven." The club's website only had pictures of partying kids and visiting bands. I couldn't find his whole name anywhere. I did find an article in the Parkland Chronicle that quoted the owner, but the picture was of a slender blonde guy named Tom Winger. So Carl wasn't the owner. I tried "Warehouse Eleven Carl" but still found nothing. So much for that.

"I can't find anything," I told Natalie. "Can you go there with me and see him again? Preferably after I buy a baseball bat."

"I don't think I can travel that far," she said. "I was following Michael earlier when he came to get you, but it was like I hit a brick wall right before the Silverlake exit."

"That sucks," I said. Maybe I could follow Carl and somehow signal Natalie when he got closer to our side of town. And maybe he lived on the opposite side of town, which would put him twice as far outside of her range. As I puzzled through the situation, I got an idea. "Natalie, how far *can* you go?"

"Not sure yet," she said. "I've never really tested it."

"Do you feel bound to a certain place?"

"Not really," she said. "I usually can tell where Michael is, like a thread tugging me toward him. Even once I hit that wall, I could still tell which way he went."

"Okay," I said. "I have an idea. I need you to figure out how far you can go in all directions. Just start traveling and go as far as you can, then do it in the opposite direction."

If I got a city map, I might be able to figure out where Natalie had been killed. I may have been a D student these days, but I knew my math, and this was basic geometry. If I could find out the boundaries of where she could go, then theoretically the site of her death was at the center of that circle. That was assuming that there was some logic to ghosts, of course.

"Okay," she said. "If I go now, I'll have a good few hours. It's hard for me to move during the day."

"You didn't have any trouble the other day at school," I grumbled.

"Michael was there," she said with a shrug. If she'd felt guilty for her scary act, she didn't show it. "If you want me to go off on my own, I feel the strongest at night."

"Okay," I said. "This is a good idea, Natalie."

"I guess," she said.

"So, should I tell your mom, or Michael, or—"

"Please don't. Screw my mom, but Michael..." She sighed. "Don't tell him. I wish he didn't have to know at all. I wish—"

"It hadn't even happened," I said along with her.

The temperature dropped again as she bowed her head, both on screen and in real life. I mimicked the gesture, rubbing my eyes hard as a familiar melancholy settled over me. In a perfect world, I would find Natalie's killer along with undeniable physical evidence that would put him in prison for the rest of his life, if not in the fast lane to the electric chair. But when it was over, Natalie was still dead before her life had gotten started. Her brother would always carry the awful weight of his sister's brutal murder. We might find justice in legal terms, but it would never be right again, not for anyone. Maybe I was doing good, but it would never be good enough.

When I raised my head, she was gone.

I spent most of Sunday actually doing what I claimed: reading *Hamlet* and taking notes. I finished the play sometime around four, and started reading the Spark Notes to make sure I had really gotten it. I took a practice test online and passed, so I figured I'd probably be okay for Mrs. McDaniel's test.

After my practice test, I took a break to walk up to the Kwik-Stop and bought a map of the city. The little container next to the cash register was crammed full of them, and I realized there probably wasn't a big market for maps of Parkland. While I was there, I picked up another can of salt; I didn't want to get caught unprepared again.

Natalie returned around seven, just as it started to get dark. I already had the laptop open and ready for her. It was a good thing, because she was already talking even as she materialized. "Okay," she said. "I was all over the place. Get ready."

Sitting on the floor with the map spread in front of me, I had a pink highlighter at the ready as she talked. "I got to the lake, but apparently I can't go across water, so I don't know how far I really could have gone. Then I just started going as far as I could in a big circle. I made it to Mount Sharon High but I couldn't get out to the football field there." As she talked through the landmarks, I drew pink X's on my map. I had to stop her a few times to look up locations online before marking them. When she was finished with her travel report, I carefully connected the X's. It formed a squiggle that came pretty close to being a circle, and I sat back and looked at it with a triumphant smile.

"This is good. Hand me the ruler." She just gave me an incredulous look. Okay, that was a sure sign that I hung out with ghosts too much. "Oh yeah. Sorry."

I got up and grabbed the blue plastic ruler off my desk, then started measuring. I lightly penciled in the points of the compass and found a rough estimate of the center. The area I estimated was partially in Fox Lake and partially in the next suburb over, Marymount. I wasn't sure what was there, but this was the first solid lead I'd found yet.

"Let's go," she said, flickering over to my bedroom door.

"Are you serious?" I asked her incredulously. "It's almost eight at night, and it's dark."

"And?"

"And *you're* already dead," I said. "I'm not walking into a psycho's lair right now."

Remember that thing I said about ghosts not being very rational? Natalie was the poster child for the emotionally unstable ghost.

The screen went white. It felt like someone dumped a bucket of ice water over me. Natalie's hands reached for me, but she'd gotten me too many times already. My ghost bag was on the floor, with the holy water in the mesh pouch on its side. I grabbed it and turned to spray her in a single sweeping motion.

"Stop," I commanded. An ungodly screech issued from the computer. I reached for my other weapon, the new can of salt. I brandished the holy water with one hand while I poured a thin line of salt around my bed.

"Bridget, you're a fucking coward," Natalie screamed from the computer.

"Yes, and I'm also alive and prefer to stay that way!" I retorted as I finished making the line and jumped back onto my bed. "I promise you I'll go tomorrow, but it would be insanely stupid for me to go right now."

"Don't you care that he's going to kill again?"

"Of course I care," I replied. "But you said yourself he kills on the full moon."

"But—"

"And it's not the full moon. What it is, is eight o'clock at night and dark. I'm not going to snoop around alone tonight looking for a killer. Now get over it."

The computer screen went dark, and I turned to face Ghost Natalie. She shot me a glare that was actually frightening against the mutilated canvas of her face, and then disappeared in a cold gale. I was sympathetic. I *really* was. But it wasn't happening tonight. I may be a little nuts, but I'm not stupid.

Still, part of me couldn't let it go. What if he already had his next victim? What was he doing to her? There could be a girl, like me in every way, crying for help when no one even knew she was gone. Wouldn't I want someone to be brave enough to face the dark and save *me?*

CHAPTER THIRTEEN

I SKIPPED LUNCH MONDAY to retake my test on *Hamlet*. Mrs. McDaniel was in her classroom eating a microwave dinner and grading papers when I walked in.

"Are you prepared?"

"Yes, ma'am," I said. "I even put the phone in my locker."

She smiled wryly and handed me a test. "Good luck."

This time, the test seemed to be in English. I breezed through it, though there were still a few answers I couldn't remember. My essay was a pretty clever exploration of whether Hamlet was truly insane or simply feigning madness. I had a spring in my step as I handed the completed test back to her. Mrs. McDaniel glanced over it and gave me a quick nod.

"Let's see if we can stay on top of things from here on out, all right?"

"I will," I replied. "Thank you."

The bell rang before I could get back down the hall to my locker, so I just waited in Mrs. McDaniel's classroom for the rest of my class to arrive. Allie Williams was one of the first to arrive, and based on the nasty look she shot my way, she hadn't gotten over her outrage at not being voted onto the Fall Court. I thought about telling her that it was all Valerie's fault, but that wouldn't exactly help my case on the crazy front. I chose to ignore her instead, and imagined her expression when she had to hear them call my name and watch me walk across the field. It was beyond petty, but that didn't stop me from smiling.

"Bridget, you broke my heart," John Chang said as he sat in the desk across from me. "The movie was awesome and you missed it."

"Sorry," I stammered. What was my excuse? Right, Colin. "Couldn't get out of babysitting."

He smiled and shrugged. "Maybe another time. We're going to Giavino's after the game on Friday to celebrate the Fall Court business for Kristen. You should come." I started to answer but he held up his hand and said, "No pressure. Don't decide now. Just think about it and tell me after the game, okay?"

With all the drama of Natalie's situation, I hadn't thought at all about the game and Fall Court since dress shopping with Mom. I instinctively wanted to turn down John's invitation, but that was Freak Bridget talking. By next Friday, I'd be a normal teenager again, or at least in theory. Going out for dinner with other kids–*living* ones–was what normal people did.

"Afternoon, everyone," Mrs. McDaniel said after the tardy bell. She handed out the graded *Hamlet* tests and took questions for a few minutes. Macie Reynolds argued with her for five minutes straight about a wrong answer that had brought her grade all the way down to a ninety-seven– gasp!–before McDaniel finally told her to put her big girl britches on and study a little more next time.

"Our next novel assignment will be *1984*, as those of you with functioning optic nerves have no doubt figured out," she said as she distributed yellowed paperbacks. "Before we begin our discussions, I'd like to discuss the term dystopia. What does the word imply to you?"

"A failed society," Macie Reynolds said, her face still set in a pout.

"Dictators," Zach Waters said, prompting a chorus of responses from the class.

I didn't really know much about dystopia or myopia or cornucopias, so I tried to make good on my promise to Mrs. McDaniel by listening attentively and taking notes.

Wasting time

I frowned and looked what I had just written. I was trying to write "futuristic." How had I gotten it so wrong? The fine hairs on my arm stood on end as I went back to write.

What are you waiting for

My stomach plunged as I looked up. This time, the cold sensation wasn't just a chill; it was a bone-deep freeze. I gasped in surprise and realized I couldn't breathe. No, it wasn't just a shock thing. This was hand on the throat, iron band on the chest, complete inability to inhale. When I smacked my desk involuntarily, the entire class went silent, turning to look at me in surprise. All I could think as Mrs. McDaniel ran over to me was *I must look so crazy right now.*

"Bridget?" John exclaimed as he leaned over my desk. "Uh, Mrs. McDaniel?"

"Chang, buzz the office," she barked. "Now."

It's not real, I tried to tell myself, but my lungs didn't get the message. They stubbornly refused to inflate. My head pounded from oxygen deprivation. Then the world went black as I slid out of my desk and onto the cold tile floor.

When I awoke, I was in a dark place. Tiny slivers of bright light filtered through the open weave of the scratchy cloth covering my eyes. Something sticky tugged at the dry, chapped skin on my lips, and I tasted something like motor oil on fabric in my mouth, choking and dry. My mouth and nose were full of the stink of something old and burnt. Panic hit me like a wave at high tide, and I flailed in vain, discovering my wrists were bound behind me.

The sudden movement made my whole body hurt. Just moving my jaw a little to shift the cloth in my mouth made me dizzy with pain, and I could feel a stinging ache as wounds in my cheeks tore open again.

"Time to go," a calm male voice said. Someone picked me up, threw me over their shoulder like a sack of garbage. I tried to scream, but my raw throat barely produced a whimper. My head felt like a sack of concrete.

I blacked out again and awoke when something sharp nipped my wrists. My arms went free, and my shoulders screamed in protest as they were released from the tense position. Light flooded my eyes, and my vision was overtaken by pulsing dark spots. When it cleared a few seconds later, I looked up into a pair of cold brown eyes. Around the edges of his face, the full moon was a sinister silver halo.

"Good night, sweet princess," the man said. There was a sharp pinch in my neck, and he planted his hand on my chest and shoved me backwards. My feet slipped, and I fell back and back. When I hit the ground, it knocked the wind out of me.

"Please," I gasped. The roughly dug hole around me was shallow. If I could have stood, I could have climbed right out. But there was something icy bleeding into my veins, and I was so heavy.

"You won't be alone for long," he said. I saw one lean arm, sleeved in dark green, reach across the rectangular opening. The dark line of his arm cut the full moon in two, blurring so I felt like my vision was doubled.

The arm came back with a shovel. I didn't understand until the first clump of dirt fell onto my face. Wet grit filled my mouth as I cried out. My vision was already blurring, but I couldn't help screaming.

"Someone, please help," I croaked as my fingers clawed into the sides of the grave. Cold dirt cascaded down my naked arms. My hand found a solid root. *Thank God!* I started to pull myself up, even though my body weighed a thousand pounds. But a sharp blade fell like a guillotine. Blood sprayed my face as the shovel split my hand open down to the bone. The pain made me want to puke, but that was still a distant second to the panic that was overwhelming me. I was really about to die. "Oh God!"

He must have decided to grant mercy, because he grabbed my shoulders and shouted "Bridget!" But instead of the stink of motor oil and wet dirt, I smelled perfume and dry-erase cleaner.

I snapped my eyes open to see Mrs. McDaniel looking terrified as I begged her to help me. I just stared at her, breathing hard as I looked around the familiar classroom. Bright lights, ceiling-high bookshelves, whiteboard...no open graves in sight.

My heart pounded. I was drenched in sweat. My classmates were gathered around in a tight circle staring down at me. Kill me now. I couldn't even begin to recover, so I just lay there in silence, my lips clamped shut for fear of screaming again. Maybe I could play dead until they went away.

"Give her some room," Mrs. McDaniel said, gesturing back. "Sweetheart, are you all right?" She helped me stand up, not even flinching as her hand closed around my sweaty arm.

There was a damp outline of my body on the tile floor, glistening bright in the fluorescent lights. The sight of it, like a neon sign reminding everyone that I was still a freak and always would be, was too much. I burst into tears and shoved past Mrs. McDaniel to run out the door. As I sprinted to the bathroom down the hall, I heard her yelling at my classmates to get back in the room, followed by the chirp of the office intercom activating.

Great. Hadn't I already done the crazy girl act my freshman year?

I locked myself into the handicapped stall and pulled my knees up. The cold breeze across my clammy skin told me Natalie had arrived. My sweat-soaked t-shirt turned into an icepack, but I didn't care. I didn't even look at her.

"Go away," I said. "I got your message."

More than ever, I couldn't wait to be rid of this curse. Maybe it was selfish, but I didn't care anymore. Natalie was driving me crazy. I could barely sleep, and now I was freaking out when I was awake. Why was it fair for me to sacrifice everything for someone who was already dead? I mean, it sucked for Natalie, but she was dead and nothing was going to change that. The whole justice thing...hello, we had an entire *justice system* for that. Since when was I responsible for finding and punishing a killer?

Thursday night was like a beacon of hope, my lighthouse in the raging storm that had become my life. Kale would show up with the final instructions, we'd do the ritual, and I'd say goodbye ghosts, hello normal high school life. I just had to make it that long. That was going to be a challenge in itself.

A staccato rhythm of heels clattered against the tile. They were still for a moment, letting silence fill the room. Then a feminine voice said tentatively, "Bridget, it's Ms. Hughes."

"I'm fine," I said. Please just leave me alone in here. Maybe I'll come out in ten years when the embarrassment passes.

"Sweetie, you should probably come up to the office," she said. "Please?"

I sighed. I had to come out eventually, and forcing a SWAT team to come in after me would only mean more embarrassment in the long run. I looked up to see Natalie looking smug. If I could have slapped the smirk off her spectral face, I would have, traumatic death or not. I pointed at her and said in a low voice, "You stay the hell away from me, you awful bitch."

When I emerged from the bathroom stall, the counselor was standing at the entrance to the bathroom. I knew her well. She had worked with me right after Val died. Like Emily, I used to visit her a few times a month to make sure I wasn't losing it.

Yeah, *that* system was obviously flawed. Like Emily, I had learned to say what she wanted to hear.

"Do you want to talk about what happened?" Ms. Hughes asked as I followed her out of the bathroom. Her smart little heels clicked noisily up the hall, and I turned away as we passed Mrs. McDaniel's door. The entire class would be staring, and while there was nothing I could do about *that*, I didn't have to see them.

"Nope," I said.

"Fair enough. May I?" She held her hand out, and I followed it with my eyes as she held it in front of my face. I nodded, and she pressed the back of her hand to my cheeks, then to my forehead. "You're burning up."

"Must be getting sick," I said, already shaping my cover story. Did the flu cause hallucinations?

"Must be," she said. "Let's have Ms. Britt check you out."

Ms. Britt was the school nurse, a stout blonde in head-to-toe purple scrubs. Apparently business was slow, because she was organizing an enormous box of Band-Aids by size and putting them in a set of tiny, labeled drawers on her desk. She looked relieved to have someone walk in. After one look at me, she pointed to the little cot. "You look awful."

"Thanks, I try," I said as I lay down on the cot. Even though I knew it was because of Natalie, I felt heavy and exhausted. My stomach churned like a blender on high speed. I didn't protest when Ms. Britt stuck a thermometer in my mouth and stepped out to talk to Ms. Hughes quietly. I didn't have the energy to eavesdrop. I probably wouldn't like what they had to say anyway.

"Are you okay?"

"No more ghost crap today," I murmured as I looked up at my sister's glowing green eyes over me. Her left was now ringed in shadow. She'd struck it on the steering wheel in the accident, but her face had always been unmarked before. I was too tired to consider *that* new development.

"It's just me," Valerie said.

"The point stands," I said. She recoiled but I ignored her.

The thermometer beeped and I examined it, 101.8. I held the thermometer out for Nurse Britt as she walked back in.

"Girl, you're going home," she said. "I'll go call your mother."

She disappeared again, and Ms. Hughes sat down in her chair with a fretting look on her face. Her jewelry jangled as she crossed her legs and folded her hands over one knee. "Do you want to talk?"

"Not particularly," I said. She looked stung. Hey, she asked. "Nothing personal."

"I'm just concerned for you," she said. "Your grades have really slipped this year, and it's getting close to the anniversary of Valerie's death. I know you struggled this time last year."

"I obviously just had some freaky fever dream," I said. "That's a thing."

"Bridget."

"Look, what do you want me to say?" I asked, propping myself up on my elbow. "I just fell out in the middle of class and freaked out, and I don't know why. And now I'm going to have to go back into that class tomorrow when I know everyone thinks I'm a total freak."

"You know how people are," she said. "They'll forget within a day or two."

"No, they won't," I said. "They won't forget, just like they didn't forget when Valerie died. People still call me Girl Interrupted after freshman year, and that wasn't even at school."

"You can ignore what they say," she said. "Don't give them that power."

"No, I can't. You say that, but it doesn't work," I said. I realized hot tears were streaming down my face again, which just made me angrier. "And I just want to be normal again. I want people to see me and not even notice me, honestly. I would be okay if people looked at me and didn't know who the hell I was. I want them to quit thinking, oh, there's Valerie's little sister, you know, the one who lost it two years ago."

"I know this has been hard on you—"

"No, you don't," I snapped. "No one does. You have no freaking idea what I'm dealing with."

"Bridget—"

"And now you're going to call my mother, which means another six months of therapy I don't need, because I understand she's dead. I. Get. It. Valerie's dead and she's not coming back," I said. I looked up to see Valerie pacing behind Ms. Hughes, her head turned away so I couldn't see her face. It afforded me a picturesque view of the fatal wound in the back of her head, which really helped matters. "I don't want to talk about my feelings anymore, because what's the point?"

Ms. Hughes just gaped at me, and Ms. Britt looked around the door. "Everything okay?"

"I'm fine," I practically roared. Ms. Britt's nostrils flared as she gave me a refined stink-eye. I shrank back. "I'm sorry. Please don't call my mom."

"Just tell her Bridget had a fever, and she'll be spending the rest of the day up here," Ms. Hughes said. Ms. Britt raised one eyebrow and shrugged before walking out again.

"I'm sorry I yelled at you," I said. Ms. Hughes probably meant well, but I didn't want her help or anyone else's. The only person I wanted getting in my business was Kale, and from him I only wanted the promise that this would really be over on Thursday.

"It's okay," she said. "But it seems like you're having some difficulty coping with things, even if it's not directly related to Valerie. Do you want to start coming to see me again? We can talk about whatever you want."

"No offense, but no," I said. "I just want to let it all go. I want to go to sleep and have all of this be gone. I just want to be normal."

There was a rush of cool air, and I realized too late what I had said. When I looked up, Valerie was gone. Great. Now I had two upset ghosts on my hands. All I had to do was piss off Kale and Sal, and my life would be a double helping of awesome.

John Chang came up to the office with my copy of *1984* and a packet of work from Mrs. McDaniel with a Post-It that said, "Page 1 and 2 for Homework—Take care, worried about you. McD." Thankfully, he didn't gawk as he handed me the work, and I mumbled a "thank you." I spent the rest of the day staring at the clock over the blurry first pages of the book.

Ms. Hughes called Emily up to the office and let us leave a few minutes before the bell rang. Usually I hated special treatment, but I was willing to make an exception this time. I didn't want to hear the gossip that would be flying in the halls. I was fine, but Emily insisted on carrying my backpack and holding my elbow like I was an invalid. We hadn't even made it out the front doors when Emily started interrogating me.

"Everyone's talking about it, aren't they?" I asked.

"Yeah, pretty much," she said. That was one of my favorite things about Emily. She didn't sugarcoat things.

"Awesome," I said. "That's great. I'm moving to Japan. They like foreigners, right?"

"If it makes you feel better, I told them you weren't crazy, but you would kick their asses if you heard them saying that." We reached her car, and she tossed my backpack into the backseat as I slumped into the passenger seat.

"I'm not sure how that helps," I said, although the fact that Emily thought it did made me smile.

"So really, what happened?" she asked as she got into the driver's seat and buckled up.

"I don't know," I said. "I started getting like, cold sweats in class. Then I passed out and had this crazy nightmare. But it was so real."

"Allie Williams says you were possessed and then you were speaking in tongues," she said. She cranked the car and immediately reached out to turn off the radio. That was how I knew she loved me. Emily didn't t turn down her music for *anyone*.

"Well, Allie is an asshole," I said. "The only tongue she knows about is Josh Bailey's."

"Ooh, say it again," Emily said, giving an exaggerated shudder of excitement. Her glittery eyelashes fluttered dramatically.

"Gossipy bitch," I said, feeling better. "With cheap hair extensions."

"That's my girl," Emily said, pointing one zebra-striped nail at me. "Whatever. I'll tell everyone she has herpes if you want me to."

I laughed despite myself. Emily was the best friend you could ask for. If spreading rumors about STDs wasn't friendship, I don't know what was. "I think I'm okay," I said. "But I don't want to go to school for the rest of my life."

"Maybe Barb will let you transfer."

"Yeah, right," I said. "I'd have to go move in with Dad to get away from this one, and we both know he won't go for that. Might as well just deal with it."

"Can I ask?" she said tentatively. "*Are* you okay? I mean, it's that time of year and—"

"I'm fine," I said. I swear, was there some official Bridget Young Mental Health Calendar I didn't know about? "It's a perfectly logical question, but the answer is yes, I'm fine."

But was I really?

CHAPTER FOURTEEN

COLIN HAD BOOK CLUB after school on Mondays, so I had the house to myself. I walked in and headed straight to the fridge for a bottle of water. I tentatively said, "Hello?" just to make sure I was really alone in the house. When I got no response, I bellowed, "Come out, you bitchy-ass ghost."

Natalie met me halfway up the stairs. I shoved my finger in her spectral face. "What the hell is wrong with you, beyond the obvious?" A cold chill ran down my back as I walked right through her and into my bedroom. "Yeah, ice me again and you'll find out what a holy water enema feels like."

She was already talking as I opened the laptop for her. "–do it to someone else."

"Start over," I said as I sat down as angrily as I could manage on a pillow-top mattress. The salt circle was still intact, although I was going to have some explaining to do if Mom came in here. I took a long drink of water and then pressed the cold bottle to my feverish cheek.

"That was my death," Natalie said. "And he's going to do it to someone else in three days, and you're just carrying on like nothing's wrong."

"I told you last night it was dark and late and–"

"I don't care!" she said, and the room went chilly. The bottle in my hand grew painfully cold, but I refused to put it down even as the water froze and crackled. "You think that's scary? Try being kidnapped, tortured, and murdered. You're worried about your fucking reputation, and I'm dead. I would literally kill to have your problems, Bridget."

Then it really sunk in for me. I'd figured out as soon as I woke up from my "nightmare" that those had been Natalie's final memories, but it hadn't really registered for me what that meant. She'd experienced God only knew what over the course of days, maybe even weeks. He'd cut her free, giving her one tiny spark of hope, only to snatch it away. Her final moments had been filled with terror, panic, and the absolute certainty that she was about to die.

"I'm sorry," I finally said. "I really am."

"You're the only one who can do anything," Natalie said. "You can't ignore this."

"I'm just a kid," I said.

"So was I."

I didn't have a good response for her, so I just stared down at my hands for a long time. This wasn't fair, not for Natalie or me.

Yeah, and...?

Pity party adjourned. I set the frozen water bottle aside, reached for the rolled up map by my bed, and spread it out. "Then let's get back to work."

Half an hour later, I had mapped out the center of Natalie's haunting grounds. I'd already figured out it was somewhere around the northern edge of Marymount and Fox Lake, but still didn't know what was in the area. This time, I used Google Earth to look at it, but nothing screamed "Killer's Lair." But then, that wasn't quite right, was it?

Natalie had died in her grave, not wherever he had first taken her. I shuddered again at the dream-memory of dirt in my throat, and shoved it back down. If I found the spot of her death, I'd also find her body. And then I could call the police and have this out of my hands. Surely, there would be enough evidence, especially with my tip. This would actually get something accomplished.

The problem was getting there. Emily was grounded, and I couldn't very well call Michael to help me find his sister's body. It was only a few miles from my house, but I definitely wouldn't make it home in time by curfew.

But Natalie's words were haunting me like a song stuck in my head, so I called Mom. Ms. Britt must not have called her after all, because she didn't ask how I was feeling. With disturbing ease, I lied and said, "Hey, I have to go do some Fall Court stuff. Me and Michael are going to do our sponsorship stuff, so is it okay if I come home a little late?"

There was a long pause, but she finally said, "Okay. Just keep your phone on you, and call me if you're going to be later than seven."

"Okay," I said. "Thanks, Mom."

After hanging up, I loaded my bag with my ghost supplies, adding the map and Valerie's laptop. The hand-me-down purple backpack would barely zip around the computer, but I wanted it in case Natalie needed to talk to me. I threw on the ratty jeans and Valerie's hoodie, like big-sister armor.

I was halfway to the exit of our neighborhood when I stopped midstride. "What the hell am I doing?" I said. Was I seriously about to go find a dead body? What if the killer was hanging out there?

Natalie was close behind me, so I turned to speak to her. "Can you press send on my phone?" I asked. She shrugged. I took out my phone, dialed a random number and held it out to her. Freezing air buffeted me as she furrowed her brow and prodded the phone. It took her a few seconds of work, but she managed to press the button. I hung up right after seeing it had gone through.

"When we get there, I'm going to dial 911," I said. "If something happens, you have to make sure it goes through." She nodded, and I stuck the phone back in my sweatshirt pocket. That was the best I could do. I couldn't very well call the police and say, "My ghost friend helped me find her dead body, now go check it out!"

Hell, the police might think I had done it if I gave them a tip without "accidentally finding it" myself. That would introduce a whole new level of suck to this situation. No, I needed to get some kind of confirmation. And when I had it, I would run my stupid little legs to the nearest public place to call the cops.

As we walked, Natalie changed subtly. Her ghostly body seemed more solid, her steps more natural. Like when she was upset, the air around her got colder, and the decaying smell sharpened. This was new ground for me, but that seemed like a pretty good indicator we were getting close.

The first stop within the "body zone" was an abandoned Fuel'n'Go gas station. Its windows were boarded over with plywood, with a rusted *For Sale* sign nailed to one of the boards. The gas pumps had been removed. The dirty shell of the car wash was a yawning mouth of black. It was creepy as hell, but there was nothing that looked suspicious. Natalie didn't seem interested, so we kept walking. I hoped she would react somehow when we got close, like a spiritual Geiger counter. Otherwise I might just walk past it without even noticing.

Next, we passed through the parking lot of Creekview Baptist, where I had sent Anna off a few days earlier. Past the church was a chain link-fenced lot with signs that said, *No Trespassing* and *Private Property*. There was a gravel access road beyond a padlocked gate, but the land was so thickly forested that it was impossible to see anything beyond the road that sloped up to blend with the dark pine trees.

I looked over to see Natalie so solid that she looked real. Considering her condition, that wasn't exactly an improvement. Instead of a ghost, I appeared to have a zombie companion. Her steps quickened, and she was soon ahead of me. I took my phone out and said, "Hey Kale. If you're hanging around, I could use some backup."

He *really* needed an answering service. Then it occurred to me that even if he was listening, he couldn't get close because of Natalie. And I needed her to get me there.

The chest-high fence and gate were more of a psychological deterrent than a physical one, so I tightened my backpack and started to climb. My toe got stuck on one of the diamond gaps in the fence, but I yanked it free and dropped down clumsily in a carpet of pine needles. Natalie simply passed through.

"Cheater," I said. The humor in my tone fell flat.

She shrugged and pointed ahead, giving me a solemn nod.

"This is it?"

She nodded again, and something flared deep in the cloudy white of her eyes. What did I expect? It wasn't like this was some happy homecoming.

We walked side-by-side up the gently sloping gravel driveway. Every footstep was a noisy crunch announcing my intrusion. If I had any plans to be sneaky, they were gone after my first steps. The driveway sloped up into the wall of trees, and I couldn't see what was at the top.

"This is such a stupid idea," I muttered.

Just like when we went to Warehouse Eleven, I realized I was doing something so far beyond stupid and dangerous that there wasn't a sufficiently strong word in English for it. But this time, I had to for Natalie. I knew that I had to be sure about this before I tipped the police. If I was wrong and they investigated, that might blow my one chance for them to take an anonymous tip seriously.

The driveway ended suddenly at a plateau of land surrounded by a tall wooden privacy fence. The gate stood open, and there was a deep crescent of damp red earth carved from its frequent use. Coming here in the day wasn't a huge improvement over coming at night. It was silent dusk beneath the deep shadows of the dense forest. When I looked back over my shoulder, I could barely see down to the main road through the trees, just slivers of sunlight and blacktop. If something happened up here, no one was going to see it.

My heart skittered, and I clutched my phone like a security blanket. "Are you sure about this, Natalie?"

She brushed past me, and I followed. Except for a gray-sided storage shed toward the back, most of the area was flat and carpeted in crunchy fall-brown grass. No kidnapper van in sight. A firm hand shoved me, sending an icy chill up my spine. My phone flew out of my hand as I tripped and slammed down on my hands and knees.

The grass where I knelt was greener than the rest, with straight lines where someone had laid down strips of sod, like the weirdly carpet-like stuff Mom had put down at the new house. I started to pry up one corner, then stopped with my fingers squishing into the cool dirt beneath. I didn't want to leave any sign I had been here.

Then I noticed the marker.

Barely visible in the unnaturally thick grass was a flat rectangle of stone, too smooth and perfect to be natural. It looked like a piece from one of the sample displays at Home Depot. Under a piece of clear packing tape, a date had been written in dark brown. As I leaned in close to read the date - October 19, 2013 - I realized it wasn't written in paint or ink. It was dried blood.

"Is this—" I started as I looked back at Natalie. She wasn't alone.

I clapped my hand over my mouth to muffle the scream. Natalie was flanked by at least two dozen other girls, each of them bloodied and dirty, each of them staring down at me with glowing white eyes. I saw the tattered remains of a cheerleading uniform, the spangles of a prom dress, and a dozen other garments too ruined to identify. Most of them resembled Natalie: tall and thin, with dark hair that had been cut short. The cold surrounding them was nearly unbearable.

I couldn't breathe. There were so many.

Natalie gestured to them in a *get back* motion. Standing at the head of the triangular formation, she looked like the leader of a tribe of vengeful ghosts. The silence was thick and tense as I stood, the only living soul in a host of the dead. Natalie's lips moved, and though I heard nothing, the girls dispersed throughout the flat area, moving slowly until they stopped suddenly. Then each of them pointed down to the ground.

My legs felt rubbery and useless as I slowly walked across the grassy area. I wanted to run away screaming. *Don't make me see this,* I thought. But I couldn't walk away any more than I could sprout wings and fly away. Someone had to see. Someone had to remember.

Each girl stood over a flat stone, pointing down to the marker that was the only acknowledgement of her death. Most of their graves had long grown over, concealing the lines of new grass. Many of the stones had long been washed clean by rain, and someone had engraved the dates in a steady hand instead. I quit counting after twenty because I could taste the vomit in my throat.

"Oh my God," I whispered. "Oh my God."

The ground rushed up to meet me as I sat down heavily. I barely registered the sharp pain as a stone marker dug into my thigh. All of them had been warm and alive like me, and now they were here, decaying and forgotten with no one to cry for them. Wrong place, wrong time, lights out, kids.

Please, no. Just wake up.

Natalie moved in front of me and pantomimed typing. My hands did the work of unzipping the backpack and opening the laptop. Even once it was on, I couldn't understand a word she said over the panicked roar in my head.

Something cold touched my shoulder. Natalie's grimy hand rested on my arm. I stared at her for a long time before I understood her. "Bridget? Are you okay?"

"No…I am not okay," I said slowly. "There's so many."

"I told you he was bad."

"Not this bad." I stared at her numbly. "Natalie, there must be fifty graves here. I have to call the police right now." I looked around and found my phone glinting in the grass by the gate, where Natalie's body was buried. She was the newest, but she was about to be old news. *Oh God.*

I scrambled for it and dialed 9-1 before they surrounded me. Icy hands seized my wrists. Something pinched my shoulder. I released the phone involuntarily as a shock ran down my arm. "What the hell?"

A spirit wearing the torn remnants of a green and white cheerleading skirt shook her head violently. I was transfixed by the blood staining her mangled fingers—she must have fought so hard—as she gestured to Natalie and spoke silently. Natalie nodded in understanding. "Sarah says that you can't call the police."

"Why the hell not?"

"Because if he's already taken his next victim, then he'll kill her if he thinks the police are looking for him," Natalie said, glancing back and forth between me and the cheerleader. *Sarah,* I told myself. She still had a name.

Sarah's face grew increasingly distressed as she told her story to Natalie. Lightning flashed behind her cloudy eyes, and the temperature plunged even further. Every hair on my body stood on end when Sarah drew her thumb across her throat in a gesture that didn't need any translation. Natalie said, "She says the police almost found her, but he convinced them to go away. As soon as they left, he killed her ahead of schedule and left town."

"What can you tell me about him?" I asked, turning to the other girls. "A name, where he took you, anything?"

Natalie turned to the spirits, but they just shrugged. A few of them covered their eyes and mouths; like Natalie, they must have been blindfolded. Natalie confirmed that with her translation and continued, "They say you have to find him and bring the police right to him. Don't scare him off, or they'll never find him, and this will never end."

"I'm a kid," I said for what felt like the hundredth time. "I can't do this, Natalie. I just—"

"You don't have a choice," Natalie said. "You *have* to do this."

"Natalie, I can't—"

"Bridget, you gotta go," a male voice said. I recognized that rich voice, and I looked up to see Kale looking terrified. The sight of his eerie blue eyes, wide with panic, sent a lightning bolt down my spine and into my bladder. I looked back to see Natalie had disappeared. So they could both push each other away somehow.

"Nice of you to show up," I said. What exactly made an untouchable spirit look like *that*?

"Bridget, shut up and go," he snapped. His head whipped around to look over his shoulder—down to the road—and back. Kale reached for me, but his hand passed through my arm uselessly with a sensation like cold rushing water. "Come on! I can't carry you, but you have to go." My heart stopped when he said, "He's here."

Two words were all it took to dump a BP-sized oil spill of adrenaline into my veins. I almost tripped over my own feet in my hurry. My toe caught Valerie's laptop, which was the only thing that reminded me to pick it up.

"Bridget, come on!"

"I can't leave it," I snapped as I scooped it up. Clutching it to my chest like a life preserver, I sprinted after Kale down a narrow side path winding down the slope through the trees. As I ran, I heard the rumble of an engine and the dry crunch of tires on gravel. Kale was like a beacon ahead of me, gleaming bluish-white as he floated ahead of me in the trees. All I could think of was Creepy Carl, glinting needle full of poison and shovel poised to bludgeon me if I fought back. "Oh God," I wheezed as I pushed my rubbery legs even faster.

I barely touched the fence as I vaulted it like an Olympic star. I didn't stop running until I passed the church and reached the abandoned gas station. Chest burning, eyes flickering with black spots, I felt like I was going to die. My stomach lurched, and I threw up noisily on the sidewalk. "Oh God," I moaned as I braced my hands on my knees. I realized a bit too late that I had dropped the laptop when I puked, and it wasn't looking good.

"Come on," Kale said. "We need to get you home."

I didn't even remember the rest of my walk home. Kale could say he wasn't an angel, but he played the part well enough. That was the only explanation for how I got home without walking into oncoming traffic. When I walked in the door, the house was quiet. The fan was running in Mom's bathroom, and Colin's door was shut. I dashed up the stairs and into my room.

What I had found wasn't a ghost–infinitely worse, and that was really saying something–but I grabbed my salt and holy water anyway and curled in a tight ball on my bed. I had just been within touching distance of a serial killer. The thought of it was so ridiculous that I wanted to laugh and scream at the same time.

Had I left footprints? Dropped some slip of paper with my name? Had he followed me home? Was there a white van driving slowly through my neighborhood?

There was a quiet knock on my door. I gasped as Mom stuck her head in. Her hair was all bound up in a twisted towel, and I suddenly had the urge to throw my arms around her and beg her to protect me. "How did it go?" she asked. She immediately frowned. "What's wrong? You look awful."

"I think I must have eaten something bad at lunch," I lied.

"You want me to make you some soup?"

"No, I don't think I can keep anything down," I said. That wasn't a lie. Just the thought of eating made my stomach start turning flips again. "Probably just need to sleep it off."

She looked a little suspicious, but she finally nodded. With a hesitant expression, she asked, "Bridget, are you okay?"

"Just sick to my stomach."

"Besides that, I mean," she said. "You just seem...never mind. I'll come check on you in a bit."

"Okay," I said, watching as she closed the door. For a second, I thought about calling her back and telling her everything. If she thought I was crazy again, so be it. I just wanted it off my shoulders. Instead, I listened to her footsteps walking away.

The door had just clicked shut when Kale walked right through it. He normally looked like an average spirit, a little translucent, but mostly human. Now he was brighter, like some internal light source was making him glow. He looked unearthly and inhuman now, which wasn't exactly comforting. "Kale, what the—"

"Listen, kiddo," he said. "You're on dangerous ground."

"Where angels fear to tread," I murmured. "Heh. I learned something in English after all."

Kale looked at me like I had just started speaking Chinese and shook his head. "You have to be more careful than that."

"But what Sarah said...I have to find him myself. Don't I?"

He gave me a long look, then sighed and sat down on the end of my bed. "I don't know," he said. "I'm not psychic."

"What are you, exactly?"

"How often are we going to have this conversation?"

"Until you give me a decent answer."

"I'm a Guardian. I watch over you," he said. "And as the one who watches your back, I think you're in too deep."

Kale had been around almost as long as Valerie. A few weeks after I saw her spirit the first time and thought I was losing my mind, he appeared to me. At first, it wasn't comforting to see another ghost, just the opposite, in fact. But he'd stuck by me, assuring me I hadn't gone off the deep end. He was the one who explained how it happened.

When I had surgery on my knee, my heart stopped. They said it was an unusual reaction to the anesthesia, and I'd been dead—scientifically, at least—for twenty-eight seconds. There was no going toward the light or choirs of angels. But that had been enough, Kale said, to make me a "sensitive." Once I finally accepted that, he'd taught me all about ghosts. But more importantly, he told me that I'd be okay, and even when I didn't believe it, it was nice to know that he did.

And at the end of the day, I had to admit I trusted him. When a suspected higher being said I should walk away, I was inclined to listen. But I would never forget those girls, all standing there over their own shallow graves. I'd seen a lot in the last two years, but something irreversible had changed in me tonight.

"But Natalie—"

"Will not be your concern after next Thursday."

"But she—"

"Is one vengeful spirit out of thousands in the universe."

"That finishing my sentences thing—"

"Is really annoying?" he finished, lips curving into a coy smile.

"Yes," I said, pointing at him irritably. "Stop it."

He chuckled, then got serious again. "Bridget, you can't fix everyone's problems."

"I think problem is kind of an understatement when it comes to a serial killer," I said. "Catastrophe. Maybe crisis."

"Your levity is cute but inappropriate," Kale said.

"You think I'm cute?"

"Bridget. Case in point."

"Well what about me earning my way clear of this? That's always been your deal."

Kale shook his head and said, "This one is beyond your reach. You've earned enough Frequent Flyer miles already. Go through with the ritual and go on with your life."

"But I'll know," I said.

"You don't have to," he said. "There are ways to forget."

"Really?"

He just gave me a calm expression, with no indication of what he thought about the matter. It had also been Kale that had told me I could earn my way free of this curse. Do enough good, and I could go back to normal. He never came out and said it, but he didn't deny either that this was how I could make up for what happened to Valerie.

"I don't know," I said. But it sounded like heaven. Memory wiped of all the darkness of the last two years, I could be a normal girl again. I could close my eyes without seeing Natalie and Sarah and all the girls who'd died in those shallow graves. I could believe the world really wasn't full of monsters. But someone owed it to them to find this guy, and that someone, by default, was me. "I'll do what I can until Thursday."

"Fine," Kale said. "I found out there's another sensitive in town."

"Like me?"

"Like you," he said, nodding. "Probably not as cute."

"Flatterer," I said. Was it completely absurd that despite the circumstances, my cheeks flushed at his compliment? Damn.

"She may be able to make contact with the spirits."

"Why can't I?"

"You already did," Kale said. "But they couldn't speak directly to you. From what I've heard, the other sensitive is very strong. She may be able to find out information you can't."

"Okay," I said hesitantly. "What's her name?"

"I'm not sure," Kale said. "I've only heard of her. Spirits aren't huge on particulars. But I know she's in town, working as a psychic. Find her, and you may find the information you need."

CHAPTER FIFTEEN

S WEETIE, MAKE SURE you stay in bed and rest today," Mom said, standing in my doorway as she put her earrings on. "You don't want to miss out on the Fall Court."

"I will," I said. Way to have priorities, Mom.

"There's soup and sandwiches in the fridge. Call me at noon to update me, and I'll get Dr. Anderson to write a script for some antibiotics just in case. If you're not feeling better by tonight, we'll go to the doctor in the morning."

"Got it, Mom," I said, nodding my head quickly as she went down her checklist.

"Are you sure you don't want me to stay home with you?"

Oh, I was sure. "I'll be okay."

"All right," she said. "Love you."

"Love you too."

Once I heard her car pull out of the driveway, I launched myself out of bed. I was already completely dressed and had been since six in the morning. I hadn't *really* lied when I told her that I still felt sick and didn't want to go to school. I didn't want to go to school for the rest of the year after what happened yesterday, and I felt like projectile vomiting every time I thought about what I had seen out on Woodlake Road yesterday. But I had better things to do than lay in bed today.

Emily was "sick" today too. She had an acute case of Kari being out of town. Treatment involved a day at the mall. I wasn't one to criticize, because she was going to drive me downtown to try the psychics I'd found. She picked me up ten minutes early–Emily was serious about her shopping–and dropped me at my first stop by eleven-thirty. It was too far away from the killer's graveyard for Natalie to join me, but Valerie appeared at my side when I got out of the car. I hadn't spoken to her since my outburst in the nurse's office, but if she was upset, she hid it well as we walked down the sunny sidewalks of Main Street.

Downtown Parkland was nice, at least in small sections. It wasn't a booming metropolis with skyscrapers packed tight and crowded sidewalks. Run-down neighborhoods sandwiched a recently revitalized area with restaurants and stores, with the occasional art gallery thrown in to spice things up.

"How are you feeling?" Valerie asked as we walked past a pair of smokers sitting outside the Aces Low tattoo parlor.

"Nervous," I said. "Like this is the stupidest idea ever."

Valerie didn't laugh, just nodded solemnly. "I've got your back."

"Like always," I murmured.

We skirted around a chalkboard sign advertising a soup and sandwich special at the Half Moon Cafe. I hadn't eaten today, but I didn't feel hungry at all. After last night, I probably wouldn't be hungry for months. "We're looking for Madam Zanka's," I said, staring up at the signs as I walked down the block.

A woman pushing a stroller smiled and raised a hand to wave. As I waved back, I suddenly felt a nervous thrill of paranoia. Did I have a big neon *TRUANT* sign over my head? If Mom found out I was doing this, she would string me up by my toes. But in the grand scheme of things, that was near the bottom of my list of worries, or at least should have been.

Madam Zanka's was another block down, nestled between a vintage clothing store and a coffee shop. I almost missed the entrance, drawn in by the rich aroma of coffee drifting out of the Average Joe's storefront. A flourish of sitar music caught my attention. I turned toward the source of the music and saw the graceful white calligraphy on a black sign: *Madam Zanka's.*

The window displays were draped in bright purple and blue silks, glittering with colorful crystals. The door was propped with a geode that had been sliced open to reveal its spiky crystalline interior. Bookshelves lined the walls, and the floor was crowded with tables covered in candles and incense.

Madam Zanka was a pale, blonde-haired woman in jeans and a filmy white blouse. She stood behind a case filled with silver jewelry, flipping idly through a catalog. Not to be judgmental or anything, but she looked about as mystical as a piece of white bread.

A floorboard creaked as I stepped into the shop, prompting her to look up. She smiled and said, "Welcome, sister. Would you like—"

I didn't have the time for politeness. We were on a mission. On the way downtown, I'd planned a quick-and-dirty litmus test. "Do you see her?" I asked, tipping my head toward Valerie. My sister grinned and waved.

Zanka hesitated, her dark brown eyes still fixed on me. "Who do you—"

"All I need. Have a nice day," I interrupted. Madam Zanka called after me as I turned on my heel and walked out of the shop.

"That was kinda rude," Valerie said as we continued down the street to find psychic number two, Miss Jasmine.

"I have two days to find a serial killer, Valerie," I said. "I think God will forgive me for being a little rude."

"Good point."

There were two more psychics in the metro area, including Miss Jasmine and Bonita Travis, both of whom seemed like perfectly nice ladies. But neither acknowledged Valerie's presence, so I crossed them off my list. If they couldn't see my sister, they couldn't help me. I stopped at noon to call Mom, faking a cough and my best pitiful voice. She seemed to buy the act, so I continued on.

Bonita Travis was the last of the psychics working downtown, and my last lead was all the way across town in Marymount, which was close to home. I didn't want to call Emily for a ride, because she was already prying about what I was doing downtown. My story was that I was hunting for the perfect "abandoned place" for shooting pictures. One day she'd figure out I didn't know an aperture from applesauce, but that day wasn't today.

Instead, I called a cab, which cost me almost thirty dollars of my laughable cash reserves. Once I was done in Marymount, I could walk home with some time to spare before anyone got home to wonder where I was.

As I watched my hometown rolling by outside the taxi windows, I had a terrible thought. What if Kale's information was wrong, and the other sensitive wasn't actually working as a psychic? What was I supposed to do then, put an ad in the paper for a ghost whisperer? No, I couldn't think that way just yet. I still had one to go.

Fingers crossed.

Our final stop, Ms. Tara, billed herself as a medium. That was promising, at least. Her "office" was a little white cottage just off the main road through Marymount. There was nothing fancy or New Age about it, and I almost thought we had made a mistake. Her yard was neatly manicured, with a bed of bright red tulips on either side of the clean-swept sidewalk. A pair of concrete rabbits flanked the red-painted door, giving the whole place the look of a kindly grandma's house, not a psychic's. But down in the lower corner of one of the front windows was a little handwritten sign that said, *Miss Tara - Medium; Weekdays 9:00 - 3:00. Walk-Ins Welcome.*

The door opened before I could grab the brass knocker. Okay, that would be impressive if not for the newfangled invention called a peephole. Tara poked her head out around the door and said, "Good afternoon, ladies."

"Holy shit," Valerie said.

"Ah, language, young lady," Tara said as she waved us in. "Watch your step."

"Sorry," Valerie said, staring in shock as she walked past Tara.

Tara was tall and heavyset. Coarse salt-and-pepper hair was braided down her back; the color seemed at odds with her smooth, tanned skin. She gestured into a living room just off the foyer. "Ladies, please, sit. Can I get you something to drink, Bridget?"

My mouth fell open. "How did you—"

"Rumors abound, dear," Tara said. "Something to drink?"

"No thank you," I said, still trying to wrap my head around the very promising Miss Tara. She gestured again to the living room. She had two big blue-checked couches and a pair of easy chairs sitting around a coffee table. I didn't hear the sounds of anyone else moving around in the house, and there were no family pictures on the walls. Tara was alone here.

At Tara's prompting, I sank into one couch with Valerie next to me. I brushed my fingers over the kitten-painted tea set on the end table next to me and said, "So, you're psychic?"

Tara just smiled. "Did I say psychic? I do believe my ad says medium." She patted one broad hip. "Though I'd say I'm more of a large." She laughed at her own joke, then shook her head. "I apologize. What is it you need?"

172

"Okay," I said. "It's going to—"

"Sound insane?"

"You really are psychic," I said with a little laugh. "The spirit of a girl named Natalie appeared to me. She was murdered, and she helped me find her body. But she wasn't the only one. There were dozens. And they say the killer is going to kill again, we think on the full moon."

"So you're Natalie?" Tara asked skeptically.

"No, I'm her sister," Val said. "Valerie."

"Another spirit told me about you," I said. "The other girls' spirits said he'd kill his new victim if the police start sniffing around, and he may disappear and start killing somewhere else. So I need to know exactly where he is before I call the police."

"That sounds awfully risky," Tara said.

"That's because it is," I said. "But I don't know what else to do."

"What do you think I can do to help?" Tara asked.

"Well," I said. "I don't really know. Maybe you could speak to the girls for me. They couldn't talk directly to me, and Natalie just keeps telling me to find him without giving me any more details."

"I could try," Tara said. "What do you want to know?"

"Anything," I said. "Names, where they went to school, where they were taken from, anything, really."

"All right," she said as she stood and walked into her kitchen. I watched curiously as she retrieved a plastic box like one of those shoeboxes Mom used to store her nicer shoes. Inside were white candles, bundles of herbs—probably sage—incense, a lighter, and a length of silver chain. She arranged the chain on the coffee table in the middle of the room, nudging it outward until it formed a neat circle. After placing the candles at five points around the circle, she burned the sage in puffs of fragrant smoke around the room.

The smoldering remains of the sage went in a ceramic dish in the center of the circle.

When she was ready, she glanced up at Valerie. "You should probably go," she said. Valerie gave me a questioning glance. I hesitated, then nodded my approval.

"I'll be fine," I said. But I still felt a chill run down my spine as Valerie disappeared, leaving me alone with Tara.

Tara reached over and took my trembling hand. Her skin was dry and warm against mine. "Do you have the full name of one of the spirits?"

"Natalie Fullmer."

Tara nodded. "This could be a little scary. Why don't you go into the kitchen?"

"Why?"

"Because once I open the door, you won't be safe from what comes through," she said.

I didn't like the sound of that. "Where should I go?"

"Step into the kitchen. There's a protected circle around the table. Sit there with your back to this room."

With my heart pounding, I followed her instructions and walked through the kitchen. It was long and narrow with a cozy breakfast nook at the end. A blue-curtained window let the sun shine onto the tiny cafe-style table, which was surrounded by a silver circle line inlaid on the floor. A triangular arrangement of half-melted candles stood in the center of the table.

I pulled out one of the chairs and sank into the blue gingham cushion, turning the chair slightly so my back was to the living room. Her instructions to not look back only made me want to look back more. Like she sensed my apprehension, she called out a reminder. "Whatever you hear, don't look back."

As I let out a shaky sigh, Tara began murmuring, so soft I couldn't understand what she was saying. A few moments later, she gasped sharply. Dishes clattered as a tremor shook the kitchen. A cold wind gusted, carrying scents of old books and decay. The candles in the center of the table ignited on their own. My eyes went wide and I passed my hand over one of them just to be sure I wasn't seeing things. The flame singed my fingers. My jaw dropped as I yanked it back.

Holy. Shit.

"Natalie, speak to me," Tara said in a rich, powerful voice. There was a roll of thunder and a choked scream that made my skin crawl, but Tara's voice remained steady as she said, "I understand. I'm so sorry, sweet girl. Go back. Tell the others to come." Her voice rose in volume. "I command you, Natalie. He cannot harm you now."

The kitchen lights flickered, and my chair vibrated as the entire house shook on its foundation. I braced my hands on the table, murmuring, "don't look, don't look." The curiosity was killing me, but the very tiny rational part of my brain kept me looking out the darkened window. The sun was still shining, but it was like a thick gray curtain had fallen over it, casting the room in deep shadow. There was another thunderous boom, followed by a gust of icy wind. Despite the wind, the candles burned bright, their flames going pale blue as the noise rose.

"Tell me everything," Tara said. Then her voice was lost in a chorus of wails and screams. It was all I could do to keep myself from turning around to see what was going on. Something *had* to be wrong. But like she had read my mind, she called out, "All is well, Bridget."

I squeezed my eyes shut and buried my face in my hands as the screams scraped at my ear drums. It was like taking a helicopter tour of Hell.

A hand fell on my shoulder. I screamed and Tara chuckled. "It's all right, dear."

I slowly opened my eyes to see the candles had been extinguished. Tara was standing in front of me, looking a little windblown, but perfectly healthy. My legs wobbled as I followed her back to the sitting room and slumped onto the couch. If Tara was that casual after all of *that*, then she had a lot more juice than I ever did. I felt a little wary of her suddenly.

"Here are some of their names," she said, pushing the legal pad across the table with one hand as she smoothed her braid with the other. "Some of them were still too tormented to think clearly enough for their names. They came from all over, but they were clear about one thing. The last thing they saw was a full moon. I think you were correct that he kills on a schedule."

I reached out for the piece of paper, where the names were written in a dozen different scripts, like each girl had written her own name. I didn't even bother saying it was impossible. After what had just happened, I knew better.

"How did you do that?" I asked. "Is that something I could do?"

Tara pondered for a moment, then walked into the kitchen to brew coffee. As she pulled down cups, she talked. "You could. But it's not something you just do once."

"What do you mean?"

"Do you see him?" Tara asked, pointing to the kitchen table. "You don't strike me as rude, so I'm assuming you haven't spoken because you don't see him."

"Who?" I asked, staring at the empty seat. A second later, the candle closest to that seat ignited again. "Holy crap!"

"That's Jeremy."

"But—"

"Right now, you see just the tiniest glimpse of the spirit world," Tara said. "Do your spirits have something in common? Suicides, diseases—"

"Wrongful deaths," I murmured. Like my sister. Like Mia. Like Natalie. Maybe even Kale.

Tara nodded. "That's how it starts for most people. Something specific, your own little niche. And that's how it stays for most. Right now, it's like you're peering through a peephole, and you can only communicate in the most limited ways with the spirits."

"But you?"

"I've opened the door," she said, shrugging casually. She took canisters of powdered creamer and sugar from above her stove.

"What does that mean?"

Tara just shrugged. "What does any of it really mean? It's not a science," she said as she poured a cup of coffee and added cream and sugar to it. "I reached out to them, allowing them all to come to me. Now, I see them all. And I can understand them."

I accepted the coffee as she handed it to me and found—without surprise—it was mixed just right. It was sweet enough that it could pass for melted ice cream. "So you never really answered my question. Is that something I could do?"

"With time. But once you open the door, it stays open. Permanently."

I nodded slowly. "You said most people. Does that mean there are a lot of people like me—like us, I guess?"

"There are some," she said. "I've only met a few here and there myself. But I'll admit I don't get out much."

"Can I ask you something, then?"

"Of course. Jeremy, put that out," Tara said. I squinted to see, but there was no sign of the ghost that extinguished the candle. A tendril of smoke snaked up to the ceiling as I shook my head in wonder. "You had a question?"

"Oh, right." I shook myself from a daze and took another sip of coffee. "A spirit told me there was a way for me to get rid of it. I guess, to close the door permanently."

Tara cocked her head. "Why would you want to?"

I just gaped at her. I didn't want to hurt her feelings, especially after she had just helped me, but really? Was she serious? "I don't think I can do this anymore."

Tara looked at me for a long time, and I could practically see her balancing the scales of judgment. Finally she shrugged her broad shoulders. "I don't know if there is. But you should consider the fact that you, of all the people in existence, were given this gift. Surely, there's a higher purpose."

"Well, no offense, but I'm not really a believer in higher purpose."

Tara snorted a laugh, then put up her hand apologetically. "I'm sorry to laugh at your plight. But you communicate with the dead and think there's nothing larger going on?"

"Well it would have been nice if something larger hadn't taken my sister, wouldn't it?" I snapped.

"The Lord works in—"

"Mysterious ways," I said. "Heard that one a thousand times, and it still doesn't make me feel better. And besides, what good am I even doing? I mean, I can't bring any of them back. I don't even know what the hell I'm doing half the time."

"Language," Tara said in a motherly tone.

"Really?" I sputtered. She raised one gray eyebrow, and I bowed my head. "Sorry."

"You're setting them free," she said. "And while you may not think that's important, that is of the utmost importance to a spirit who's stuck here, unable to pass on."

"What happens if they don't? Pass on, I mean?" I asked. This was a rare opportunity for me. This was the only person I'd met besides Kale who knew anything about this stuff. And he was infuriatingly reticent about details, especially when I really wanted them.

"They get ugly," Tara said. "Especially wrongfuls."

"But I've never seen one," I said.

"Because you've been sending them on before it gets that bad," she said gently. "They start out almost human, but the longer they stay, the worse they get. They start showing their deaths, getting restless and volatile. Eventually they get so tormented…well, they all eventually end up far worse than your friend Natalie. By helping them resolve whatever pain was holding them here, you're helping them finally rest."

I was silent for a long time after that. Maybe she was right. Still, her words were troubling. The bruise on Valerie's eye, the trickle of blood down the back of her neck, sprang to mind. After two years of apparent serenity, she was showing her death. Was she going to end up like Natalie?

"How long have you had it?" I finally asked. "This curse, I mean."

"It's not a curse."

"You sound like Kale," I said.

"He sounds wise," Tara said. "I've had it since I was a little girl. I nearly drowned swimming, and when my brother brought me back with CPR, I could see them."

That sounded familiar. "How did you deal with it?"

"It was hard," she said. "In and out of hospitals for my whole childhood...I learned quick to lie about what I saw. But when I was older it was easier."

"Yeah, well how many serial killers have you run into?"

"Oh, sweet Bridget," she said with an indulgent smile. There was something chilling about the expression, despite her sweet demeanor. "You have no idea the things I've seen."

My throat went dry. My phone vibrated against my leg. I was thankful for the interruption as I looked at the screen. "Oh crap," I said. I had a text from Emily saying, *I'm out of here.* What the heck? I shook my head and set the coffee cup aside. "Thank you for all your help. I have to go."

"Good luck, dear," Miss Tara said. "Oh, and Bridget?"

"Yeah?"

"Believe it or not, I understand your anger. Quite well, in fact. But the universe can be cruel to one while still being kind to many. You just have the misfortune of being on the wrong side of the equation," she said.

"Uh, okay," I said. "Thanks?"

"Think about it," Tara said. "And you come back and see me again if you need help."

"I will," I said, but I had no intention of crossing her doorstep again. In two days, Miss Tara and I were going to have nothing in common. It was good to have some answers, but they were going to get filed away in my *Things to Never Think About Again* file come Thursday night.

As I walked outside, I called Emily. She was already ranting as she picked up the phone. "Whoa, whoa," I said. "What's going on?"

"Kari called and told me I better get my ass home."

"How did she—"

"Apparently the credit card company called her to verify one of my purchases, and she was all 'why are you out shopping when you claimed to be sick?' and then said I was grounded for the rest of the year. So I'm out. I'm going to Stacey's."

"Emily, don't do this," I said. I really needed a ride home. Her drama could wait.

"No," she said. "This is ridiculous."

"Emily, why don't you grow the hell up. Some of us have *real* problems, you know," I snapped, my face reddening with anger before I even realized what I had said.

Long silence. "What did you say?"

Our friendship worked because when she got worked up over stupid things, I just played along. But all I could see was Natalie, whose mother didn't even care enough to keep searching for her while a serial killer was burying her alive. Natalie would have been ecstatic to be grounded for the rest of her life.

"I said grow up," I said. In for a penny, in for a pound, right? "Your mom lets you do whatever you want as long as you follow her rules, and you're bitching because you got caught skipping school. *Seriously?*"

"You don't know what she's like," Emily said. "But you know what, whatever. I'm so sorry I interrupted your earth-shattering drama with my stupid problems." And then she hung up on me. When I called back, it went straight to voicemail. I tried again and left her a message asking her to call me back. She didn't.

Awesome. Life just kept getting better.

CHAPTER SIXTEEN

WHEN I QUIT FUMING, I checked my texts to find a new message from Michael:

Michael: Left school early today—up for a ride?

Did the Pope wear a funny hat?

If I had to go on record, I'd admit that I cheered a little in Tara's front yard when I read his message. Hey, he was cute, and I was human. Instead of texting, I called him back.

My cheer evaporated when he answered. "Hey, are you feeling any better? I heard this morning about what happened—"

My face was already flushed before he finished the sentence. I had held out hope that he was somehow the only person at school who hadn't heard about the Great Freakout of 2014. Optimism was stupid. Case in point. "I'm fine. What did you have in mind?"

"Oh, I was thinking we could go try for some donations today," he said. "We're supposed to turn in something tomorrow and I got nothing."

"Me either," I said. "Sounds like a plan."

He picked me up at Miss Tara's half an hour later. I watched him squint to read the sign in her window. To his credit, he wiped the incredulous expression from his face as I sank into the passenger seat. He looked over and asked diplomatically, "Psychic, huh?"

"Medium," I corrected without thinking. "Uh, she's an old family friend. She's going to make a donation."

"I see. You think she could...never mind."

"What?" I asked, though I already knew where his train of thought was heading.

"You think she could find out something about Natalie?"

I shook my head and said, "To be honest, she's a fake." Lord, forgive me for all the lies I was telling these days. "She just does a great act."

"Oh," he said, looking disappointed. "So what happened yesterday?"

"I just passed out," I said. "I was kind of dizzy and feverish, and then I passed out and had a crazy dream."

He quirked an eyebrow. "People said you were seriously freaking out. Are you sure you're okay?"

"I'm sure," I said. "Honestly, I want to forget the entire thing happened. Like, total amnesia would be welcome at this point."

"Fair enough," he said. "So I already called Hometeam Advantage, but they said no donations. That was my only idea. What have you got?"

"I was thinking about Giavino's and Vanilla Dipper," I said.

"Cool," he said. "Let's go, then."

It took us ten minutes to drive back to Fox Lake, where we stopped at the strip mall across from Wal-Mart. Our first stop was Giavino's, a Parkland tradition. It was a new location, but the restaurant itself had been around for years. I remembered going to the old Giavino's in Marymount when I was a kid, back when we were still a normal family. The last time we had been was on my eleventh birthday, just after the new location opened. Giavino's had been Dad's favorite place to eat back when he still lived here in town, but Mom never wanted to go anymore. As if their separation had something to do with the alfredo sauce.

The new location was much nicer than the old one, which had this old brown seventies lodge look. The new one had a black and white tile floor with gold-flecked green walls and art canvases of Italian monuments. Butter, garlic, and basil were all the air fresheners it needed. I felt like a cartoon puppy following my nose in pursuit of a good scent.

Michael greeted the hostess politely and asked for the manager. "Hey, look at this," he said as he pointed at a plaque on the wall. "It says they just baked their five thousandth pizza. They still use the same brick oven that they installed at the original Giavino's. Just tore it out and moved it here."

"Interesting," I mumbled as I eyeballed the glass case full of cannoli and cheesecake. My stomach had finally gotten over its acrobatics, and I was ravenous. I thought about reaching into the bread basket of the closest table, but I resisted the urge. Invading the customers' personal space just might discourage management from making a donation.

A tall man in a crisp blue polo shirt waved a greeting as he emerged from the kitchen and approached us. "I'm Dennis. Can I help you?"

"Hi Dennis, I'm Michael Fullmer, and this is my friend Bridget Young," Michael said, extending his hand to shake. He had a natural, easy charm about him.

"A pleasure," Dennis said, shaking with each of us. As he gave my hand a firm squeeze, I noticed a row of brown scars up his forearm—pizza oven burns, probably. Ouch.

"We're on the Fall Court at Fox Lake High, and we were wondering if you would be willing to make a donation to support the school," I said.

"Oh, sure," he said. "We donate every year. Hold on." He disappeared into the back, leaving us waiting again.

"Well, that was easy," I said with a nervous laugh. Michael just smiled and looked back at the pictures. My stomach sank as I followed his gaze to a familiar sight. Under a framed picture of a Little League baseball team was a picture of the Fall Court from Valerie's senior year. She was shaking Dennis's hand, her smile even brighter than the sparkling crown on her head. I wondered if she had any idea what was going to happen just weeks after that picture was taken.

"Here," Dennis said as he came back with two white envelopes. "Here's fifty each, and a couple gift cards you can raffle or something. Sound good?"

"That's great," Michael said as he accepted the donation. "Thank you so much."

"No problem, kiddo," he said. "My kids start going to Fox Lake next year, so I try to do my part. Good karma, am I right?" He laughed heartily. "Good luck, guys."

After Michael handed me my envelope, we walked down to the ice cream parlor next door. The Vanilla Dipper was decorated in an outer space theme, with dark blue walls and silver stars all over. It was childish, but it was so familiar that I loved it.

"Hi," I said to the girl at the silver-painted counter. The sign behind her was shaped like a cartoon rocket ship, with the flavors painted in white down its length. Paper bowls in each size hung from its sparkling blue tail fins.

The cashier looked up from her cell phone and smiled. "Cuporcone?" she said, so fast I wasn't sure she was speaking English at first.

I toyed with a pink sprinkle that had fallen on the counter and said, "Neither. I was wondering if your manager was here."

Her face fell. She jammed her phone into the pocket of her space-silver uniform apron and straightened her posture. "What's wrong?"

"Oh, nothing," I said. "I wanted to see if they would make a donation for Fox Lake High School's Fall Court."

"Oh," she said. She winced and said, "Honestly, he probably won't. His niece or cousin or somebody is on the court, so he already made a donation the other day. But if you wanna leave a letter or something, I'll put it in his office."

186

"Oh," I said, feeling deflated. "No, but thanks anyway."

"You want some ice cream?" Michael asked. "I could eat."

"Sure," I said. "Um, how about a cup with a scoop of...um, Galactic Strawberry?" I used to think the flavors were the coolest thing ever until I realized they were just regular flavors with weird names.

"Cool," the girl said. "You?"

"Double scoop of Out of this Swirled," Michael said, reaching for his wallet. He made the hokey name sound cool when he said it.

"Okay, that's five eighty-seven," she said.

I quickly dug for the crumbled wad of cash in my pocket. "Wait, it's separate."

"No it's not," he said, pushing his arm gently in front of me to block me. "I got it."

I tried to hand him a couple of ones, but he just rolled his eyes and handed his debit card over. When we got our ice cream, he led the way to one of the glittering red booths by the front window. "You didn't have to do that," I said as I took a little bite of the ice cream. It was sweet and fruity and tasted extra good considering who had just *insisted* on buying it.

"I know," he said. "But I wanted to."

"Well, thanks," I said, taking another tentative bite of ice cream. "My dad used to bring me and Val here when we were really little."

"Natalie was always in trouble, but she used to take me out for ice cream after every single football game. Never missed one, even when I was warming the bench all freshman year," he said, staring off into the distance as he fiddled with the paper sleeve on his sugar cone. He suddenly shook himself and snapped back to focus with a little laugh. "She might have been drinking under the stands for the whole game, but she was there."

"She sounds like a good sister," I said. My stomach was churning again. The ice cream was suddenly sickeningly sweet. He deserved to know what had happened to Natalie. It was so screwed up for me to act like everything was going to work out.

"She is," he said. "Well, sometimes. Other times, she's awful, but she's my sister either way. Did I tell you she texted me finally?"

"No," I said slowly. This killer was too smart. He must have figured out Michael wasn't going to let it go until he heard from Natalie. Did he have a whole box of dead girls' phones somewhere, ringing as their families kept trying in vain to make contact?

"Yeah," he said. "Said I better leave her alone and she was better off now. I just don't get it." His face was stony, but I could see how much it hurt him to repeat it.

I wished Tara was here to talk to Michael just then. What trite crap would she tell him? What was the good that came out of Natalie's death?

Oh, right. There wasn't any.

"I'm really sorry to hear that," I said. I couldn't keep lying and telling him it was going to be okay. It *wasn't*.

Instead I stared at the table and wrestled with my conscience. My cheeks were so flushed they must have been the deep pink of my ice cream. If I told him the truth, he'd think I was crazy and probably hate me for making up such a screwed-up story. And if he happened to believe me, he'd probably still hate me for keeping the truth from him. I was screwed either way.

"Hey, I'm sorry," he said. "I didn't mean—"

"You're apologizing to *me*?" I asked incredulously.

"Yeah, I didn't mean to make you uncomfortable."

"It's okay," I said, forcing a smile to my face. "I was thinking of something else."

"Oh. You know, you do that a lot," he commented. "Sometimes it's like you're on another planet."

"So I've moved up to being an alien," I said. "Great."

"Did I say that? You shouldn't keep knocking yourself like that," he said. "I know we're getting to know each other under pretty weird circumstances, but you seem cool. I just wonder what you're keeping hidden from everyone." I couldn't think of words as his warm brown eyes looked me over, creased by his easy smile. I felt self-conscious, small and insignificant.

"Thanks," I finally said. Then I took a deep breath. "You know it's almost the anniversary of Valerie's death?"

"Really?"

I nodded. "I know it's just a date. It's not any more significant than five months or seven hundred hours, or anything else. But every year it hits me all over again."

"You know that's okay, right?" he said. "You're *allowed* to be sad."

I just nodded and looked out the window, feeling the warning sting in my eyes. Tomorrow was going to be it for me and Val. And I was sitting here eating ice cream with Michael like I didn't have more important things to do. I suddenly pushed the ice cream away. "I've got to get home."

"Did I say something? I didn't mean—"

"No, it's not you," I said. "I just need to get home before my brother does."

He looked disappointed, and on another day, that would have made me so happy I could have danced. But today I just felt dread weighing heavy in my gut as I wondered how much he would regret coming to know—and trust—me in the days to come.

Chapter Seventeen

I TOLD MICHAEL I was supposed to be home in bed, with the sort of conspiratorial wink and nudge that had him smiling in amusement instead of being suspicious. In the grand scheme of things, the lie was hardly a blip on my bad karma. He got me home by three forty-five, just ahead of the middle school bus. I even got another hug before I got out of the car.

After I ran in the house, I dumped part of the soup and one of the sandwiches in the garbage disposal so it would look like I had eaten. Like lying to Michael, wasting food seemed a minor sin considering I was trying to find a serial killer.

I was barely tucked back into bed when I heard the hissing brakes of the school bus outside. The house shifted a little as the door slammed. I heard the refrigerator, then the load screen music for Colin's game. I wouldn't see him for a good few hours.

But to my surprise, his spiky head poked in my door. "Are you awake?"

"No," I said. "Try again later, Captain Obvious."

"Do you want a snack?"

"What?"

"Do. You. Want. A. Snack?" he repeated, doing an exaggerated pantomime on each word.

"Are you attempting to be nice?"

"No," he said, looking embarrassed as he rolled his eyes.

"Aww, look at the baby monkey acting like one of the humans," I said, puffing out my cheeks in my best monkey face. "So cute. Does it know sign language?"

"Shut up," he said, his cheeks turning red.

"I'm okay," I said. "But thanks anyway, monkey."

He just shook his head and closed the door behind himself.

Once I heard the onslaught start downstairs, I tossed off my blanket and pulled out the folded yellow sheet Tara had given me. Spreading it out next to my laptop, I pulled up Google to start looking up contact information. Tara had gotten several full names from the dead girls, and hopefully at least one of them would lead somewhere. If I was a TV detective, I'd start by looking for what connected the girls.

The first girl was Tabitha Turner. I tried searching her name with "missing" and instantly found an article about her being reported missing about two years ago from the nearby city of Winder. There was little information about her disappearance, and a six-month update in the local paper only confirmed that they hadn't heard anything from her. That article linked to a simple website run by Tabitha's parents. Featuring a big senior portrait that showed off a pretty smile and light brown eyes, it was a heartbreaking plea for help. The site hadn't been updated in over six months, which sent a knife of sorrow into my gut. Had they given up hope? The site still had an email and phone number for tips, so I jotted down both and went on to the next name on my list.

Carmen Pagani had gone missing from here in Parkland three years ago. Several friends were quoted in an article about her disappearance. Carmen had been a student at Marymount High, but had transferred there from Fox Lake. Valerie could have known her, a thought which made it seem that much sadder. Several "persons of interest" had been detained for questioning about her disappearance. I instantly wondered if Creepy Carl had been questioned. No names were listed in the paper, but I wondered if Sal could get access to the information. In any case, without a body or any evidence a crime had even been committed, there was nothing the police could do.

The third girl was Sarah Ketter, who was reported missing in Atlanta just over six months ago. I gulped. Sarah, in the tattered cheerleading skirt. Sarah, with her hands split open from trying to protect herself.

There were at least a dozen articles about Sarah's case. Her mother was trying to sue the state for not issuing an Amber Alert. Every article I found had the same quote from her mother: "her blood is on their idle hands." Ouch. Then again, maybe Mom hadn't been wrong.

There was still an active Facebook group for Sarah, much like the one Michael maintained for Natalie. It offered a $10,000 reward for anyone with solid information on Sarah. Well, *there* was some easy cash, but my information wasn't going to be what they wanted to hear.

After an hour of searching, I had phone numbers and contact information for three of the girls' families. The others had never been reported missing. I tried looking for their Facebook pages, and found an ongoing flame war on Lilly Hanson's page, saying that she had just run away again. Except for the names, it could have been Natalie's, complete with accusations of being a drama queen who thrived on attention.

I stared at my list blankly for a few minutes. I had three phone numbers, two e-mails, and one seriously heavy heart. It was Tuesday. The first day of the full moon was Thursday. What the hell was I doing? I wasn't a detective. This guy could already have a girl, tormenting her like he had Natalie and all the others. This was a matter for the police, not for me.

Instead of dialing the number for Tabitha Turner's parents, I dialed the police station. Before I called, I took a long look at the purple backpack that contained my ghost kit. I laid the phone down and dug out my holy water and can of salt. I poured a new salt line around my bed, then put the holy water on my nightstand. If Natalie showed up, I had no intention of playing another round of her favorite game, *Let's Terrify Bridget.*

Safely inside the salt circle, I called the police. As I listened to the phone ring, I rolled the edges of the phone number list between my sweaty fingers. By the time a polite female voice answered, my paper was curled like a scroll. I recognized the voice before she identified herself. She said, "Byron County Police Department, this is Donna speaking, how may I direct your call?"

"I need to talk to whoever is in charge of homicide investigations," I said. My voice sounded small and immature in my ears, like a little kid trying to approach the adult table to ask for more dessert. I hoped it came off more confident on her end than on mine.

There was a long pause, and she said, "May I ask what it's regarding?"

"It's regarding a homicide investigation," I said. "It's important."

There was another long pause, and the phone went silent like Donna had covered the receiver with her hand. A few moments later, a male voice said, "This is Detective Fulbright, can I help you?"

"I need to talk to someone. I have information about a murder," I said.

He paused. I wondered what his face looked like. Did he believe me, or was he rolling his eyes, pointing to the phone while making a silent comment to his buddies? "May I record this conversation?"

"I don't care as long as you use what I tell you," I said. A boom shook the living room, and I heard Colin screech in delight. Idiot.

There was a click, and then the cop said, "For the record, this is Detective Fulbright recording a call on November 18, 2014. Go ahead."

I took a deep breath. *Here goes,* I thought. "I know it's going to sound crazy, but everything I'm about to tell you is true. There is a serial killer in Parkland—"

"Whoa," he said. "Sweetheart, that's a big—"

"Just listen," I said sharply. The line went silent as I continued, "There are dozens of victims, and I can give you names for at least eight of them. Many of them were never even reported missing. His most recent was Natalie Fullmer, who died almost a month ago. You all assumed she was a runaway, but she's dead. Some of his other victims are Tabitha Turner, Rosie Wilkes, Lilly Hanson, Gabriella Phillips, Carmen Pagani, Sarah Ketter, and Rae Wallace."

"Miss, how do you know all of this?"

"You wouldn't believe me if I told you," I said. "But they're all buried here in town."

"Where?"

"Here's the thing," I said, ignoring his question. "He kills on the full moon. But he'll kill early if he thinks you're onto him."

"Do you have any identifying information on this…killer?" I could just picture him making air quotes around the word "killer," and it made me angry.

"I left an anonymous tip the other day. Did you not check it?" I asked incredulously.

"Uh, I'll have to check into that."

I sighed. Sal's faith in his colleagues was seriously misplaced. I rattled off the description Natalie had given me. "I think it could be a guy that works at the Warehouse Eleven club downtown. His name is Carl, but I don't have his last name. Natalie was seen there before she disappeared."

"I see," Fulbright said. There was a long pause.

"Look, I know it sounds crazy," I said. "But I promise it's all true."

"How do you know? Are you connected to the killer in some way?"

"No!" I almost shouted. "I just have feelings." *I have feelings? Really, Bridget?*

"You have…feelings," he said slowly, like he would say *You knit sweaters out of your cat's hair?*

"Yeah," I said. "It's kind of like I'm psychic, but I'm not really. I just…I just know things."

He sighed heavily. "If this is a prank—"

"It's *not.*"

"All right. So do you have a *feeling* about where the bodies are buried? If you know where they are, that would let us start an investigation," he said.

"But he goes there," I said. "He was there yesterday. If he sees you—"

"If he goes there, we could catch him," the man said gently.

"Oh," I said. "Right. But you have to be subtle. If he figures out you know about him, then he'll kill whoever he's got to keep from getting caught."

"Sweetheart, we know what we're doing," he said.

"Do you? Because Natalie Fullmer died almost a month ago and you guys closed her freaking case," I snapped. My face was hot with anger. "You do realize any dumbass with thumbs can send a text message from someone's phone saying they're alive, right?"

There was a long pause, and I had the awful suspicion that he was going to hang up on me. "I'll look into the handling of that case," he said finally. "What's the address?"

My heart pounded as I looked over the list of victims' names. Was I about to add someone to that list?

Honestly, I wanted this to be someone else's burden. If they failed to catch him, it wouldn't be on me anymore. Even so, I couldn't forget what Natalie had told me. If I told them what I knew, then I would bear partial responsibility for whatever followed, good or bad. Then again, if I didn't tell, and he just kept on killing...I would share in the responsibility for that as well.

I took a deep breath, then exhaled in a trembling sigh. "3487 Woodlake Road. Please, don't let him see you. You'll get someone killed."

"We won't," he said. "Look, I'm going to trust you, but you're looking at jail time if it's a joke."

"It's not," I said. "I promise it's for real. Please find him."

"Thank you," he said. "Listen, do you need protection? We can help—"

But I didn't hear the rest. I hung up and tossed the phone away. It bounced and slid between my pillows. Out of sight, out of mind.

I had barely hung up when Natalie snapped into existence and headed straight for me. She came up against the salt barrier, pounding against the invisible wall with one dirty fist. Even through the barrier, I felt the glacial intensity of her anger as her eyes flared lightning white. I gave her a triumphant grin. Finally, a victory for me.

"Don't. I know you're angry, but I had to." She gestured angrily toward the closed laptop on my desk, but I shook my head. I'd had enough of her ordering me around from beyond the grave. It sucked, but she was dead. I was alive, and I was going to carry the weight of this decision for the rest of my life, not her. "No. This guy is going to kill in the next few days. I had to call them."

Icy wind whipped my curtains in billowing waves. Natalie swept the laptop from my desk. It made a crunching noise as it hit the ground, but didn't break. A rustle of school papers followed, raining down slowly as the cold wind died down.

"Are you done?" I asked her. It's possible that I was a little smug with her. Possibly. It was easy to do within my line of salt.

Her eyes flashed again as she stuck up both middle fingers. I flashed one back. She stared me down with wide cloudy eyes. I expected her to start throwing around my clothes or hurling books from my shelves. But instead, she shrank back, defeated. She just shook her head and sat on my desk, arms folded across her chest as she stared at me. My triumph was short-lived as the familiar old guilt returned. Beating a dead girl in a battle of wits was like beating a toddler at arm-wrestling.

To pass the time and soothe my guilty conscience, I started calling the numbers on my list. I had seen enough crime TV to come up with a passable cop impersonation—I hoped. I started with Tabitha Turner. A woman answered after two rings, sounding tired. "Yes?"

"Hi," I said. "I'm calling from the Winder Police Department to follow up on your daughter's case." My hands were sweaty and shaky as I smoothed out my rolled paper. Was this illegal?

"I thought her case was closed," she said. "Have you found something?"

"No ma'am, but I wanted to follow up on some of the reports from earlier. May I ask you a few questions?"

She sighed heavily. "I answered all of your questions a hundred times, and they still didn't help you find my daughter. Why are you dragging it out again?"

"It won't take long, I promise," I said. My mouth went dry and sticky as I said it. She had been through hell already. I'd seen Mom go through it herself. I was grabbing a rusty knife and ripping open every half-healed wound Mrs. Turner had.

"Fine," she said, and I could hear the icy wall going up in her tone.

"Did Tabitha ever hang out in Parkland?"

"What? I guess so, once in a while," she said, like it was a stupid question. "Her and a friend would sometimes go to that club, what's it called...Warehouse something?"

"Warehouse Eleven?"

"That's it," she said. "But I took away her car after she ran away, and she hadn't been to the club for a good year before she disappeared."

"She ran away?"

"She had some personal issues when her father and I divorced. Hung with a bad crowd. She ran away a few times, but we did some family therapy, and that seemed to help."

"And you don't think it's possible–"

"Do not ask me that question again," she said in a cold voice that made my guts twist up in knots. "My daughter didn't run away."

"I apologize," I said. "Um, I think that's all. Thank you."

She hung up without saying anything else. Ouch. I hoped I had enough karma built up to make up for probably costing Ms. Turner another few months of therapy. It was for a good cause, which was what I had to hold onto. Guilt aside, I had gotten something from the call. The signs were pointing to Creepy Carl after all.

Natalie was still sitting on my desk, arms folded across her chest as she glowered at me. I carefully tiptoed to the edge of my circle and reached out for the laptop. After opening it and setting it on the chair, I leapt back onto my bed within the safety of the salt circle. I eyeballed Natalie, who paced a tight path in front of the desk as the computer powered on.

As soon as the computer powered on, she bellowed, "What are you thinking?"

"I'm thinking that you can quit being a backseat detective," I snapped back. "I'm doing the best I can."

"Your best is going to get her killed," Natalie said.

"And if I don't find him by Thursday, she's *still* going to get killed," I said. "And I'm sorry, but I'm pretty sure the police have a lot better chance of finding him than I do."

"You better be right," Natalie said. "Because if you're not, her death is on your hands."

And if I was wrong, Natalie wouldn't be around to give me a hard time about it. I would have to live with the guilt, but so be it. I was already used to that. At least I wouldn't have a ghost following me around like a macabre conscience that choked me or gave me nightmares every time she didn't get her way.

I sighed and went to the next number on my list. A male voice answered. "Hello?"

"Hello, may I speak to Mr. Roberto Pagani?"

"This is he," he said, his speech faintly accented. "May I help you?"

"Mr. Pagani, I'm calling from the police department about your daughter Carmen," I said. Here I went with the rusty knife again.

He took a deep breath before continuing. "Yes?"

"I just have some questions, sir. We're investigating another disappearance and wanted to follow up some loose ends with Carmen."

"I see," he said. In that long pause, I could picture him closing his eyes, steeling himself for what came next. *It's for a good cause,* I told myself. "All right."

"I was wondering if Carmen ever went to a club called Warehouse Eleven."

"Not that I know of. But she was not very close to me then."

"I see. Did Carmen ever run away from home?"

He hesitated again. "Several times," he said finally. "She used to fight all the time with her mother. Then she came to live with me, and she seemed fine. She was going to school, starting to bring her grades up, really getting back on track, you know? Then she just disappeared one day."

"All right," I said. That was disappointing. There was still the runaway connection, but no hard connection to Warehouse Eleven. "Thank you for your time."

My last call was to Sarah Ketter's mother. Her voice was full of hope as she answered. "Yes?"

"Ms. Ketter? I'm calling—"

"About Sarah, I know," she said. What the heck, was she psychic? "This is a dedicated line. What have you found?"

"Oh," I stammered. "I'm with the police. I'm trying to follow up on a lead. Did Sarah ever go to a club in Parkland, Georgia?"

"No," she said. "Which police department did you say you were with? Fulton County closed the case a month ago."

"Uh, GBI," I said, my stomach twisting in anxiety. I vaguely remembered discussing the state's investigative bureau in middle school social studies. *What the heck?* I was supposed to be asking the questions here.

"Really," she said. "They said they had insufficient evidence to investigate."

"Well, something new has come to light, and we're taking a look again."

"And your name was..."

"Salazar. Natalie Salazar." Natalie raised an eyebrow as she watched me crumple the paper, ink smearing like watercolor on my sweating fingers. Ms. Ketter knew exactly how the system worked, and she knew I was lying.

"All right, what is it you want to know?"

I had to take a minute to clear my head. My best bet was to ask my questions directly and then get off the phone before she got suspicious enough to call the real police. Could they trace my phone? Shit.

I shook my head and plowed forward. She had my number. I took a deep breath and asked, "Uh, did Sarah have a history of running away from home?"

"She did once," she said. "But we worked through it. I put her in therapy, and she seemed to be doing well. She was looking forward to the retreat this summer."

"Retreat?"

"Yes," Ketter said, like I should have already known what she meant.

"What is that?"

"I told you all about it before," she said. "She went to a girl's camp over the summer as part of her therapy. It really helped Sarah find her balance again."

"Can you tell me more about it?"

"It's called Skybridge. If you look it up, you should find it online. Or in your case files," she added, her tone taking on a sharp edge. "Since we've discussed it. I even gave you contact information for the program director."

"And she was in therapy as well?"

"Yes," Ketter said. "Her therapist recommended the program and made sure our insurance covered the cost."

"Okay," I said. "That's very helpful."

"Wait," Ketter said. "Do you have a case number, so I can call and follow up?"

"Uh, not yet," I said. "I'll call you back with it."

"Wait—"

I hung up before she could ask me any more questions I couldn't answer. For a minute, I waited for a return call from the police demanding to know why I was not only tormenting traumatized parents, but impersonating law enforcement to do it. But it didn't ring, so I finally let out a shaky sigh and quit ignoring Natalie. To her credit, she had waited patiently without doing any of her poltergeist tricks.

"Natalie, two of them mentioned something about being in therapy. One of them went to this camp or something called Skybridge. Do you know—" I froze, as her face went slack in surprise. "You've heard of it."

"I went to Skybridge two years ago," she said. "It was so lame. It was all group talk, you're okay, I'm okay, let's hug it out bullshit."

"But you went," I said. "Did you go to a therapist here in town?"

"Used to," she said. "But she was a little old lady, not a serial killer."

"What was her name?"

"Nancy Rogers," she said. "I quit going because it was a waste of time."

"Oh, it's not a waste of time at all," I said. "This might be exactly what we need."

CHAPTER EIGHTEEN

WHEN WEDNESDAY ROLLED AROUND, I took one look at my phone and stuck my head under the covers. It was November 19th, and if there was a day I could get away with skipping school, it was today. It was two years ago today that Valerie died.

Most people–Mom included–would dread the day. Considering I saw Valerie almost every day, it didn't have the same significance to me as it did for Mom. No, I dreaded for another reason entirely. The reminder that popped up on my phone calendar said simply this:

Sending V.

It was time to pull that splinter and hope it didn't kill me.

"How are you feeling?" Mom asked when she stuck her head in the door. Her eyes were already red, but her face was perfectly made up. That was Mom, always put together. No falling apart in this household, or at least where anyone could see it.

She could have meant my feigned illness or Valerie's death, so I gave her a vague answer. "Like crap."

"Do you want to stay home?"

"Yes," I said quickly.

"Okay," she said. Normally she wouldn't have dreamed of letting me be out two days in a row, but today was an exception. "I was thinking we could spend some time together tonight, if you want. Maybe order out and watch a movie or something?"

"Okay," I said. "Sounds good."

But it sounded awful. I didn't want to sit and cry, only to pretend that things were okay again tomorrow. Mom had this weird way of compartmentalizing, where she could pull out her grief like an old scrapbook from the closet. She could run her hands over the old pictures and cry over her losses. Then came the part that utterly baffled me. When she was done, she somehow closed it up, all neat and clean, to put it back on the shelf until the next time she was ready. For me, it was a floodgate. Once it was open, there was no closing it.

"All right, well get some rest," Mom said. "I'll call the school and tell them you're still sick."

"Thanks," I said, tugging up my covers as she closed my door. I immediately dove out of bed and watched from the upstairs window until her car had cleared the driveway.

Fifteen minutes later, I was out the door and on my way to the park to meet with Sal. He was already there when I arrived, his face alight with excitement. All things considered, I doubted he was excited about a new snack machine in the station lounge. He made a *hurry up* gesture.

"Something's going down at the station," he said as I walked up and switched on the radio. "Everybody's talking about this mystery informant. They're talking stakeouts, opening up all these cold cases. They're ono the horn with GBI and the Feds. It's insane. Nothing like this has ever happened in Byron County."

"Shit," I moaned. "They were supposed to keep it quiet."

"They're putting a hush order on it," Sal said. "If they talk to anyone outside the department, they can lose their jobs."

"It'll just take one to run their mouth," I said. My stomach twisted into knots. "Sal, was this a mistake?"

"No! You did the right thing," Sal said. Then again, he was kinda biased.

"Okay, so help me out on this," I said. "I got in touch with three families yesterday."

"You did *what?*" The radio screeched with feedback. With my ears ringing, I fumbled to turn the volume down. "Bridget!"

"I called them and said I was the police."

"Oh Jesus, Mary, and Joseph. It's a crime to impersonate a police officer."

"Seriously, Sal? This guy is killing people and you're going to give me a hard time about a couple of faked phone calls?"

"Okay, fair enough," he said sheepishly. "Did you get anything?"

"Affirmative, Officer Salazar," I said. He grinned. "One of the girls used to go to Warehouse Eleven, just like Natalie. But the others, at least as far as their parents knew, didn't. But, two of them said they had to go to therapy, and one went to a retreat called Skybridge. Guess who else went?"

"Natalie?" he said. I just nodded slowly. He punched the air triumphantly. "You need to call the police again and tell them."

"Are you sure?"

"Absolutely," he said. "They're still getting organized. It'll be another day before they move on anything."

"Okay," I said. I dialed the number again. When I told Donna I was their mystery tipster, she immediately transferred me.

"What do you have?" Detective Fulbright asked. I heard the click of the recording halfway through his question.

"Several of the girls went to this camp called Skybridge," I said. "They went there because they had a history of running away from home. I think that's the connection between them. That's important, right?"

"It's something. Could be useful," he said. "Thank you."

"Hey, can you tell me what's going on?"

"Sure, come on into the station and tell me how you got all this information. I think that's a fair trade." I just sat in silence. "Didn't think so."I hung up, and looked up at Sal. "What do I do now?"

"Pray?" he asked.

Not really my thing.

Instead, I walked back to the gas station near the killer's graveyard and sat down inside the abandoned shell of the car wash. Except for the faint rushing sound of the road noise outside it felt quiet and isolated from the rest of the world. The dingy cloth fingers let in stripes of light, leaving deep pockets of shadow inside. I sat down in one corner and set out Valerie's laptop. The webcam light didn't come on automatically, so I guessed Natalie wasn't lingering around.

"Natalie?" I said hesitantly. The salt and holy water were in my backpack for protection, but I really needed to see her. I sat staring at my collection while I waited for her to show up. Maybe she was giving me the ghost version of the silent treatment.

While I waited, I tried to figure out what I was going to do for Valerie that evening. I wanted to make sure I got to say goodbye to Valerie properly before I lost my power for good two days from now. It was a weird coincidence that I'd end up saying goodbye on the day of her death, but Kale had just said, "He works in mysterious ways." As usual, he was vague on who *he* was.

Valerie's final sending was supposed to have been something special, with pictures and music and flowers and everything I could think of to show her she was loved. I had intended to plan it down to the word so that she'd go in peace, with no regrets about leaving me behind. But I'd been so wrapped up in helping Natalie that I had forgotten about it entirely. Now there was no time left. It felt wrong that I had spent more time preparing to send off a stranger like Anna Cole than I had for my sister, who had been my whole world. But I couldn't put it off. Today had to be the day, or I risked leaving Val her here. Tara's words about what happened to spirits who lingered too long echoed in my mind. I couldn't let that happen to my sister.

With Valerie gone, all I had left was Emily. That was, if she ever quit being mad at me. I realized with a little surprise that I hadn't spoken to her since she hung up on me yesterday. I guess trying to find a serial killer made you forget everything else. I checked my phone, but I didn't have any messages from her. She didn't answer when I called, so I sent her another text.

I know you're mad, but please just let me know you're okay.

No response. Maybe I really was alone now.

A sudden chill in the air told me Natalie was here. Not alone then. I had a pissed-off ghost for company. Great. I looked up at the computer to see Alive-Natalie glaring from the monitor. She snapped, "What?"

"I need your help."

"What do you want?"

"I'm thinking that the police may find your killer, but they might not be fast enough."

"Gee, I wonder who else thought that," she said.

"Anyway," I said, "I need you to get the others. Figure out what they remember of where you were kept. Was it always the same place?"

"Hold on," Natalie said. She faded until I could barely see her in the shadowed interior of the car wash. A few minutes later, she solidified again, with half a dozen of the other ghosts flanking her.

"I need to know what you remember," I said, looking up at them. They gestured wildly, but Natalie held up her hand to silence them.

"They're upset," she said.

"Gee, you think? Can they show me their memories like you did?"

Natalie turned to them. As she spoke, I felt the cold breeze that always accompanied her flaring emotions. In the presence of so many agitated spirits, the temperature plunged. The shell of the car wash crackled and popped as it grew painfully cold. Did I need to be afraid of them? Their eyes were like stars in the darkness, but they were a distant, cold reminder of how insignificant I was, not the serene twinkling of wishing stars. I was very small in the deep shadow of that "something larger" Tara had talked about.

Finally Natalie turned back to me and shook her head. "They can't reach you. They're trying, but they say it's like there's a wall around you."

Tara's words about opening the door came back to me then. There was a way to speak to them, but I might never be able to turn it back off. There had to be another way. But there was so little time left. The full moon started tomorrow, and someone was about to die.

CHAPTER NINETEEN

ON THE WAY HOME, I stopped at a grocery store and wandered blankly through the aisles to clear my head. If I could have, I'd have put this off. One more day, so I could pick the right song to sing to her, maybe gather some of her things so we could take one last look at them together. It wouldn't be perfect, but it would be better than this. I just needed one more day.

But this was it. God, it was unfair.

I got a cheap bouquet of pink-dyed daisies and a Milky Way Dark—Val's favorite—before leaving the store. My feet turned to lead as I approached home, and I had to stop several times along the way to coax myself into going on. It was like walking to my own funeral. Instead of crossing the street and taking the left into our neighborhood, I kept walking down to the old neighborhood where she and I had both grown up.

Our old house was in a single-street neighborhood called Foxwood. It was a single dead end street that formed a horseshoe around the lake. A gazebo jutted out into the water on one side, and that was where I headed. Valerie and I used to play there for hours when we were little, pretending to be princesses, pirates, and everything in between. I'd always known this was where I wanted to send her off, not from that awful place on the interstate.

Dead leaves crunched underfoot as I trudged onto the short wooden bridge to the gazebo. Murky lake water rippled faintly in the breeze, sunlight glittering in blinding beams. As I looked around, I was struck with a dozen memories at once: a Peter Pan and Captain Hook style stick fight; jumping around on the railings until Dad shouted at us to get down before we fell in the damned pond; running and dancing around the benches like

Liesel and Rolf after we saw *The Sound of Music* for the first time; feeding the new ducklings until Mom figured out why the bread was running out so fast.

"Is it time?" she asked, jolting me out of my memories.

"Yeah," I said, turning to watch her approach. Like always, she wore her favorite jeans and the black sweater she had worn the day she died. She looked luminous, almost angelic, with the sunlight passing through her. "I'm doing the ritual on my birthday."

"I'm glad," she said, but her face was solemn.

As she drew closer, I realized she *didn't* look the same as always. Her blue eyes were clouded in blotches of gray. Dark trickles ran around her neck like a crimson necklace. The legs of her jeans were soaked through with blood, and glass glittered against the fuzzy knit of her sweater. She was dying all over again. And just like before, I couldn't stop it.

"I wish I could have it both ways," I said, laying out the flowers in front of me. "But Tara says the longer you stay here, the worse it gets for you. Eventually there won't be anything left of you."

"Bridget, I'm scared," she said, sitting down in front of me. "I don't know what's next."

"Me either," I said. "But it has to be better than staying here. You're gonna be okay."

I remembered the last time I had told her it would be okay, and how that had worked out. I didn't have the first clue if she was going to be okay, and I had to do it anyway. Even worse than sending her off was the thought of her following me, alone forever as I went on with life, completely blind to her.

"Okay," she said. She forced a smile to her face, the kind that you wore to make someone else feel better, not for any real personal sentiment. "I love you, Idget. Don't ever forget that."

"I love you too, Valley," I said, using our old childhood nicknames for each other. "I'm so sorry. For everything."

"You didn't do anything wrong," she said.

"I let you down," I said, still afraid to tell her what really weighed heavy on my heart. We had no secrets but this one.

She shook her head. "Not possible. I've always been proud of you. Take care of Mom and Colin, okay?"

"I will," I said, tears streaming freely down my face now. "I don't know what else to say. I can sing, or whatever you want me to do. With Natalie, I just—"

"I already know," she said. The breeze picked up then, strangely warm, and I smelled the faint smells of grass and the flowery perfume Val had worn before she died. And just under that, the burning rubber that made my throat close up. "Don't forget to smile on Friday."

"Val—"

"You're going to be okay," she said. "I promise."

And with that, I couldn't keep back the tears. I covered my face, shoulders shaking as I cried for the big sister that I let down the one time when it counted.

"You're going to be okay, I promise," I told her. The car was upside down, the horn was blaring, there was glass everywhere. It was chaos. I was crumpled in a ball on the roof of the car, which had swapped places with the floor. It was cold. My leg hurt.

"Don't leave me," Valerie said weakly, her voice pinched tight with pain. Her manicured nails were bloody as she reached for me. Shards of broken glass bristled from the back of her hand like scales.

"I won't," I said. "You'll be okay."

My head hurt. There weren't words for my leg, which looked like the aftermath of a chicken dinner. Sharp stings pricked my palms as I slid backwards out of the car, purse in hand. Had to do something. Call the police. Call Mom. Get Val out.

My fingers left bloody streaks on the face of my phone as I dialed 911.

"Bridget, help me," Val moaned. She tried to reach out for me, but she cried out before her hand got past the window. Her body was contorted around the steering wheel. The highlights in her hair were streaked violent red, dripping at the ends.

"You're going to be okay," I told her again as the dispatcher picked up. "Please help us. We're on the interstate."

"What is your location?"

"Uh, it's near the billboard for the Hardee's," I stammered.

"Are you hurt?"

"My sister, she's stuck," I said.

"Bridget, come back," she wailed.

"Are you in a red car?"

"Yes," I said, trying to keep my cool.

"Someone else just phoned in. An ambulance is on the way. You need to get out of the road if you can and wait for help."

"Please come get my sister," I said. "She's stuck."

"I'll stay on the line with you," she said.

"I'm fine, just come help Valerie," I said, setting the phone aside as I crawled back to the car. My hands stung as I got down to peek in at Valerie.

I had to help her.

I had to get her out.

But it was already too late. Through the fractured kaleidoscope of the back windows, I saw a glow, and thought in that fuzzy head-injury sort of way, "what a pretty light." I kept thinking that right until the pretty light struck the overturned car, flipping it through the air to land in a mangled heap in the middle of the interstate.

We shouldn't have been out. I begged her to take me to the mall before it closed. I insisted that she drive faster on roads that were still slick from an afternoon thunderstorm. She died because she didn't want to disappoint me by telling me no. My whining got her killed.

They said that she would have died instantly, that she would have felt no pain. They said this as if it was some sort of consolation that my world ended quickly instead of dragging things out. But there was nothing that made it better, and nothing that ever would.

She didn't even make it out of the car. They said I was touch-and-go for a while, and they thought they had lost me for real in surgery. They were calling it a miracle that they brought me back. But I didn't make it back entirely, because something in me died forever when Val did.

Wind whipped around me, cooling the tracks of tears on my face. I got a strong whiff of Val's perfume, and I realized too late that she was moving on without me. I opened my eyes to see her gazing out on the lake, her body slowly fading. Her head was tipped back, her face up to the sun that could no longer warm her skin. She was smiling, arms open wide to whatever waited.

There was still so much to say, and the time was running through my fingers like so much water. "Don't go! Please, Valerie, don't leave me here alone!"

I stumbled to my feet, flinging myself against the railing of the gazebo as she faded into the sunlight. With huge, gulping breaths, I took in the last of her scent as the wind died. Within moments, all that was left were the fishy smells of the lake and old wood, drifting on a gentle breeze.

And then my sister was truly gone.

As I walked home, I realized with vague dismay it was past my curfew. Mom would be home and demand to know where I had been. Not that it mattered.

But when I stumbled in the front door, my mother took one look and threw her arms around me. Her eyes were red, and I briefly wondered how she knew that Val had finally gone on. Then my brain caught up. *Duh.* For me, mourning Valerie was just getting started. The last two years had just been a warmup.

"Oh, honey," Mom said, squeezing me painfully tight. I didn't bother trying to hold it back anymore. My breath hitched as I sobbed into my mother's shoulder. She wore the same perfume Valerie did. The scent just made me cry even harder. "It's gonna be okay."

"She's really gone," I said.

"I know, I know."

"I'm alone now," I said, not caring that Mom had no idea what I was really talking about. She pulled away from me, giving me a sad expression. Her makeup was streaked down her face, her eyes puffy and bloodshot.

"Sweetie, you're never alone," she said. "I will always be here for you."

"It just didn't hit me before," I said. "She's not coming back."

Mom just nodded. We'd had this same conversation a dozen times, but she just went along like it was the first time. "I know, sweetie. And one day, it won't hurt as much. That's what they keep telling me, at least."

"But it still hurts," I said. It hurt like it had right when she died, and any illusion that I was okay was gone. I would *never* be okay. Not after this.

"Yes, it does," she said, scrubbing away a fresh spill of tears. "It hurts every day. And I think it always will."

I was never going to see Valerie again. I was never going to fight with her over the bathroom or get advice on my makeup. I was never going to ride in a car with her, or try on her old clothes. I was never going to wear an ugly dress in her wedding, and I was never going to be an aunt for her undoubtedly gorgeous kids. I was never going to hear her laugh or hug her again. A million possibilities died when Val did, and the thousands of futures I had once pictured with her were gone. It was all gone.

"I'm going to order some dinner," Mom said. "Do you want something?"

"I think I'm just going to go to bed," I said. "Sorry."

I left her sniffling in the kitchen as I trudged up the stairs. For once, Colin was in his room; he usually steered clear of Mom and me on days like this. If he was upset, he hid it from us in true family tradition. I dropped my book bag without looking and flopped onto my bed. I curled up under the covers with my shoes still on, staring at the foot of the bed like Val might magically appear. I knew better, but my heart still clung to a stupid, lingering hope that she'd come back to me.

The tears came again, trickling steadily down my cheeks as I stared blankly at the stars on my ceiling. *Come on. Haven't I done enough? Can't I have just this one thing?*

I wasn't alone for long. Kale appeared around midnight, his face sympathetic as he perched on the edge of my desk where Natalie usually sat. He just watched me quietly for a few minutes without speaking, which made me inexplicably angry. "What do you want?" I finally snapped. "I'm kind of having a moment."

"You did it, huh?"

"No, I'm crying because I just watched *Bambi*," I said, turning onto my other side so that my back was to him. My pillow was damp and cold against my cheek, and little flyaway strands of hair were sticking to the wet spot on my face. I didn't bother trying to wipe them away, just closed my eyes to block out the rest of the world.

"Okay," he said. The sound of his voice, trying to be comforting when my world had just ended, was like hearing Alvin and Chipmunks singing "It's a Small World" at a funeral. He obviously didn't find himself nearly as annoying as I did, because he said, "You know it was the right thing to do."

"Was it?"

"She was already suffering. She hid it to keep you from worrying, but it was well past time for her to go," he said. "I know you're in pain, but you set her free."

I didn't care if he was right. That didn't put my heart back together. I tugged the covers up over my face as the tears started again. "I can't do this anymore, Kale."

"It's almost over," he said.

"No it's not," I said, my voice muffled by my comforter. "I'm not going to find this guy, and he's going to kill someone tomorrow. And even if I really can get rid of this curse, I'll always know that I failed." And that was the worst of it, wasn't it? Even if I got rid of this, I'd never really be free of it.

"I told you I could make you forget." I flipped back my covers. Cool air flowed into my blanket cave. His blue eyes were solemn as he looked down at me. "I wasn't lying to you."

"You could really do that?"

"It's dangerous, but I could."

"All of it?"

"You'd forget everything you've seen, all the ghosts, everything," he said. "You'd be completely normal again."

"I don't know…" I said. Playing around with my memory sounded sketchy. Then again, amnesia might be nice after the week I'd had.

"Just think it over," he said. "You can tell me tomorrow."

Tomorrow. When the end of the world would get that much worse.

CHAPTER TWENTY

THE THOUGHT OF GOING BACK to school on Thursday morning made me feel sick again, and the thought of what was going to happen when the full moon rose was enough to push me into projectile vomiting territory. I was thankful I hadn't eaten in a while, or my room would have looked like a scene out of *The Exorcist*. When I got up to use the bathroom, the sight of my own pale, blotchy reflection startled meme. My eyes were puffy and shadowed with exhaustion. Hell, I looked worse than Natalie.

But none of that convinced Mom to let me stay home again. She'd put her grief back on the shelf like she always did, so she checked my temperature and proclaimed me healed. I tried using Emily as an excuse, since she wouldn't answer her phone to confirm whether she was picking me up. Our neighborhood was the first stop on the bus route, so it had passed the house a good ten minutes before I even got up. Undaunted, Mom got ready two hours early to drive me herself.

I smoothed on a light layer of foundation and some mascara to try to balance out the aftermath of my crying jag the night before. When I went to put on Valerie's old sweatshirt, I could barely look at it without my throat pinching tight. Instead, I pulled out a pretty blue hooded sweater and tugged it on over my head. I even put in a pair of earrings. If I had to go to school and face the crowds of people staring at me, I wasn't going to do it looking like a zombie. I looked borderline presentable, if a little tired and sad.

Mom was still getting ready by the time I finished, so I opened my laptop and checked the Parkland Chronicle website. There was no *Serial*

Killer Caught Red-Handed headline blasted across the front page. So much for a lucky break. I wanted to call for Sal and find out what was going on, but Mom knocked on my door to let me know she was ready.

She looked me over and raised her eyebrows. "Well, don't you look nice."

"Thanks," I said, trying not to be insulted that she was so surprised.

I couldn't help smiling when she handed me an insulated lunch bag, unbalanced by the weight of a soda can tucked into one end. She hadn't made me lunch in years, and she didn't say anything as I took it. "Thanks."

"Sure," she said.

We were silent on the ride to school, but I could tell Mom wanted to talk about yesterday. She kept glancing at me furtively, her earrings tinkling as she looked back and forth. We had just passed the student parking lot when Mom finally took a deep breath and spoke up. "I know we've been kind of distant since Valerie died, but I want you to know I'm still here for you," she said as she pulled into the long line of cars dropping off students.

"I know, Mom," I said absently.

"Seriously," she said. She put her hand over mine and squeezed. "I can't imagine what it's been like dealing with this at your age. Plus with your dad...but I'm always here."

"Thanks, Mom," I said, giving her a quick smile for her benefit. "I know you are." That seemed to ease her tension a little. Like I said, I was getting pretty good at lying. She leaned over to kiss my forehead, which was unusually affectionate for her. "Thanks for the ride."

"Have a good day," she said as I got out of the car.

Yeah, right.

The stares started the instant I walked in the door. Like a cold rain on bare skin, it was impossible to ignore as each one hit me. I tried to pretend it was positive, like everyone was noticing my new and improved look. Yeah, right. After I heard a girl whisper, "That's her," I made a beeline for the library.

On my way past the office, I saw a newly posted bulletin board with the Fall Court pictures. A banner saying *Vote Friday Morning!* hung just above the board. The ballot boxes sat on a table directly below the board. On the bulletin board, there were six gorgeous girls and one that looked like she was getting over the flu. Well, at least I stood out.

The library was empty except for a few students playing games on the computers. I retreated to the back corner, where a few computers had been wedged in between the reference and periodical sections.

The stares were already fading into distant memory. At this point, being a social outcast was a non-issue. Trying to find a serial killer before he serial-killed again had a way of putting life into perspective.

So why was I even at school? Another absence was hardly a blip on the radar compared to what was going to happen tonight. I mean, what teacher was going to refuse to excuse an absence for tracking down a serial killer? I should have said, "Mom, I'm sorry, but I have to save the day today. School just doesn't fit my schedule."

Clearly, I was getting delirious.

The problem was that I was operating entirely on an education from crime TV shows. Considering it took the detectives an average of forty-five minutes to solve a case, I'd have to say that my education was lacking, or that they were in on some secret I had yet to learn.

"Okay, what do you know?" I asked myself, digging in my backpack for my notebook and pen. I smoothed out my creased notes and reread the names of the eight victims. I already knew the connection: Skybridge. That was where I had to start. I did a quick search on the school computer and immediately found the camp's website.

Based on my highly scientific TV education, it was possible and even likely that a Skybridge employee was the killer. In their *About Us* section, I found a picture of the two female founders–both decidedly non-serial-killer looking types–and another picture of the counseling staff. They were a mix of male and female, mostly young, all friendly looking. No one came close to the description of the killer. There might have been other staff, but I didn't have the time or the access needed to find out. By the time the police maneuvered through that labyrinth of connections, his next victim would be dead.

I shoved my chair back and stared up at the ceiling. I felt myself verging on an epic whine, the kind that seemed like the only logical reaction to being completely overwhelmed. A brief fantasy flitted through my head– flinging myself onto the floor, pounding my fists as I screamed at the top of my lungs.

Instead of acting out my immature, if enjoyable, fantasy, I just sighed and shook my head at the ceiling. Divine intervention wasn't coming, it seemed. "Think, Bridget," I said quietly. "There has to be something."

I knew where the killer's victims were buried, but unless they found his driver's license on the ground, that wasn't an instant win either. If they'd even moved on my tip, they obviously hadn't found a smoking gun yet, or I'd have read about it in the papers that morning. None of it was enough, and the killer was going to strike again because I didn't know–

"Where he took them," I said aloud. I glanced over at the librarian, who was up to her elbows in the book collection bin. She apparently hadn't heard me talking, which was good. I was so used to talking to what would appear to be thin air. That was going to be a hard habit to break.

222

A few years ago, I had watched this serial killer marathon on TV, fascinated and creeped out at the same time. It was sad, but I remembered more about that than I did about anything I'd learned in biology class this year. Serial killers were all about routines. The fact that all the girls were killed on the full moon, then buried at the same place pointed to my guy being set in his ways.

Natalie died at the grave site, but maybe one of them had surprised him by fighting back sooner. Or maybe one of his early kills had died early, before he figured out his technique. If one of them had died at his hiding place instead, I might be able to get something solid for the police.

And for that, I needed Tara's help again. I had Natalie's memories of her death—and no matter what Kale said, I'd never get them out of my nightmares—but I needed the other girls to tell me what they knew about his lair. If one of them had died there, I could find the location just like I had the graveyard. It was a long shot, but it was all I had.

I slipped out of the library to call Tara, and realized dimly that the homeroom bell had already rung. "You're tardy," one of the assistant principals shouted across the commons. "Get to class."

"Yes sir," I said, waving as I darted down the science hallway. My homeroom was on the math hall, but I didn't have any intention of being an attentive student today. I kept walking to the exit doors at the end of the hallway. As soon as I was outside, I whipped out my phone to call Miss Tara. I hoped she was a morning person.

As the phone rang, I leaned against the cool brick and tried not to let my imagination run wild. *Come on, come on.*

"Hello?"

"Miss Tara, it's Bridget Young. From the other day."

"I remember," she said.

"I need your help."

"What can I do for you, dear?"

"I need you to speak to the girls again," I said. "I need to know if there's something different from what I saw already."

There was a long pause. "I see."

Okay, not the reaction I was hoping for. "I can't get there in time," I continued. "I need you to come here to do it. I'll be happy to pay for your cab fare, or gas, or whatever, but—"

"No," she said, and while her tone was still polite, there was a definite finality to the word.

"What?"

"I said no," she repeated. "This is my safe haven, and I will not call up a host of angry spirits outside these walls."

"But the girls—"

"I've said no," she said. "Please don't ask again."

"Then can I come to you?"

"I never said you couldn't," she said in an annoyingly sweet voice.

Seriously? I took a deep breath and reminded myself that swearing at the only person who could help me was a poor course of action. "I'll be there soon," I said and hung up before she said goodbye. Great, now how was I going to get across town? I was in good shape, but it was a good five miles to Tara's, and I didn't have the time to waste walking. After buying flowers yesterday, I only had ten dollars to my name, so another cab was out. I was still weighing my options when my phone rang. I answered it without looking, expecting it to be Tara calling me back. "Hello?"

"Hey, Bridget, it's Kari," a woman's voice said.

I frowned in confusion. Why was Emily's mom calling me? "Hey, Kari. Uh...what's up?"

224

"Shouldn't you be in class?" she asked.

"Oh, I've been really sick," I said. I faked a cough but it was probably a little late.

"Is Emily there with you, then?" she asked, apparently unconcerned with my health.

My stomach twisted with a feeling I couldn't quite place. "No…"

There was a long silence. "Be honest, Bridget, I won't be mad at you. My daughter, on the other hand…"

"I'm serious, Kari," I said. "I haven't even talked to her since Tuesday. She got mad at me and said she was going to Aunt Stacey's."

"Oh my God," Kari said. "She wasn't home when I got in last night, so I called her. She texted me back saying she was staying with you last night. I was trying to stay out of her way and let her cool down a little before we had World War Three over her skipping school."

My stomach fell out and hit the ground that time, or felt like it did. "Kari, have you actually *talked* to Emily? Like heard her voice?"

"No, she won't answer my calls," Kari said. "And I just got a call from the school saying she's been out of school since Tuesday. I mean, really, all I ask is that she goes to school and doesn't completely flunk out. Is that so much to–"

"Kari, shut up," I said. My heart felt like something was kicking my sternum from the inside.

"Bridget! There's no need–"

"Kari, shut up," I said more vehemently. "You need to call the police right now." Another awful thought occurred to me, like some twisted form of divine inspiration. "Have you ever heard of something called Skybridge?"

Say no, say no.

Kari's long silence was all the answer I needed.

225

"Oh God," I murmured. "Please say she wasn't going."

This is not happening.

"I just got confirmation a few weeks ago that she made the waiting list. How do you even know about that? I haven't even told her yet."

"I can't explain," I said. "Call the police. Tell them Emily is missing, and it has to do with Skybridge. They'll know what it means."

"Bridget, you're freaking me out," she said.

"You *should* be freaked out," I practically shouted. What the hell? If it had been my mom, she would have pounded down doors until she found me. Then I would have been on my way to the ICU after the royal ass-whipping she dispensed. I used to think Kari was the coolest mom ever, but now her cool act might have let Emily fall into serious trouble. "Go call 911. Now!"

My whole body was rubbery with anxiety as I paced the sidewalk in front of the school. I had to get to Tara. I had to call Kale for help. I had to do something. It was possible that Emily really was on her way to Stacey's and ignoring all of our calls, and it was just as possible that she was tied up somewhere, terrified and alone as a killer–

"Stop," I said aloud. I could already feel my heart racing, my skin breaking out in a cold sweat as hysteria loomed. Breaking down right now wasn't a luxury I could afford. I had to think outside the box.

It didn't take many steps outside the box to find an idea. It was a terrible one. Okay, actually, it was a fantastic idea, but I was a terrible person for coming up with it, and even worse for actually doing it. What was it we kept talking about in history class–*The end justifies the means?* These were going to be some seriously mean means, so I hoped the end was really worth it.

My conscience had to take the backseat as I dialed the school's front office. I pressed *1* to get to the main secretary. In a breathless rush, she said, "Fox Lake High School, this is Ms. Brown speaking. How may I help you?"

I was so going to regret this. Dropping the pitch of my voice, I said, "This is Michael Fullmer's mother. I need you to call him out and tell him to meet me out front to speak to me. I just got some news about his sister. I'm not sure if you knew, but she was missing. I want to fill him in."

"Oh, that's wonderful, Ms. Fullmer," the secretary said. "What is—"

"Just call him," I said sharply. "I'm out front."

Finding Natalie's killer had to make up for what I was about to do to Michael. If this led to finding her killer, then he would *have* to forgive me. Assuming I could even tell him what I had done, and that he believed me, that was.

As I paced up and down the sidewalk out front, an awful thought struck me. Even if Kale could make me forget, Michael would still remember. He'd be stuck with these memories forever, and because of them, he'd hate me for what he would see as a borderline psychotic manipulation of his love for his sister. For a split second, I thought about running away and letting him think it had been some twisted prank call.

But I couldn't do it. This was the best solution I had, and I couldn't back off because it would be a little painful. I would sacrifice the fragile seed of our relationship, would never kiss those lips if it meant saving Emily's life. A few minutes after my call, Michael came sprinting out of the school. His face fell when he saw me. That was minor compared to how he was about to react, but it still stung.

"Bridget?"

"Michael, I'm so sorry about this."

"What the hell is going on?" he said, looking around me like he was expecting Natalie to pop out from behind me.

"I…I needed you to come outside," I said.

His jaw dropped. "So you used Natalie?" I felt like something was stabbing my gut as I saw his face shift from confusion to rage. "What the hell is wrong with you?"

"You want me to make you a list? Look, I don't have time to explain."

"You better find time," he said. "This is sick."

"Okay," I said. "I see dead people and I know there's a serial killer on the loose. And also I need your car keys."

He just stared at me. "Do you really think that's funny?"

"No, I really don't," I said. I stepped closer and grabbed his arm. It was tense and trembling under my grasp, just like it had been when he wanted to smash Carl's face in. "I know you're going to hate me forever. I don't like it, but I can live with it. What I can't live with is knowing I could have done something to stop this guy and didn't. So you can either drive me or you can give me your keys."

"What do you mean, you could have done something to stop—this guy who? Bridget, I'm not taking you anywhere until you explain."

"Michael, I don't *have* an explanation other than what I just told you," I said.

"Fine," he said. "If you think this is funny, then you're ten times as crazy as anyone thinks. You can go ahead and delete my phone number, and don't ever speak to me again. I would think you of all people would understand what this is like."

"I *do* understand," I said. "And that's why I have to do this."

"You know what?" he said. "Go to hell."

He yanked his arm out of my grasp and turned away. He paused, and turned back like he wanted to say something else to me. That moment of hesitation was what I needed. As he stood there, trying to find the perfect words to tell me what an asshole I really was, I did something I'm not proud of. I mean, I wouldn't even do this to Colin on his most annoying day, and my little brother would be an Olympic contender if being obnoxious was a sport. But Michael was the only thing standing in my way.

With that in mind, I wound up and gave Michael a UFC-worthy kick to the nuts. He was a big guy, but apparently a good kick to the family jewels was the great equalizer. His shocked face went slack as he hit his knees. His fingers curled up as he moaned in pain. I was so shocked that I just stared at him for a solid ten seconds. *Did I really just…no way.*

"What the hell, Bridget," he moaned, bracing his hands on the sidewalk.

The words jarred me out of my daze, and I remembered there was a reason I had just completely incapacitated my former crush. I dropped to my knees on the sidewalk and reached out for Michael's keys. They were a sharp-edged bulge in his jeans pocket. I snaked my fingers in to grab them. He made a half-hearted attempt to stop me, but I slapped away his grasping fingers easily and backed out of arm's reach.

"I'm *so* sorry, and I hope I can make it up to you someday. I know this doesn't mean anything to you right now, but if this works out, you'll understand why I had to do it. You might even thank me, though I won't hold my breath," I said as I fumbled through to the black-capped car key.

Without looking back, I ran for the parking lot and prayed I wouldn't have to lose any more friends today.

CHAPTER TWENTY ONE

THANK GOD MICHAEL'S car was an automatic.

I didn't drive. Theoretically, I knew how, thanks to Val sneaking me off to the school parking lot right after she got her license. But ever since she died, the last thing I wanted to do was get behind the wheel of a car. I still got nervous just being a passenger. Sitting in the driver's seat alone, my heart was trying to burst out of my chest *Alien*-style.

My phone buzzed angrily, and I took it out to see Michael's picture on my screen like an accusation. He had recovered enough to call me, which alleviated the fleeting fear I had really hurt him. I ignored the call and eased the car out of the parking space.

Okay, so far, no fiery death. Good.

"He is going to hate me," I said. "Shit, this is car theft. Shit." So in addition to impersonating a police officer and contaminating a crime scene, I was now a car thief. This was going to look *awesome* on a resume. Did this make me a badass?

I drove all of twenty miles an hour as I pulled onto the main road outside the high school. The car was struggling to go. I had to jam my foot down hard on the gas just to get it up to twenty-five. Whatever. I was okay with slow. It was hard to flip a car and die horribly by going slow.

My arms were locked tight as I gripped the steering wheel mercilessly. Someone leaned on the horn as they passed me. I hoped that my scowl sufficiently conveyed my irritation. I didn't dare take my hand off the wheel to flip them off. The good part of my terror was that I had to focus so intensely on not crashing the car that all my other fears had diminished into background noise.

"Jesus, take the wheel," a male voice crooned from my right.

I yanked the wheel to the right and skidded in the gritty mud of the shoulder before I corrected. "Kale, you creepy son of a—"

"Hey," he said. "I'm trying to help you. Take the parking brake off."

I looked down and saw the handle sticking straight up like the proverbial sore thumb. The car jolted forward when I released the brake. "Oops."

"You're a mess," he said, shaking his head. "Do you even know how to drive?"

"It's not rocket science."

"Apparently it is, Einstein."

"Look, you either have the best or worst timing ever," I said. I filled him in on my conversation with Kari. "It can't be coincidence, Emily just disappearing like this. Although it would be really awesome if you could convince me it is."

"I don't know either way," he said. "You know, you're really cutting it close. We're supposed to do the ritual tonight."

"Kale!" I snapped. "Hello, priorities? Can't we just do it tomorrow?"

"No," he said. "It has to be tonight."

"But why?"

"It just has to," he said sharply, eyes flaring bright. "That's how it works. Seventeen is a special age for a sensitive. It's tonight by midnight or never."

"Well you're just a big fat load of useless," I said irritably. How was it that he couldn't budge on this? What happened to doing the right thing?

"Stop sign." I stomped on the brakes and scowled at the smug expression on his handsome face. I've never wanted to punch a ghost so bad in my life, not even Natalie, and that was saying something. "Useless, huh?"

"Shut up," I said. "Then help me do this before it's too late."

"What do you need me to do?"

"Find where he takes them," I said. "Do something useful other than remind me of the freaking ticking clock. In case you haven't noticed, I've got that part figured out."

"I don't know if I can find him just like that. Right," he said. "Right. Turn the wheel to the right, Bridget!"

With tires screeching, I turned abruptly and narrowly missed a stray black cat scampering across the street.

Come *on*, universe.

I slammed to a halt at the foot of Tara's driveway. When the metal death machine was safely turned off, I turned to glare at Kale, and got even madder at the angelic expression on his handsome face. How was he so damn calm? "Then what the hell can you do? I'm a seventeen year old kid—"

"Sixteen."

"Sixteen! Even better! I'm practically flunking out of high school, and I've managed to turn up more evidence on a freaking serial killer than the police have. You're a Guardian, whatever the hell that is, and you can't even find out where a bunch of girls were taken? Seriously?"

"Well there's no need to be nasty about it," he said, folding his arms across his chest.

"Oh, go cry about it!" I shouted. But he was already gone, and I thought I smelled smoke in his absence. "Great! Is there anyone else I can piss off today?"

I kicked the door open hard enough to make it swing back on my leg with a painful crunch—instant karma—then slammed it shut behind me. With my backpack bouncing against my back, I stomped up Tara's yard. I was so mad and worried at the same time that I probably could have picked up the car and thrown it. Instead, I ran right up to her door and pounded on it.

She yanked it open and ushered me in. I didn't bother with pleasantries, just shoved past her as I said, "It's my friend Emily. She's missing. I need to know right now where he takes them."

"Bridget, I already got all I could from the girls," she said, shaking her head and setting her silver ponytail swinging as she followed me into the sitting room. As I plopped down onto the couch, I smelled cinnamon rolls. The sweet, spicy scent set my stomach churning again. How could people be eating breakfast when a girl was *missing*?

"There has to be something else," I said. "There are like sixty of them, and all you gave me was eight names."

Tara frowned and shook her head as she sat down on the couch across from me. "Those were the only ones who spoke to me. It's possible that some of them didn't make it this far. Most spirits can't venture far from the place they died."

I resisted the urge to smash her adorable kitten tea set like a rampaging Godzilla in a china shop. "That's why I wanted you to come to the grave site," I said slowly, spitting every word so I wouldn't scream at her in frustration.

Her face darkened like a storm cloud had passed across her eyes. For a moment, I realized that she was quite a lot bigger than me, and she had the ability to summon a horde of angry ghosts away from their graves to get up close and personal with me. And considering Natalie—that would be *choked me half to death and made me hallucinate* Natalie—was the most even-tempered one of the bunch, that could have made for a very bad day indeed. "And I told you no."

"But why?"

"Because that's a whole lot of angry spirits, and I can't control them all at once," she said.

"But they want to help," I protested.

"Not all of them," she said. "Some of them have lingered far too long. Their pain has driven them mad, and they'll hurt anything that comes near them, including me and you. Reaching out to them is like locking yourself in a room with a rabid dog."

"But—"

"Bridget, I'm sorry," she said. "It's too dangerous. For both of us."

"Then just tell me what to do," I said. "I'll do it. What do I need? Candles? The silver chain? I'll do whatever you say."

"Then you should leave," Tara said. She put up her hands defensively. "I admire your zeal, but you have to know when you've done enough. That's my advice to you. Call the police and move on."

Like I had done enough for Valerie? If ever there was a time to earn peace, this was it. This was the first time I'd be able to help someone *before* they died. "Miss Tara, I'm begging you to tell me. Please."

"And I'm telling you no, no matter how politely you ask," she said, her voice rising. She stood and pointed firmly toward the front door. "Now please leave, or I'll call the police myself."

"Do it," I said, folding my arms as I wiggled down further into the couch. "Tell them you refuse to help find a missing girl. That's aiding and abetting. Maybe accessory to murder. Don't you watch TV?"

"Bridget—"

"Tara, I'm not leaving until you tell me how to open the damn door! What happened to all that crap about higher purpose and mysterious ways? Maybe all of this has happened to both of us so that we can save Emily's life."

Her eyes softened for a minute, but then she shook her head vigorously. "Please leave."

"Nope."

"Fine," she said. She took a step toward me, and I prepared to fend her off if I had to. But she skirted around my chair and headed into the kitchen for the blue plastic phone on the wall. There was a thunk as the phone hit the floor. "Oh my…"

I stood to see what had startled her and gasped myself. There was a brilliant light in the kitchen. It took me a full five seconds of staring to realize it was Kale, but not the Kale I knew.

Holy…

His blue eyes were painfully bright, and he had sprouted a massive pair of feathery wings. They curved up and over his head, gleaming like there was a spotlight behind him. His face was carved from silver-flecked stone, and his voice sounded like three voices speaking at once. "Taralynn Bledsoe, I command you."

Her eyes went wide, and she backed into the kitchen counter. "I can't–"

"You would disobey a messenger of the Most High?" he bellowed.

The echo of his voice shook the house, sending the china set rattling toward the edge of the table. One kitten-painted cup toppled over the edge and landed safely on the fuzzy knotted rug underneath. Tara didn't even notice; her eyes were locked on his terrible gaze.

"I'm sorry," she said weakly, tearing her gaze away to look at her feet. She hurried out of the room, then came back with a notepad and a pen.

As Tara wrote, I just gaped at Kale. *Was* he an angel? He may have been beautiful, but there was something deeply unsettling, even frightening about him. He wouldn't meet my eyes as he glided silently to loom over Tara. Her hands shook as she wrote. Every few lines, she sneaked a furtive glance at him.

Fifteen minutes later, I had a set of written instructions to call up the spirits and command them. I glanced over it, and it seemed relatively simple. Then again, there was no section saying, *What to Do if the Dead Turn on You*, either. Easy didn't mean safe.

"Do not interfere with the Lord's work again," Kale said to Tara. "Or I will return."

Tara's eyes went wide as she cringed and cowered. Then as quickly as he had appeared, Kale was gone, leaving Tara trembling. A quiet sniffle made me realize she was crying from fear.

"Thank you for this," I said after a long, awkward silence.

She didn't acknowledge me, just trudged into her kitchen. I heard the sound of cabinets opening and closing. She returned a minute later with a plastic grocery bag full of candles and sage. Without looking at me, she pressed the bag into my hands. "Bridget," she said in a small voice.

"Yes?"

"I don't know if you remember what I said before. But once you open this door, you can't close it. This is not a game," she said. "You'll never be the same. You'll see them everywhere, and not just the nice ones. They're not all sweet like your sister."

I chewed on my lip and shook my head. "I guess I have to take that risk."

"Well, don't say I didn't warn you," she said quietly. Her voice had regained some of its strength. "Now please go. And don't ever come back."

I left her house without another word. There was no mistaking the cold hand—Jeremy the ghost, maybe?—that shoved me out the door. The brass knocker jangled as she slammed the door behind me.

There was something inherently wrong about terrorizing Tara, maybe even worse than what I had done to Michael. Whether it was justified or not, it wasn't fair that people like Michael and Tara had to be hurt because of this. As I replayed my Greatest Hits in Asshole Behavior over the last few weeks, I realized I had been doing a lot of wrong in the name of good. Would it all balance out in the end? Or was I eventually going to have to pay for all this? If it was true that what goes around comes around, then I had some bad days coming.

"Yeah, well, life's not fair," I said as I got back into my stolen car and set the bag of candles in the passenger seat. Fueled by my success, ill-earned as it was, I was adventurous enough to drive the speed limit through the suburb of Marymount to the abandoned Fuel'n'Go just outside the killer's graveyard. When I stopped, I checked my phone and found I had fifteen missed texts and calls, but I ignored them all. I didn't need Kari or Michael or anyone else distracting me.

Nothing was going to stand in my way now.

I went inside the car wash shell again and set out Valerie's laptop, which was battered after my graveyard flight and Natalie's temper tantrum in my room. After powering it on in case she made an appearance, I arranged the candles and silver chain to match the sketched diagram in Tara's instructions. Once they were set up, I read carefully over her written instructions.

There was a simple little speech—I couldn't bring myself to think of it as a spell—then I had to reach out to the spirits. It didn't sound difficult, but I couldn't stop thinking about what Tara said about opening the door. I was so close to being rid of this curse, and now I was going to make it worse, like picking off an almost healed scab.

"I'll be fine," I said to myself. Yeah, I didn't even convince myself.

"No you won't," Kale said, appearing in a rush of cool air. He had returned to his usual appearance.

"You need a bell," I said irritably. "Like a sneaky kitty."

Usually he was good for a sarcastic response, but he didn't even seem to hear me speak. "I'm serious," he said. "If you—"

"Kale, what are you?" I interrupted. "What the hell was that at Tara's? And if you say 'I'm just a Guardian,' so help me, I'll—"

"What, this?" His eyes closed for a moment. A cold blast of wind whipped my hair around my face as a pair of huge white wings materialized, arching gracefully around him.

"Holy balls," I murmured.

"It's just a parlor trick," he said. He spread the wings wide, casting an eerie glow on the metal walls of the car wash. With a little shake of his head, his dark hair grew into a long white mane down his back. "It's not real."

"But—"

"I'm a spirit, Bridget," he said gently. "I just played a trick on Tara." He shook his head again and returned to normal Kale, with his casual clothes and a pair of eyes that didn't hurt to look at. But it wasn't just a trick, and we both knew it. Maybe he wasn't an angel, but he wasn't *just* a spirit either. Now that I had seen what he could do, there was something about his casual, easy personality that worried me. The fact that the wolf looked so convincingly like a sheep was the exact opposite of comforting.

"Good trick," I finally said, avoiding his direct gaze.

He shook his head slowly. "Bridget, if you do this, I can't guarantee my ritual is going to work afterward. You could be stuck like this forever."

I just stared at him blankly. That was what I was really afraid of, wasn't it? That was what Tara meant when she said I couldn't close the door once I opened it.

238

"I can make you forget," he said gently. "All of it. Natalie. Mia. Even me." Now that I had seen his little show at Tara's, I believed him.

For a moment, I entertained a guilty fantasy. I'd forget *all* of it. My sister would just be dead and gone, and I'd have been through the grieving process like any normal person. It would suck, but people had gotten over much worse. I would be as surprised as the rest of the world when the front-page headlines read: *Serial Killer Apprehended, 60 Victims Found!* I could gasp in horror when I saw the news footage of them exhuming bodies and interviewing the grieving parents, without the heavy burden of guilt and wondering what I should have done differently.

And I wouldn't have to know how I had walked away from my best friend, knowing I was the only one who could stop what was about to happen.

I wished I could say it was a no-brainer, that I chose the right thing without hesitation. I liked to think I was a decent person, and this was an easy choice for a decent person, right? But it was difficult as I weighed the options of each choice. I could let Kale take my memories and not have to do that impossible thing they call *living with myself* after. I'd never even have to know about how guilty I *should* have felt. It would be so easy.

But I'd walked away once. I made the wrong choice with Valerie. It was my fault we'd been on the road, but I'd still had a chance to make it right. I could have gotten her out, but I was so scared. Selfish, childish, cowardly; I'd called myself all three and worse. But it all came down to this: I should have helped her first. She had begged me to help her, but I got myself out first. The time I wasted calling 911—when someone had already called—would have saved her life. Her death had come down to one split-second decision, and I had chosen wrong.

I wouldn't choose wrong again.

"If you're going to help me, then help me," I said. "This is what I choose."

He bowed his head, then nodded. "I'm your Guardian until the end. For better, or for worse."

I didn't like the way that sounded, but I nodded and said, "I'm ready."

As I reread Tara's instructions, I took out a small silver cross I kept in my ghost kit and laid it in the center of the circle of candles. It said I needed an item of faith. I hesitated, then took off Valerie's dragonfly necklace and added it.

"Archangel Michael, I implore you to watch over me as I open the door. Protect me from evil and guide my hand to do your work. I give myself freely. Spirits of the wrongful dead, I command you to appear before me," I said, my voice shaking as I envisioned myself grasping a door handle and flinging it open. The candles ignited suddenly. My voice faltered at the sight, my heart racing at the sight of the flames. Tension built in my chest, ready to explode with the slightest spark. "I open the door for you. I open the door for you. I open the door—"

The world went white. My heart pounded, each beat an explosion that threatened to shatter my ear drums. I fell backward through screaming wind, and the blinding light slowly faded. My fall slowed until I simply stopped, but there was no impact or sensation that I stood on anything solid. I looked around in wonder and found myself standing in a featureless gray expanse.

The untouched apparition of Natalie Fullmer stood before me. "Nice trick," she said. She was beautiful, her face free of the traumatic injuries that had marked her before. Her long wavy hair was back to its natural chestnut brown, her eyes as blue and clear as the afternoon sky.

"Where am I?" I asked her.

She shrugged. "Somewhere between," she said. I followed her gaze upward to the distant image of the cloudy afternoon above us. I was afraid to look down. Like it sensed my fear, the ground trembled a little under my feet. "It's all right. You're just visiting. For now."

"If that was supposed to be comforting, it wasn't," I said with a nervous laugh. There was a thunderous boom from overhead. The resonating echo of it left me feeling dizzy. What was that?

"Why are you here?"

"I need to see them. All of them," I said. She hesitated, then disappeared for a second. There was another roll of thunder that nearly knocked me over. What the hell? I closed my eyes, but realized that had been a mistake as the world began to spin around me. I opened them quickly, then let out a clipped shout of surprise as I saw the host of spirits. Dozens of girls stood behind Natalie.

Like her, they all appeared alive, but there was something otherworldly about them. Their eyes were like colored flame, their skin pale and luminous. I recognized a few of them from before. Sarah Ketter stood right next to Natalie, staring at me with the same intense green gaze I had seen staring off her mother's website. As each of their faces seared into my memory, I imagined their loved ones forever lost in limbo as they wondered what happened. I couldn't forget this, no matter what Kale said.

I felt like the littlest gazelle in the herd as the spirits stared, glowing eyes sharp and predatory. "I need you to think. I need to know where he took you. I know he has another girl now, and you're my only chance of stopping him in time. Please."

Just using the male pronoun made them uneasy. Shoulders tensed and eyes winced. A low murmur rose as they shifted in place. Lightning arced across the gray landscape and I staggered as another thunderous drum beat—*boom boom*—sounded. My chest ached as the sound echoed. Exhaustion hit me like a wave. I had to concentrate hard to keep my eyes from closing. "We don't know," Natalie said.

"No," I said. I had *not* just done a bunch of ghost hoodoo for nothing. "*Think.* I know most of you died in the graves, but did anyone die somewhere else? Did you see anything that would help me find where he kept you? I know it's awful, but please think."

I heard a moan of anguish, and like a yawn in a crowded room, it spread, until it was almost deafening. A chill ran down my spine. I took a tentative step back. Like a pack of ravenous lions, they moved closer, and I could swear some of their eyes darkened to blood red.

"Please, anyone?" I pleaded. "My best friend is going to die if we don't do something. Please help me save her."

The wails stopped as if someone had yanked out a speaker cable. The crowd of spirits parted to leave a single girl isolated at its center. She was tiny, with a thick dark braid over one shoulder. Her eyes were downcast, but she walked slowly toward me, her steps small and unsure.

"I remember," she said, and her voice was dry and choked. When she raised her head, I saw that her eyes were completely black, like her pupil had taken over her entire eye. She reached out for my hand, and I hesitantly let her take it. As soon as her cold fingers closed around mine, I felt that sense of falling again. This time, I hit the ground with a bone-cracking impact.

When I landed, I was lying on my side, my head throbbing.

Where was I?

The last thing I remembered was sneaking out of the football game to smoke with my friends, when something hit me hard in the back of the head. Now my hands and ankles were stuck together, tied with something I

242

couldn't loosen as I struggled. Panic exploded through me in an electric shock. I flipped over on my side, and the motion made me realize something was tied over my eyes. The cloth shifted slightly as I rubbed my head. I saw a sliver of light and rolled over to try to see more.

But there was a metallic scrape and a rush of humid air as the van door opened and someone reached in for me. I tried to scream, but there was something sticky covering my mouth. I fought as much as I could, fishtailing against the man and driving my knees into his chest. He grunted in pain, and suddenly I was flat on my back on the concrete, staring up at the stars. In the struggle, the cloth had fallen off my eyes, and my vision filled with the sight of the nearly full moon against a blanket of black.

I strained to look around. There were old, mildewed cardboard boxes stacked against a brick wall. *Bulk Spaghetti* and *Diner Napkins* were all I could make out before he picked me up again. As he did, I read the plastic sign next to the door.

Giavino's Employees Only.

Seeing the name jolted me, and I suddenly had the bizarre sensation of sharing the dead girl's memory. Until then, it had been like I was reliving my own memory.

But I couldn't break free of the memory any more than she could break free as the man dragged her into the kitchen of the abandoned restaurant. She—we—fought him the whole way, and he reached out for a heavy wooden rolling pin. He brought it down on one of her arms with a sickening crunch. I cried with her in agony as the bone snapped. He brought it down again and again until she quit struggling. Her neck was rubbery and weak as she slumped on the ground, staring up at a strangely stained wall, all grimy except the precise edges of a white square halfway up.

"You never could stop fighting me, Caroline," he said in a curiously high voice. What was he calling her that for? Her name was Nadia, which I knew as surely as I knew her favorite color and the brand of cigarettes she smoked. "Just do what you're told," he said as he swung the pin again. Black bloomed in her vision. Her body went numb, which was a mercy. "It will be so much easier when you learn to mind me. Just listen…"

Then something grabbed me and struck me hard across the face. That hadn't gone numb. My face was hot and stinging as something struck me again. I opened my eyes to a pair of strange blue eyes. "Breathe, dammit!"

My eyes widened, and I suddenly realized I was dying for air. I gasped for breath and coughed violently. "Giavino's," I wheezed. The strange gray landscape and the spirits were gone. I was back in the metal shelter of the car wash. Kale was standing over me, his eyes glowing bright as he stared down at me.

"Are you all right?" Kale asked. He hunched over me, looked into my eyes like he saw something hiding there.

"No," I wheezed. I slumped back against the cool metal wall. My cheek stung where he had slapped me. He was one hell of a strong spirit. "She died at Giavino's. The old one. The brick oven. The freaking wall. Five thousand pizzas."

"What?"

"The wall Natalie saw," I said again. "The brick oven used to be there, but it was clean in one spot where there was some kind of vent before. They must have patched it up when they moved."

That was it. I had found it. So why didn't I feel relieved yet?

"Okay," Kale said. "Then you need to call the police and get out of here."

"Yeah," I said. I finally brought my hand up to rub my face. "Holy shit."

244

"Don't do that again."

"I don't plan on it," I said. As I stood up to dig in my pocket, I got a warning throb that preceded the worst headache I'd ever had. I staggered and pressed my hand to my forehead. "Holy–"

"Yeah," he said, catching my wrist and righting me as I stumbled. It was like he was completely human and alive, a thought that scared the hell out of me because Kale hadn't changed one bit.

I had.

"Bridget, you were dead for at least a minute."

I just gaped at him. "It was just a hallucination."

"Bridget, I know dead when I see it," he said. "You were close for a few minutes, and then it just stopped. You quit breathing, and your heart just stopped."

"No way," I breathed. The thunder, the drum beats I heard...that had been my brain processing my own death.

"You didn't just open a door," Kale said. "You tore the damn thing off its hinges."

CHAPTER TWENTY TWO

I WAS ABOUT TO CALL the police again when a new text message arrived and covered my screen. It was from Mom, saying, *Where the hell are you? Call me right now.*

Had she heard something? If she had, this was about to get messy. Mom answered halfway through the first ring, and her voice was just a shade shy of hysterical. "Bridget, where the hell are you?"

"I'm at school," I said, leaning against the cool hood of the car as I brushed my fingers absently across my cheek. My face was still hot and stinging from the impact of Kale's slap.

"Like hell you are!" she screamed. I yanked the phone away from my ear as she bellowed. "Emily is missing, and you're not at school, and I've been worried sick!"

Wait, what? "What do you mean, Emily's missing?"

"It's all over the news," Mom said breathlessly. "I wanted to make sure you were okay, only for the school to tell me you never showed up today."

"Mom, I can't explain," I said. "I'm fine. I have to go."

"Bridget Leanne Young, don't you dare hang—"

I hung up. The phone instantly began buzzing in my hand like an angry bee, but I ignored the call, and the one that came right after that. If I didn't get killed by a serial killer or arrested for one of my many petty crimes or accidentally strangled to death by an angry ghost, I was going to be grounded for the rest of my life. The Cave Man treatment didn't even begin to touch how much trouble I was going to be in.

But I had bigger things to worry about. If Emily's disappearance had made the news, then the killer had to know they were onto him. I pulled up the browser on my phone and opened the newspaper website. They didn't have anything yet, so I checked the news station's website. The top headline read: *Breaking News: Local Girl Feared Kidnapped.* My stomach dropped when I opened the article and continued reading.

An anonymous police contact confirmed that they are currently investigating a series of disappearances previously thought to be unconnected or runaway cases.

My stomach heaved as I read the first line over and over. I couldn't even read the rest. Emily was as good as dead. And it was my fault. I should have never told them. What now? All I could do was call the police again and try to get them to Giavino's before he killed Emily.

I had just dialed *91* into the phone when an icy wind kicked up. The glacial air was so powerful that it was like a hand shoving me backward. The phone flew out of my hand and shattered against the metal wall of the car wash.

Natalie stood before me, looking furious. Strangely, she looked more like she had in my vision—alive and well again. I could see a trickling puncture at her neck and blood on her fingernails, but otherwise, she was untouched. With one bloody finger, she pointed to me, then to herself, then drew her finger across her throat in a fairly universal gesture.

"I didn't tell them!" I said. "It's not my—"

Cold hands shoved me back. My head smacked the metal wall hard enough to make me see stars. Natalie's sudden strength could have just been her hysterical fury with me, but I knew in my heart that it was because of what I had just done. The wall that protected me from the unhinged spirits lurking around had come tumbling down, and now I was fair game for them. "It *is* your fault," Natalie screeched.

"It is not!" I shouted back, even though I completely agreed with her. Then her hands released me. We gawked at each other. "Wait, I can hear you—"

"—without the computer. Oh my God."

"Natalie, I didn't do this. There was a leak, or something." But then I realized what I had done. I purposely told Kari about Skybridge because I knew that was the key word to make the police act quickly on Emily's disappearance. So this *was* my fault. After everything, if Emily died, it was going to be on me.

"Did you get what you needed?" she asked.

"Yes, but it's no good because some people can't control their tempers," I said, pointing to the destroyed phone on the ground. I had the one piece of information the police needed, and I was on a deserted island as far as communication went.

"Sorry," she said sheepishly. Her rage had gone, dissipating as quickly as it had come.

"Whatever," I said. "I have to call them. I need to get a phone."

Natalie hurried after me as I got into the car and pulled out onto Woodlake Road. She raised an eyebrow. "Why do you have Michael's car?"

"Um, I borrowed it?"

"Borrowed?"

"Stole," I amended. "I also kicked him in the balls."

"Wow," she said, shaking her head. "He's gonna be pissed."

"Understatement of the year," I said. "But he'll have to get over it."

There was a drugstore just ahead. Quick choice. I swerved across two lanes of traffic to pull into the parking lot. I was quickly getting over my fear of driving. Something about a serial killer about to strike made everything else seem easy.

"Park," Natalie reminded me as I tried to yank the keys out of the ignition. I jammed the shifter up into park and half tumbled out of the car.

"I need a phone," I shouted as I ran into the drugstore. There was a line of people at the checkout, where there was only one register open. The cashier looked up at me, then pointed out the door. "Phone!"

"There's a pay phone across the street at the BP," she said.

I stepped in front of a woman trying to hand the cashier a thick stack of coupons. The woman tried to protest, but I shot her a glare that was at least scary enough to make her take a big step back. Her extreme couponing could wait, dammit. I looked at the cashier's name tag, then pointed at her. "Victoria, there's a serial killer out there, I know where he's going to be, and I don't have a damn quarter! Now give me the phone!"

There was a ripple of conversation around the counter, and Victoria just gaped at me. If I had been an action movie badass, I would have pulled my gun and threatened her, but instead, I just barged around the counter and grabbed the black phone mounted on the wall behind Victoria. I hit 0 and shifted nervously in place while I waited for the operator to pick up. "Operator, please speak the name of the city."

Oh my God, seriously?

"Parkland, Georgia," I said.

"Is that—Heartland, Georgia?"

"Park. Land."

"Parkland, Georgia?"

"Yes!" I shouted. Then I had a brilliant idea that seemed fairly obvious in retrospect. I had an excuse for being a little slow, considering I'd flatlined for a minute and was currently running on high-octane terror. I slammed the phone back on its cradle and picked it back up. This time, I dialed 911 instead.

"911, what's your emergency?"

"Hi, I know where the missing girl is," I said. Victoria just gaped at me, then yanked out her cell phone and started texting. I watched as the three customers in line did the same and realized this was about to get very interesting, and not in a good way

"Ma'am, this is not a—"

"Are you listening to me?" I spluttered.

"Ma'am, this is an emergency line. If you have information for the police, you need to call the police department."

"Under what definition is this *not* an emergency?"

"Ma'am, we have to ask—"

"Oh for...can you transfer me?"

"One moment."

Victoria's phone made a harp sound, and she leaned to whisper, "Is this for real?"

"Oh yes," I said irritably. "Totes."

"Cool," she said.

"No, not cool, Victoria! This is the opposite of—"

"Fox Lake Police—" the receptionist said pleasantly.

"Donna, we don't have time," I interrupted. "It's your mystery informant. Get Fulbright."

"One moment," she said. Maybe I was getting to be popular. She didn't even question it anymore. Maybe I needed my own hotline now with a red phone.

"Did you go to the news?" a gruff male voice asked by way of greeting. "You could have just gotten that girl killed. If you—"

"No, the mother of the most recent victim did," I said, emphasizing the word *victim*. But the accusation had sunk in, gnawing at me like a rat on a good piece of rotten carrion.

"This place is a goddamned zoo," he said. "We've got tips pouring in left and right."

"He's taking them to the old Giavino's," I said. I watched as Victoria started texting again, and realized this might blow up in a bad way. I could just imagine it plastered all over Facebook, followed by dozens of people riding out to see if there was, in fact, a serial killer holed up at Giavino's. People could get hurt, namely Emily.

"In Marymount?"

"Yeah."

"How do you know?"

"I just have a feeling," I said. What the heck else did I have to lose? I might as well tell him that a ghost told me.

"Well, kid, I hate to tell you and your feelings, but I've got sixty-eight tips to get through already," he said. "I'll take it under advisement, but right now, our priority is finding this missing girl."

"Oh for God's sake," I muttered. "She's *at* Giavino's. I know she is."

"We'll send a car over as soon as we can," he said. "Thanks for the information."

And then he hung up on me. The good guy hung up on me.

I didn't waste any time getting righteously indignant. Instead, I grabbed Victoria's phone and ran back around the counter. The stunned customers didn't make a move as I dashed through them and knocked over a display of M&Ms.

"Hey!" Victoria shouted as I ran out the automatic doors. An older man started to follow me out the door, but I was already in the car and backing up by the time he got to the sidewalk. I peeled out in a screech of tires and onto the main road.

What the hell was I supposed to do now? It was already five o'clock, and it was starting to get dark. I had no business going out to Giavino's but that was exactly what I had to do. I had to walk right into the lion's den.

CHAPTER TWENTY THREE

THE OLD GIAVINO'S was much smaller than the new one, but it was still the largest building at the end of a mostly abandoned strip mall in Marymount. Dad had once explained in highly technical economic terms why most of Marymount was run-down now, but I had tuned him out in favor of a Mario Kart battle with Valerie.

The entire strip mall that had once housed Giavino's now had only one open store, a small Dutch bakery that was only open until two in the afternoon. The rest of the storefronts were hidden behind dirty glass or warped plywood. There were a few hopeful *For Lease* signs, but it was obvious that this place had already seen its best days.

Giavino's itself was at one end, a long building forming an L with the rest of the strip. I parked the car at the opposite corner of the parking lot. There were no other cars, and there wasn't another soul in sight. That boded well, right?

What didn't bode well was the quickly darkening sky, and the full moon that gleamed overhead, bright silver like light reflecting off a knife. Even in the half-light of afternoon's end, the moon was already huge and luminous, like a huge neon sign that said, "Time's up, Bridget."

But I couldn't just walk in there alone. Natalie had disappeared about a half-mile before I got to the strip mall. We must have crossed the border of where she could go. One second she was sitting in the passenger seat, and the next, I looked back to see her spirit standing in the middle of the road throwing her hands up in frustration.

Now I really was alone to figure this out. It would have been nice to have her give me pointers on what was inside. I rested my head against the steering wheel, banging it lightly. "Shit, shit, shit," I muttered in time with my head-banging.

"What's the plan?" Kale asked as he materialized. I didn't even jump this time.

"Can you go in?" I asked him. "I mean, with that whole avenging angel act you pulled on Tara—"

"Bridget. I'm not—"

"Can we not do semantics right now? I'm just *saying*," I said. "Surely you can go peek into an abandoned building."

He closed his eyes for a moment. "I can try," he said. He disappeared in a rush of cool air.

Okay, this was how it would go. Kale would find something, and I'd call 911 again to confirm she was here. The police would show up and rescue Emily, who would bounce back like she always did. Everything would be fine. This would go down in history as the most pants-wetting scary day of my life, but it was going to be okay. My heart slowed, and I felt like I could get a full breath again.

I managed to believe my fantasy for about thirty seconds, until Kale returned shaking his head. "It's like a wall around that place. Too much..." he shuddered. His face was creased in pain. "All that suffering. I can't get in there."

I sighed. "Of course you can't," I said. Of course the incorporeal spirit who could pass through walls and invisibly observe a serial killer couldn't go in. But I could.

Of course.

"Try calling Natalie," he said.

"Calling?"

"Like you called to the spirits earlier," he said. I took a deep breath and closed my eyes. But a cool hand closed on my wrist, and I opened my eyes to see him only inches from my face. Up close, his pale skin shone faintly. "Wait. When she comes, I have to go."

"And?"

"Be careful," he said. Then he did something he never could have done before. His lips brushed my forehead, cool and dry. A tingle radiated from the kiss, electrifying me all over. My heart lurched forward as I raised my head to look into his bottomless blue eyes. "Please don't get hurt."

It was hard to resist him. I wanted to lean in and kiss his lips, just to finally find out what they tasted like. But this was *so* not the time. "I'll try."

He nodded. "Goodbye, and good luck."

I closed my eyes again and felt a weird, swimming sensation. "Natalie," I said. My voice vibrated strangely as I spoke her name. Something tugged at my chest, and suddenly there was an ominous, low roll of thunder in the back of my head. A moment later, she appeared in the back of the car.

"Whoa," Natalie said. "That was weird."

"Tell me about it," I said. It felt like a string was pulled tight between us, connected at my chest. Somehow I was able to hold her here, even outside of her usual radius. "I need you to go in there and check it out for me."

She took one look at the restaurant, and her entire demeanor changed. Her usual bluster faded as she began trembling. Her shoulders hunched as she collapsed in on herself. Her face bloomed with bruises again, and I watched in frozen horror as her death replayed on her body like a horror film. "I can't," she moaned into her hands.

"Natalie, you have to do this."

"I can't!"

"Please, just try," I said. "Do it for Emily."

She glared at me, her pretty blue eyes going white again. Then she tore her gaze away and passed through the door of the car. I saw her moving in fits and starts, disappearing and reappearing in flashbulb images as she approached the restaurant. The connection between us was tense, like someone was pulling that string as hard as they could. My chest was tight and it was hard to get a full breath, but a little discomfort was worth it to not have to go inside

Natalie finally reappeared at the edge of the sidewalk, and froze, staring into the distance. Her apparition faded slightly, going dark like a shadow was falling on her. A moment later, I felt a snapping sensation in my chest. The tension eased slightly as Natalie retreated to the car. Now *that* was weird.

She was sobbing, hugging herself tightly as she reappeared in the back seat. "I can't," she wailed. "It's too much."

"You've asked me put my life on the line for this, and you won't even go look inside?"

"Bridget, you don't understand," she murmured.

Could I command her, like Tara had commanded the spirits at her house? I had already pulled her here, far from where she had died. Deep inside, I *knew* I could do it. All hyped up on adrenaline and fear, I was strong enough to force her in.

"Natalie! I–" I froze with the words on my lips. I remembered–all too clearly–what she and the other girls had been through. Dead or not, she was still human. And of all the things I had done in the name of finding this killer, this would be the one that was over the line.

"You know what, it's okay," I said. "Thank you for trying. You can go if you want to."

Her eyes flicked toward the window. I knew she wanted to leave. She pulled herself upright and closed her eyes for a moment. When she opened them again, they were clear and blue again. In a quiet but steady voice, she said, "I'll stay here with you."

Fair enough. I had one last idea.

"Sal?" I thought about his dopey smile, the polished brass of his badge and the tilted hat over springy dark curls. His consciousness suddenly awoke, like a dog perking its ears at its master's whistle. I grabbed him with my mind, imagining that I was twisting my hand in the collar of his shirt. He resisted, making it feel like pulling a knotted rope over a ledge. I gave it a ferocious tug, and suddenly Sal appeared in the front of the car. I didn't feel the weird tension connecting us like I had with Natalie. He glanced back at Natalie, who didn't scare him off like she did Kale and Valerie.

"Whoa," he said. "How did you—"

"Not now," I said. "I need you to do your cop thing and go check the restaurant out. I think my friend Emily is in there. If she is, I'll call the cops and get them here."

He cocked his head and gave a snappy little salute. "You got it, Bridget."

Thank God.

I watched him walk toward the restaurant, even reaching for the phantom gun at his belt as he walked through the front doors. Some habits didn't die, I guess. I wondered why he could approach and Natalie and Kale couldn't. Maybe it was because Sal's death hadn't been ugly; it had been tragic, but it had been quick and not overly malicious. Maybe he didn't feel all that psychic pain the way they did. It seemed like it shouldn't have bothered Kale, but maybe he was more sensitive about it because he was so powerful.

And maybe he just didn't like the smell of garlic. Who knew?

I drummed my hands on the steering wheel nervously as I waited. Sal had been gone for what seemed like hours before he finally came running back out grinning. "She's there!" he shouted as he stuck his entire upper body through the car window. It was disconcerting to have his ghost shouting in my face, but I didn't care. "Pretty girl, bright pink and black hair, right?"

"Oh my God," I said, sighing with relief. "That's her."

"Let's get her!" he said. "I'll go in first, and you cover me."

"Um, you're a ghost, Sal," I said. "And I'm unarmed. And scared out of my mind."

He shook his head, then looked down at his gun and laughed a little. "Oh yeah."

I dialed 911 on Victoria's phone. "911, what's your emergency?"

"I know where the missing girl is," I said.

"Ma'am, this is not a—"

I roared in frustration and hung up. After waiting thirty seconds, I dialed again. While it rang, I glanced at Sal and got an idea. A different operator answered, thank God. "911, what's your emergency?"

I let out a piercing scream. "Oh my god, someone's been shot at the old Giavino's in Marymount," I said. Wow, I was a terrible actress. Meryl Streep had nothing to fear from me. "There's so much blood, oh my god!"

"Just calm down, miss," the dispatcher said. "Are you injured?"

"No, but I'm scared," I said. "Oh God, he's shooting again, please send someone now!" I resisted the urge to say "bang bang!" for extra dramatic effect.

"Help is on the way," the dispatcher said. "Can you stay on the line?"

I responded by hanging up. Okay, now I just had to wait. The police would take care of it. Wouldn't they?

"What if he shows up before they do?" Natalie asked. Why did she have to keep saying what I was thinking? "You have to get her out now. It's dark now. He comes when it's dark. It's dark now," she repeated, muttering it under her breath like a mantra. As she rocked in place, the temperature in the car steadily dropped. After a few minutes, you could have stored hamburger meat in Michael's backseat without getting food poisoning.

Time was really up. If the killer showed up right now, he'd kill Emily. And the police might get there in time to catch him if we were lucky, but it would be too late for my friend. And I couldn't live with that, not even if Kale could make me forget. I sighed and pushed the car door open.

And then I went to save the day.

CHAPTER TWENTY FOUR

THIS DEFINITELY RANKED HIGH on the list of idiotic things I had done in my sixteen years. The front doors and windows were boarded over. I knew the restaurant had been closed for at least six years, because we had celebrated my eleventh birthday at the new location in Fox Lake. But the plywood covering the front windows looked like it had just come off the shelf at Lowe's. The nails were fresh and bright silver like the full moon, with no sign of the rust that streaked the fixtures on the stores further down the strip.

I pried at the boards, but they were good and tight. The killer didn't come and go through the front. I shook my head at Sal. "How about the back?"

"Let's check it out," he said.

I would have rather had Natalie for backup, since she could at least throw things around if she really concentrated. Sal was a gentle spirit, and he couldn't do much except give me a few seconds' warning if the killer showed up. I was really alone on this one.

We jogged around to the back of the restaurant. Faded yellow lines marked off parking spots against the back wall. The middle parking spot was splattered with the opalescent sheen of motor oil. Someone had been parking there recently. Shoved against the back wall of the restaurant was a dumpster streaked with suspicious dark brown stains. The cardboard boxes I had seen in Nadia's vision were gone, but the cracked plastic sign reading, *Giavino's Employees Only*, was still there. That little piece tied it together, and even though I'd never set foot back here in reality, I remembered every bit of it. I knew exactly what I would find beyond the red back door. The door was firmly locked, but I pulled hard on it for good measure. There was something in human nature that said you had to give a locked door a good tug.

"It's locked," I said to Sal.

"I noticed," he said. "You should be a cop with those investigative skills."

"Shut up," I said.

He just grinned. The weirdo was enjoying himself. "We could pry off the boards in the front. Well, you can pry. I can supervise."

I nodded, and we ran back around the front. Okay, I ran, and Sal sort of floated. When we got there, I wedged my fingers under the board on the left window. I winced as a splinter went under my fingernail, but I got some leverage. I braced my foot against the brick frame of the window and pulled as hard as I could. A couple scrapes and a stumble later, the board broke away from the window. Thankfully, it was only secured by a few nails. Once I got it off, I had a big enough opening to crawl through. I used the loose board to knock out the remaining shards of glass.

"Emily?" I called into the yawning black of the restaurant. Awesome. I had to go into a pitch black room with no weapons or even a freaking flashlight. I stopped to dig in my backpack and came up with the lighter I usually used for burning sage. It was better than nothing, I guessed. I could singe the killer's eyebrows if he got too close.

This was so stupid.

As I crawled through the open window frame, part of me was wailing a chorus of "oh God oh God what the hell are you doing?" But the other part felt like it was all just a crazy dream, so it didn't matter what I did because it wasn't real anyway. Because there was just no way I was ever going to walk into a killer's lair like I had any business doing so. I might as well just come in, kick over some tables action-hero style, and beat the killer unconscious with his own rolling pin for poetic justice.

"Emily?" I called again. Sal stopped at the window, and I gave him a thumbs up as I lit the lighter. "You stay there. Call me if something happens."

The lighter cast a tiny globe of light around my hand. I carefully tiptoed forward. My thumb was getting uncomfortably hot as the lighter burned. I made a slow pass in front of my face with it, and realized the front room was mostly empty. The tables and chairs were gone, leaving just their footprints in the dust and grit on the floor.

"Stupid, stupid," I muttered. I was going to get myself killed. But all I could think of was my Valerie, beautiful face bloodied as she reached through broken glass. When I told her it was going to be okay, and she said, "Don't leave me, Bridget." I saw her eyes on mine, the way she knew in her heart I would save her.

"I won't," I said. "Not this time."

My heart was beating so fast that I felt shaky and unsteady. My clammy thumb slipped off the lighter, plunging me into complete darkness. I fussed with it to get it lit again, and stubbed my toe. "Dammit," I hissed. Closing my eyes, I thought back to when I was younger. There was a step up in the back: on one side, there was a hallway that went to the bathrooms, and on the other was a half door that led to the bar and then to the kitchen. I swung to the right with the lighter and saw a glint of silver that had to be some sort of kitchen fixture.

"Emily?" I called.

My foot caught on something soft, and I tripped headlong to the ground. The impact jolted my wrists. I reached out for the soft thing and shook it. "Emily?"

"Mmmph?"

Oh God. She was alive. I stuck the lighter between my teeth as I ran my hands all over her, trying to find her face and hands at the same time. "Sorry, I just grabbed your boob," I said like an idiot. Tears were already streaming down my cheeks as I finally found her wrists, pulled tightly behind her back with duct tape. I ran my fingernails over the tape, trying to find an edge to start peeling the tape.

"Bridget?"

"Hold on," I said. "I'm just trying to get this tape off."

Then my blood chilled. Emily's mouth was covered. The voice was male, and it didn't sound like Sal. Had Kale come back?

The scrape of the lighter was like a gunshot as I illuminated a stubbled face. All at once I saw it: pock-marked cheeks, watery brown eyes, chapped lips.

Oh God.

The face contorted in rage. A brilliant white light shone in my eyes and blinded me. Something came down hard on my shoulder, sending an electric shock down my arm. The lighter flew out of my hand as I reeled.

"You little bitch," the voice said, curiously high for a man. Emily squealed, a muffled sound that didn't lose any of its terror through the tape on her mouth.

"Natalie," I screamed as I clutched my half-numb arm. "Carmen, Sal, Kale, anyone, help me!" I didn't know what else to do, so I closed my eyes and imagined a big door again. It was huge and black with a gleaming silver handle. With a wordless shout, I flung it open onto empty black space, and icy air blasted me from the void.

Something crashed against a wall. The beam of the flashlight bounced and ended up casting a hazy beam across the floor. The killer grunted in pain. I heard the beautiful sound of police sirens getting louder, until it was almost deafening. Blue strobes reflected off the steel fixtures.

"They're coming for you, asshole!" I shouted. The spots cleared from my vision, allowing the darkness to resolve into faint outlines. The killer shook himself and lunged for a huge rolling pin on a stainless steel table. "Is that what you do to the ones who fight back?"

He froze with it poised in the air. In the flickering blue light, I saw the dark stains on the pale wood. Rage washed over me as a dozen bloodied faces flashed in front of me.

"Yeah, I know what you did to them. I know what you did to Caroline, you piece of shit," I shouted. *What the hell am I doing?* I thought. "Girls, this is your chance! He can't hurt you anymore!"

I spread my arms wide. It was melodramatic but it just felt good at the time. Cold washed over me, whipping my hair back. This time the cold air was comforting, like air conditioning on a sweltering summer day. There was probably something mystical and powerful I could say, but I didn't know it. So I just went with efficiency and screamed, "Kick his ass!"

For once, the presence of the spirits didn't feel foreign or invasive. It was terrifying but exhilarating as they exploded into existence, thunder rolling and walls shaking. I heard the wailing voices of his victims, and I realized after a while that their words were coming out of my mouth. They were passing through me, and I realized I *was* their door.

Holy. Shit.

I watched as a row of claw marks scored his already pocked cheeks, and he clapped his hands to his face in surprise. "You're screwed. Fifty to one, asshole."

"You'll pay," he said, lunging for me. I threw up my hands, but it was a split second too late. The pin smacked the side of my head, sending stars exploding across my vision. The cold air suddenly stopped. I couldn't keep my balance, ears ringing as the world spun around me. I reached for the door again, but it was far away, blinking in and out as my head throbbed.

"Mmph!" Emily protested.

"Police! Come out with your hands up!" someone shouted from outside.

"I'm sorry, Caroline," he said, and then my world went black.

CHAPTER TWENTY FIVE

I F THIS WAS DEATH, then the afterlife looked a lot like a hospital room. It was all bland seafoam-green walls and a dizzying expanse of white square tiles. There were no heavenly choirs singing, but there was a TV silently playing *Law and Order* in the corner. And the white rectangle of light overhead was no heavenly door, but a quietly buzzing fluorescent light.

Not dead then. Good.

My head throbbed to a lazy bass beat. My mouth tasted like something small and furry had nested there overnight, then vacated after taking a morning dump. I reached up to shield my eyes from the painfully bright light. A sharp rustle of paper, like a startled creature diving into bushes, preceded a gasp.

"Bridget? Oh God," a voice squealed. I looked over slowly to see Mom standing by my bed. She burst into tears. "I thought you–it was–oh my God."

"Emily," I mumbled. My tongue felt thick and useless.

"She's fine," Mom said. "Bruised up, dehydrated, but okay. Honey, what happened? What were you doing there? How did you get there? What–"

"Whoa," a woman's voice said. I glanced over to see a doctor enter the room, flanked by a man with a badge clipped to the pocket of his blue sport coat. The cop was already pulling out his phone. He hung back by the door while the doctor approached. "Take it easy on her."

I looked over and realized without much surprise that Kale was sitting in a green plastic chair, looking at an open magazine on the table. He waggled his fingers at me. After he spared a glance at Mom, who was completely focused on me, he flicked his hand. A little breeze ruffled the magazine pages, and he went back to reading."Can you tell me your name?" the doctor asked.

What kind of stupid question was that? "Uh, Bridget," I said, surprised at the long hesitation. "Bridget Leanne Young." I saw Mom nodding behind her, grinning manically like I was spelling the final word at the national spelling bee or something.

"Okay, Bridget," the doctor said. "Do you know what year it is?"

"2014?" I said. I shook my head, which made the broken glass inside rattle around. "2014," I said, hoping it sounded more confident. What was she going to do if I failed the test?

"Okay. Do you know her name?" she asked, pointing to Mom.

"That's Barbara," I said. "My mom." Tears were trickling down Mom's cheeks. Good Lord.

"Okay," she said. "I'm going to shine a light in your eyes, and I want you to follow it." She took out a little flashlight that looked like a pen, then clicked it on. The light made my eyes hurt, but I didn't want her to recommend a lobotomy or something. I did my best to follow the light as she ran it back and forth in front of my eyes. I must have passed her test, because she clicked it off a few seconds later. A big blue strobing spot obscured her face as she loomed over me. "You're going to be okay. You had a mild concussion, but it looks like most of the damage was cosmetic."

"Doctor?" the police officer said. "Can I?"

"Take it easy," she said, backing up a little to allow the police officer to approach.

"Hi," he said. "I'm Detective Fulbright."

I just gaped at him. "Really?"

He frowned, and I realized it was a very odd thing to say. He didn't look at all like I had imagined. He was kinda short, but bulky with muscle. His dark hair was cropped short, and he couldn't have been more than forty.

Did I tell him who I was? I glanced over at Kale, who seemed to be following my train of thought. He placed his finger over his lips solemnly. I looked back to the detective and gave him a goofy smile that made my face hurt. I was going for *concussed ditz* and I nailed it, if I may say so myself.

He seemed vaguely unsettled, but he composed himself quickly. "Right," he said. "I just need to ask you some questions."

"Okay," I said.

"How did you end up at Giavino's?"

Why couldn't he start with easy questions, like my name? As I looked Kale again, Fulbright followed my eyes. Kale gave me an exaggerated shrug and shook his head. "You don't remember," he said quietly.

"I don't remember," I said.

"I see," Fulbright said. "Do you know anything about a reported shooting at that location?"

"Nope," I said cheerfully.

"That's interesting, because the call was made from a phone found on your person," he said. "So how is it you ended up at Giavino's?"

"I told you I don't remember," I said. "I remember getting up to go to school this morning, and then it's all a blur until I just woke up. I have a concussion." Kale was nodding emphatically in my peripheral vision.

"And I don't believe that for a second," Fulbright said. He knew. He didn't want to say it and look crazy, but there was something in his eyes— not unkind at all—that said *I already know exactly who you are.*

"Sucks for you," I said.

"Bridget Leanne!" Mom exclaimed.

"We found a car belonging to Michael Fullmer, who says you stole his keys. The phone belongs to a Victoria Lewis, who reported that a girl matching your description made a 911 call at her place of employment, then stole her phone. Coincidentally, the phone found on your person," Fulbright said. "So one more time, how is it you ended up at Giavino's?"

I looked at him squarely, staring into his eyes until he shrank back a little. "I just had a feeling."

"A feeling, huh?" he said, one corner of his mouth tugging up almost imperceptibly. "Ms. Young, do you mind stepping out for a moment?"

Mom gave him an incredulous stare. "You can't question her without me present."

"Of course, it's within your rights to stay, but she's not under arrest," Fulbright said.

"Mom, you can go."

"But–"

"Mom, please," I said. Mom just stared at me in disbelief, then shook her head as she walked out to speak to the doctor.

Fulbright turned to me once the door was closed again. "So, you get a lot of these feelings, Bridget?"

"Lately, yeah," I said. "Interesting how they turned out to be pretty good, huh? I'd say I told you so, but…never mind, no buts. I told you so."

He sat back a little, a faint smile on his lips as he shook his head. "What do you know about the guy?"

I shrugged and gave him the same description I'd already reported to the police. "It was weird. He said, 'I'm sorry, Caroline.'"

Fulbright narrowed his eyes and nodded. "Anything else?"

"Not that I can remember," I said. "What happened?"

"Maybe five minutes after you reported the shooting, we got another call reporting an emergency at Giavino's."

"Tara," Kale said. "Got her wrapped around my finger now."

"–had dispatched three cars to Giavino's," Fulbright said, oblivious to Kale's commentary. "We diverted all available officers over there. When we got there, we saw the boards pried off and realized someone had gone in. We came in and found you unconscious and your friend screaming."

"What about the guy?"

"He got away," Fulbright said bitterly. "We came in through the front and he ran right out the back. We got a license plate off his truck as he drove away. They're locking down the interstates now."

"And yet you're here to visit me," I joked. "I feel so special."

"You're making jokes? You realize I could charge you with half a dozen crimes right now," he said. My stomach dropped. Was he serious? I really didn't want to go from D-student to juvenile delinquent. He sighed. "It was incredibly stupid of you to go in alone."

"You didn't give me a choice," I snapped. My fear of being arrested turned quickly to anger. "I asked for your help over and over. Was I supposed to wait and let him kill Emily?"

"You realize how crazy you sounded?"

"And yet I was right," I said. "Maybe if you'd listened to me the *first* time you would have caught him."

Fulbright just stared at me, and for a second I was sure he was about to arrest me for any one of the perfectly justifiable reasons he had. Instead, he shook his head and said, "It's crazy, but you're right. And I'd love to know how you knew."

"I had a–"

"Feeling, I know," he said. "Come on. There's no way you knew all that unless you were an accomplice and—"

"Are you serious?" I screeched.

"I'm just saying. Well, kid..." He reached into his pocket for a business card. Creamy white, it read *Det. Tom Fulbright* in navy blue letters. "You call me if you get any more feelings."

"Yes sir," I said to him.

I watched him leave, then speak to Mom as he passed. Once he left, she walked back in, obviously doing her best to not look irritated. After this, I was pretty sure I deserved a get out of jail free card.

"What was that all about?" Mom asked.

"Just answering some questions," I said. "You already looked freaked out."

"Bridget…" she said helplessly. She sighed. "Well, did you do all those things he said?"

"Yes," I said without hesitation. She could get mad if she wanted.

"Why?"

I shrugged. "I can't explain it. But Emily's alive, and that's what matters."

"Bridget, that's not good enough," she said. "I mean, why did you go there? And what were you doing when I called you?"

But I couldn't answer her questions. I finally just pretended to have a headache, which wasn't much of a stretch, so she quit asking. Instead, she fussed over me, checking my face and my eyes and my arms and every little scratch she could find. The worst of it was a long gash in the side of my head, which was stitched up under a thick bandage. I had gotten off lucky.

Mom finally left me alone a few hours later and went home to make sure Colin was all right. When she was gone, I finally got to relax, and looked over to see Kale smiling.

"That was brave," he said.

"I think you meant stupid."

"They usually go together."

"Why are you here?"

"I told you'd I always watch your back, didn't I?" he said. "Now get some rest."

"Kale, what's going to happen next?"

"With the police? Not my area of expertise."

"No," I said. "You know what I mean."

"Well," he said. "I don't know on that one either. We're in new territory now, kiddo."

And that was far more frightening that anything I could imagine.

Emily had what our history teacher called a thousand-yard stare when I saw her early the next morning. Physically, she was okay except for a few bumps and bruises. She looked young and vulnerable without her usual mask of makeup. Sitting in the corner was Kari, who had the puffy, blotchy look of someone who had been crying for hours. She immediately began crying again when I came in, throwing her arms around me painfully tight.

"How did you know, my God, how did you know?" she wailed. All I could think was that she was hurting my arm and I really just wanted to talk to Emily.

I stammered something about a rumor and a weird feeling, and my mom had the foresight to rescue me from her grasp. The two of them went to get coffee, leaving me alone with Emily for the first time since stumbling on her–literally–at Giavino's.

"Bridget, how did you know?" she asked me as soon as our mothers left us alone for a minute. "I thought–"

"You wouldn't believe me if I told you," I said.

She just shook her head, staring down at her hands as she toyed with the paper tag of the scratchy hospital blanket. "He was going to kill me, wasn't he?"

"Yes," I said without hesitation.

She nodded slowly. "Last night. That's what he was coming in to do when you showed up."

"Yes," I said again. "You weren't the first. That's what happened to Natalie Fullmer."

Her eyes just got wider as she stared at me, then suddenly went blank. For a few seconds, I got the feeling of *no one's home, try again later.* Her wrists were scraped and raw in wide stripes from the duct-tape, her zebra-striped nails cracked and half broken. I knew what she had felt–experienced it right along with Nadia–but I had the luxury of waking up.

"I think I'm going to throw up," she finally said. I looked around frantically for a bin. But the place was practically spotless, and Emily was already heaving. I finally found a plastic bag from the sandwich shop downstairs and held it open in front of her. There was still a heel of bread and a ragged piece of tomato inside. She stared down at it, then looked at me. Her lips quirked up in a smile, then she burst out laughing. "Are you fucking kidding me?"

I couldn't respond, just started laughing along with her. Before I knew it, she had her arms around me, her head pressed painfully close to my stitches. But I didn't move, just hugged her and held onto her. I didn't have

273

to be psychic to know what she was thinking. Ten minutes and we'd have never hugged again.

"Bridget?"

"Yeah?"

"Happy birthday."

CHAPTER TWENTY SIX

"I CAN'T BELIEVE you're still making me do this thing," I complained.

The football game and Fall Court announcement had been delayed until Tuesday night. Considering several victims of the Runaway Killer, as the papers were now calling him, had gone to Fox Lake High School and to Marymount, our rival and opponent for the game, it seemed disrespectful to carry on with the game. Instead, they had held a candlelight vigil that Friday night for the victims. There had been a huge turnout, but it didn't come close to making up for all the destruction he had caused.

"Emily wants you to," Mom said. "Don't you?" Emily gave a thumbs up. She still looked pale, but Melinda had put on makeup for her and styled her hair so she looked more like herself.

There was a folded newspaper on Melinda's cart of clips and rollers. The huge headline across the top read: *Runaway Killer Discovered in Parkland - Police Find More Than 50 Victims.* They'd traced his license plates and discovered our killer was a computer technician named David Miles. He'd worked on the wireless network for Skybridge's offices, granting him access to an ever-growing list of victims with a history of running away from home. I looked away from the paper as Melinda gently nudged my chin back towards her.

"And so do you," I grumbled. I sighed and closed my eyes as Melinda, Mom's hairdresser, leaned in with an eyeshadow brush. I got another wave of tropical fruit in the face. Was it possible to die from perfume inhalation? My head hurt already, and adding a bunch of bobby pins and hairspray wasn't helping. Wouldn't most moms let you skip Fall Court if you got a concussion from confronting a serial killer?

"More purple," Emily directed. Still shaky and weak from her ordeal, she wasn't sleeping at all. She acted casual, but I knew that she was one wrong word from a meltdown. "And do a little of that gold in the corners."

Despite everything, I was still on the Fall Court. I just hoped that the whole student body didn't boo me for being a total weirdo. I had no idea what story was going around school, and at this point, I didn't care. The only person—besides Emily, of course—whose opinion concerned me was Michael, and I hadn't spoken to him since the whole thing blew up. God only knew what he was going through.

National media had been crawling all over town trying to get the scoop, but Emily and I had dodged most of it. At first, Kari had been ready to do an interview for every reporter who asked, but Mom talked some sense into her. Michael wasn't so lucky. His mother, who hadn't cared enough to keep her daughter's case open, was on every news channel weeping and demanding justice for her poor baby Natalie. Meanwhile, Michael was in the background of every shot looking miserable. I wanted to call him, but I knew I was the last person he wanted to hear from.

Sightings had been reported from Atlanta to Chicago, but none of them had been confirmed. An FBI agent had assured us he wouldn't come back for us. Based on his extremely careful behavior, they thought he'd never return to Parkland. But that wasn't nearly as reassuring as the young, eager agent had seemed to think. He could already be setting up shop in another city, looking for his new victim for the next full moon. But that wasn't my responsibility anymore.

Or was it?

"Quit frowning," Melinda scolded. "Look over my shoulder." I sighed and obeyed her commands. She was one bossy hairdresser. I tried to keep my eyes open wide as she applied mascara.

If he killed again, would it be my fault?

"Okay," Melinda said, pulling away from me with a bright smile. She turned the chair so I could see myself in the mirror. Despite my worries, I smiled. She was *good*.

The makeup was much heavier than I would normally wear, but it was perfect. She'd done my eyes with rich purple shades that made my light brown eyes look unnaturally bright. My hair was curled, with half of it caught up in a glamorous style and a big wavy section hiding the stitches on my temple. Melinda had stuck purple gemstone pins all through the style, so my head glittered when I moved.

Mom started crying again. I just rolled my eyes. She had been crying off and on for the last four days. Colin had made me a card, and she cried for two hours when he brought it to me in the hospital. My teachers sent my work home with a Get Well Soon card, and she cried. The neighbors brought over a lasagna, and she cried. It was like living with a leaky faucet.

"Cut her a break," Melinda said quietly in my ear. "You don't know what she's been through." I nodded and forced a smile for Mom's benefit.

"Well?" I said.

"You look like a hooker," Emily said with a devious grin. "I love it."

Mom shot Emily a glare. "You look beautiful."

I didn't feel beautiful by the time game time rolled around, however. I felt completely terrified as we walked into the stadium through a crush of people. There were police throughout the crowd, but the thing that made me feel safest was when Kale materialized at the top of the pressbox, waving down at me as I passed. We were extremely late, considering the game was already well into the second quarter. They could blame my total inability to walk in heels, resulting in me scraping my knee on the driveway and Mom crying for another twenty minutes.

"Oh my God, you look so pretty," Kristen Chang said as I hurried down the stadium steps and joined the line of girls waiting at the edge of the field.

"Thanks," I said. "So do you. You have movie star hair!"

Kristen beamed at me, shaking her dark hair and bouncing her curls. "Extensions. My sister put them in," she confided.

"Nice," I said, faking a cheerful grin.

"We love you, Kristen!" a group of kids shouted from the stands. We whirled to see John Chang at the center of the group holding a *Go Kristen!* sign. John waved at me, and I smiled faintly as I raised a hand in greeting.

As usual, I felt like the odd one out. The other girls looked like they were meant to be this way, all statuesque and sparkling like goddesses. I just felt like an impostor as I wobbled slightly in my too-high heels. There was no ignoring the stares I got as I waited on the rubbery track.

On either side of the stadium, the seats were packed with crowds wearing black armbands that bore the initials of all the identified victims. They were selling the bands at the gates and donating the proceeds for a scholarship fund. It was nice to see something halfway decent come out of all this.

Detective Fulbright was in plain clothes, sitting with my mom and Emily in the front row. He tipped his head in greeting. I responded with a little wave.

"Um, Bridget, so, what was it like?"

I turned to see Aisha Townes, senior class goddess, looking shy as she talked to me. Yes. *Aisha* looked shy talking to *me*. Were we in Backwards Land? She looked like she should have been going to the Oscars, with the orange chiffon dress that glowed against her dark skin. I would have looked like a carrot in it, but she looked incredible.

"Oh my God, Aisha, you can't just ask her that," Sierra Lewis said, smacking Aisha in the arm. She had gone with a dark blue dress, and while she wasn't as Vogue-worthy as Aisha, she looked beautiful.

I just stared at them. Was this real life?

Aisha ignored Sierra and said, "Is it true that you saved Emily King from that guy? That's what I heard."

I smiled and shrugged. "I don't know...I guess?"

Suddenly, they launched a barrage of questions at me. I did my best to answer, sticking to the story we'd come up with for the paper: after seeing so many calls and text messages from me, the Runaway Killer lured me in and grabbed me. But to his dismay, I got free and helped Emily fend him off until the police came. I didn't like having to say he'd tricked me, but I couldn't very well tell the truth. It was a flimsy story at best, but everyone was eating it up.

"That's really scary," Sierra said. "I would have been like, freaking out."

"I was," I said, which was the first entirely true statement I'd made in ten minutes. "I wish they could have caught him a long time ago, though."

"For sure," Aisha said. She perked up as Mrs. Brasco, the faculty sponsor for the Court approached. I saw Mrs. Brasco pointing to me, and Aisha nodded. "Obviously, Michael dropped off the Court, but they asked Tim Cross to do it so you wouldn't be alone. He's really cute, and–oh." She stopped mid-sentence, her eyebrows raised as she looked at something over my shoulder.

I turned to see Michael approaching. If he was even alive behind that stony face, I couldn't tell. He stopped about twenty feet away, then tipped his head slightly.

My stomach started doing gymnastics as I walked toward him. My legs were shaky on the high heels. I didn't know what to apologize for first. Kicking him in the gonads? Lying about his sister? The mere fact that Natalie was dead? Standing here in a pretty dress while his world fell to ruins?

I decided to go for the easiest. "My mom insisted. I know that it looks bad, believe me, but—"

"Shut up. I don't care about this crap," he said. I recoiled at his harsh words. The *shut up* echoed in my head, the venom soaking down into my bones. "Did you know about Natalie?"

I just stared at him, afraid if I said anything I'd start to cry. The lack of an answer was an answer in itself. I clenched my jaw instead and didn't break his gaze.

He just pursed his lips and shook his head. "How?"

"Michael, you wouldn't believe it if I told you."

"That's not good enough," he said.

"But it's all I have," I said. I felt my throat pinching tight, and the hot sting that meant tears were coming. I stared up at the waning full moon and willed the tears to go away.

A cold breeze sent a chill down my bare arms. I looked over to see Natalie flanking her brother. She looked clean and whole again, breathtakingly beautiful. I hadn't seen any ghosts except Kale since waking up in the hospital, which Kale said was thanks to the concussion and the mild painkillers I was taking. That only made me dread what I would see once everything was out of my system. But seeing Natalie like this was worth it. She looked weightless, even peaceful.

I didn't wave to her, but she smiled at me anyway. "Tell him Nanalee says she loves him," Natalie said. When I frowned at her in confusion, she repeated it. "It's okay. I want you to tell him."

"Um, this is going to sound crazy," I said. "But Nanalee says she loves you."

Michael's stoic facade crumbled. "How did you—"

"Tell him I'll never forget the way he fought off Peter Brennan in eleventh grade. And that no matter what, he's always going to be my little Mikey."

I repeated what Natalie said. Michael clamped his lips shut as he looked away from me, tears gleaming bright under the harsh stadium lights. I had to look up at the waning moon again to keep from crying.

"How do you know all of that?" he said, his voice catching in his throat. "There's no way."

"She loves you," I said without prompting from Natalie. "I can't explain it to you, but she's here. And she wants you to be happy."

He scrubbed his sleeve across his face. "She's here?"

I nodded slowly. The staging grounds for a halftime show weren't exactly the ideal place for a teary goodbye, but who was I to judge?

"Tell her…" he started. "God, I don't know."

"You can tell her. She can hear you, even if you can't hear her."

"Nat?" he said hesitantly. "I'm sorry I didn't protect you."

"It's okay, Mikey. There was nothing you could have done," she said. She gestured for me to tell him, and I complied. "I know you tried so hard."

"I don't know what to do now. You left me all alone," he said, crying openly now. People in the front row of seats were staring down at him.

Flipping my hair over my shoulder, I shot them my meanest glare. Didn't they have any decency?

"You'll be okay," she said. "I'll always love you, no matter what."

He stared at me as I repeated the words. "Please," he wept. "Don't go."

"I have to go now," Natalie said. There was a sharp crack as the drumline began a cadence. The band began marching onto the field. "Thank you, Bridget."

"But I didn't catch him," I protested.

"You scared him out of the dark. Now they know his name and his face," Natalie said. "That's enough for me. Remember when you told me you were just a kid?"

"Yeah?"

"You're a pretty badass kid. Sorry for all the scares," she said. After glancing up at the moon, she smiled beatifically. "Keep an eye on him, okay?"

Tears spilled over onto my cheeks. I didn't scrub them away, just grabbed Michael's hand. I wanted him to see her like this, but all I could do was watch her go and realize that for all I had done, she was gone just like Valerie.

"What's she saying? Bridget, what is she saying?" he begged, grabbing my arm.

But she was gone, fading out slowly until there was nothing left but a cool breeze and a whispered *goodbye*.

"She's gone, Michael," I said. His face wrinkled up in a grimace as he turned away.

"Bridget, you need to get in line," Mrs. Brasco shouted. Couldn't she see we were dealing with a first class, capital-I *Issue* here? I mean, *seriously*.

282

"Michael, I'm so sorry, for everything," I said. "I get it if you hate me, but I did it all to stop this guy before he hurt anyone else. I was afraid to tell you, and—"

"Bridget!" Mrs. Brasco called.

"Oh my God, can you just wait?" I snapped at her. Her eyes went wide.

"Come on," Michael said as he linked his arm through mine.

"What are you—"

"Natalie would have wanted me to do this," he said. There were still tears streaking down his face, but he looked defiant. "Screw the dress code."

"Michael, we've got a replacement," Mrs. Brasco said as she hurried over, looking thoroughly miffed. "I didn't think you would be—"

"His sister just *died*," I said, laying on the drama. "Could you just make an exception?"

Okay, that might have been wrong, but I knew there was no way she could say no. She sighed and gestured for us to go on. I watched her wave off Tim Cross, who did look hot in his suit. Tim shrugged and went back to the line of metal folding chairs that had been set up for the candidates along the sidelines.

The band was playing an arrangement of Aerosmith's "I Don't Wanna Miss a Thing." It was just cheesy enough for something like this. I had an earful of tuba as we waited at the back of the line. I was the last alphabetically, so it would be a few minutes before they called my name. I rocked nervously on my high heels, sinking slowly into the damp turf.

"So you see dead people, huh?" he asked.

"Something like that."

"Always?"

"Since Valerie died."

And forever, it seemed, as we had missed the opportunity to do the ritual. Kale hadn't said as much, but our window had closed. But there was no sense in worrying about that tonight, because done was done.

I grabbed a handful of my dress and pulled it clear of the grass as we moved forward in the processional. The crowd had just cheered for someone. The applause was followed by a brief pause as the band started the song over.

"So you got to know me—"

"So I could figure out what happened to Natalie," I said. "She came to me and told me what happened to her."

"And you knew all along?"

I nodded. "She begged me not to tell you until we absolutely had to."

He paused and looked over at me, then shook his head. "I don't know what to make of any of this."

"Me either," I said. "I've never told anyone about this."

"So you do this all by yourself?"

"Do what?"

"Find serial killers?" he asked. "Wow, did I really just say that?"

I let out a nervous laugh. "This was my first one," I said. "But mostly, yeah. There's a couple spirits that hang around me, but otherwise, it's just me."

"Sounds lonely."

I shrugged. "It is what it is."

"Our next candidate is the lovely Miss Aisha Townes. Miss Townes is accompanied by Will Frost. Her parents are Jonathan and Layla Townes. Miss Townes is—"

Michael extricated his arm from mine for a second and turned to face me. "Don't judge me, but I want to put all this on pause for a second. Before you kicked me in the balls—"

"I am *so* sorry. Really. That was really bad."

"Uh, yeah, you're a little crazy," he said, but he was smiling. "But before that, I was working up the nerve to ask you out."

"Really?" My heart thumped. My cheeks heated as I looked up at him.

"Really," he said. "I had just about accepted that Natalie was off partying somewhere, and I wasn't going to sit around waiting for her to come back so I could get back to my life. And then everything got so...I don't even know."

"Screwed up? Completely unfair?"

He smiled sadly. "Yeah. But pretend for just a second that none of that happened. What would you have said?"

"I would have said yes," I said without hesitating. He smiled sadly and brushed a light kiss on the back of my hand.

"—dive team in 2014. Miss Townes recently received an invitation to attend the University of Georgia on scholarship, where she plans to major in international business." There was a roar from the crowd as Aisha glided across the field like a goddess.

"Oh shit," I muttered.

"Our final candidate is Ms. Bridget Young, accompanied by Mr. Tim—" The announcer fumbled the microphone. "Mr. Michael Fullmer. Her mother is Barbara Young. Ms. Young is a junior." Well, that certainly sounded anticlimactic compared to Aisha's introduction.

But even if there had been something else to say, I wouldn't have heard it over the noise. It wasn't boos or laughs. They were actually cheering.

My heart thumped as I scanned the faceless crowd. My feet were rooted to the grass. Michael took over and nudged me forward to stand at the end of the line next to Aisha and Will. He leaned in to whisper in my ear, "You're amazing."

"Now, for the moment you've all been waiting for," the announcer said. The drumline started a noisy roll punctuated by a cymbal crash. "Our Fall Prince is Cole Charles." Cole crowed in triumph and stepped out of the line to accept the simple gold plastic crown they put on his head. "And our Fall King is Jeff Bailey!"

The crowd cheered as Jeff walked forward and shook Principal Smalley's hand, then accepted his crown. He waved to a couple in the front reserved seating and paused for his mom to snap a picture. Then he leaned over and let his parents hug him, which made me smile. He ran down the track, parallel to the student section, slapping high-fives to his friends hanging over the railing.

"And for the ladies," the announcer said, prompting another drum roll. *Kristen Chang and Aisha Townes*, I thought. "Our Fall Princess is Bridget Young."

"Called it," I muttered. It wasn't until Michael prodded me that I realized what the announcer had said. My eyes went wide. He smiled and nodded.

"It's you," he said.

"No way," I murmured.

The girls turned to wave me forward, and the crowd erupted in cheers. I walked forward in a daze to shake hands with Principal Smalley. For a moment I thought I saw Valerie smiling in the crowd, and my eyes blurred over with tears. When I looked again, there was no one there but Mom and Emily in the front row. I just gaped like an idiot as Mrs. Brasco tried to put the petite tiara on my head without hitting one of the jeweled hair pins. Finally I just took it from her and plopped it on crooked. Mom was practically dancing as she applauded wildly.

"And the 2014 Fall Queen is Aisha Townes," the announcer finished. Maybe it was just my addled brain, but the cheers didn't seem half as loud. There were dozens of flashes as people took pictures, and then the band was crowding behind us as we moved off the field to make way for the football team.

Okay, this had to be a prank. Someone had screwed with the computers. I told Emily as much when she slid down through the railing to stand with me. Had it been Kale? Maybe Valerie had given him pointers before...she left.

"No, just a little Facebook campaigning," Emily said. "It's amazing how people's opinions change when you show up and tell a serial killer he's fucked."

"You didn't," I said. "Tell me you didn't."

"I didn't do anything."

"Good," I said, letting out a sigh of relief.

"Hachi, on the other hand..." Emily said. "She made a picture of you fighting Chuck Norris and wallpapered the entire school with it. You kind of got the badass vote."

Only Emily.

I just laughed, which made my face hurt. Michael approached me again, and wordlessly wrapped me in a hug. "Do I have to unpause it?" he asked.

His arms were so tight around me I could barely breathe, but I didn't care. I took a deep breath, took in the laundry smell of his shirt and the sandpaper scratch of his cheek against mine. I wanted to remember this moment, maybe the only time I'd ever feel normal again. For just a second,

I was a normal girl, the Fall Court princess, wrapped in the arms of the guy I liked.

"I think you do," I said. "But I wish you didn't."

"God, me too."

"Michael, I'm sorry for everything. I wish I could—"

"Stop apologizing," he said. "Thank you for what you did. I'll never forget it."

Then the world came crashing back down as he brushed his lips against my cheek and walked away. As he left, I watched him look back over his shoulder to the spot where Natalie had said her goodbyes. His eyes creased in pain, then he walked away without looking back again.

I was still watching him walk away when Mrs. Brasco hurried over to me with a bouquet of flowers. It took me a second to realize they were for me, and I thanked her absently. A dozen long-stemmed red roses? I stuck my nose into them and inhaled their heavy perfume. I frowned and looked over at Mom, who still had a bouquet of purple flowers in her hands. Then who had sent these? I never got around to telling Dad about the whole Fall Court thing.

There was a little card in the flowers. I removed it and handed the flowers to Emily. I turned it over and read it silently.

Dear Bridget,

I regret that we couldn't get better acquainted. While I would certainly love to finish what we started that evening, I regret that I must move on and start anew.

You look lovely tonight.

An icy chill bloomed in my chest as I read the note. Blood roared in my ears. I whipped my head back and forth, scanning the crowd for his face. I walked back to Mrs. Brasco and grabbed her arm a little harder than I should have. She looked at me in shock. "Who gave you these?"

"Someone delivered them for you just now," she said, pointing to the retreating back of a uniformed courier. I kicked off my brand new heels and ran past her, then up the ramp behind the bandstand. Halfway up the stairs, I stopped to yank my skirt up around my thighs, ignoring the gaping stares as I sprinted like Cinderella at five till midnight.

"Bridget, it's not him," Kale said as he materialized and floated just ahead of me. But I didn't stop running until I caught up with the courier and grabbed a handful of his collar.

"Hey, asshole," I hissed. The courier turned, and I realized *he* was a pretty blonde woman with a tablet in her hand. "Wow, I am so sorry." The woman pulled away from my grasp and shot me a disgusted look as she walked away.

"Told you," Kale said.

"Not helping," I hissed.

"Company," he said, pointing over my shoulder.

I turned to find Mom and Emily at the top of the steps and Detective Fulbright running my way. "What?" I asked innocently. Emily had my shoes in her hand. She stared at me with wide eyes. I shook my head at her.

"Did something happen?" Fulbright asked. I handed over the card. After he scanned it, he yanked his radio off his belt and started running toward the courier.

"Oh, Bridget," Mom said, reaching for my hand like I was a little kid. But I gently shook her off.

"Don't worry, Mom. He won't be back."

He wouldn't dare.

CHAPTER TWENTY SEVEN

WEDNESDAY WAS THE START of Thanksgiving holidays, making it over a week since I had been to school. It was going to be a rude awakening when I had to go back Monday. Mom went back to work, so I stayed at home with Colin for most of the day watching Netflix on my laptop while he played video games.

But there was something I still had to do. I called Emily for a ride, on the condition that she didn't ask me any questions. I figured after rescuing her–kind of–she owed me one. Or a hundred.

Emily had her own condition; she had to check in with Kari every fifteen minutes. I had a feeling that would get old for both of them very fast. We still hadn't talked much about what happened to her. I had a feeling it was going to be a while, if ever, before Emily wanted to talk about it. She was like my mom in that way; she'd pretend she was fine until it became more or less true. Instead, we talked about our sudden surge in popularity. The highlight was Allie Williams adding me as a friend on Facebook, complete with a sappy apology for our falling out in ninth grade.

"You should lead her on and then crush her dreams," Emily said. "No mercy."

"I should," I said. But we both knew I wouldn't. I'd clicked *Confirm* and instantly groaned at the gushing post she wrote on my wall.

But maybe that was a good thing. Maybe it was time for big changes. Maybe it was time to for me to quit hiding out and get back into the world. I was never going to be normal again. Fact. My past hurt, and nothing would ever give back what I'd lost. I would always be sad about what happened to Valerie. But I'd realized there was room for more than just my sadness. And it was up to me what the future would hold.

The afternoon was on the verge of rainy, with that feeling of expectation that comes with a thunderstorm. The world seemed to be waiting for something. After a few minutes of driving down the interstate, we arrived at Valerie's memorial. Emily pulled off into the shoulder and turned on her hazard lights. As I got out of the car, Emily pretended to be engrossed in her phone, but I knew she was watching me out of the corner of her eye.

The memorial just a wooden cross with *V.R.Y.* engraved on the cross piece. I knelt by the cross, feeling the dampness of the grass soaking into the ratty hand-me-down jeans. Maybe I didn't have to let go of *everything* right away. I held the Fall Court tiara in my hand, then slowly set it out next to the cross. The sparkling rhinestones were completely out of place in the overgrown grass, but that seemed right somehow.

"Leaving it here?" Kale asked. "Kinda maudlin, don't you think?"

I didn't look up at him. "She liked this stuff more than I did."

"You should keep it," he said. "You deserve it."

"Not really," I said. Even so, I toyed with one of the sparkling points as Kale shrugged and sat down next to me. "She's really gone. I mean, really gone this time."

"She is," Kale said. "But you're going to be okay."

"We missed it," I said, still staring at the glittering crown in the damp weeds. "I thought I was finally going to be normal."

"About that," he said. "I need to tell you something."

My heart leapt. "You mean we didn't miss it? Kale, don't hold out on me."

"Uh," he said. "How do I put this…there was never a ritual."

I gaped at him. He looked embarrassed and apologetic at once. Surely this was a Kale joke. A very bad one. "There—what—huh?"

"I'm sorry, kiddo," he said. "But you were going to drive yourself crazy and never let Val go otherwise. You would have held onto her for the rest of your life if you could have."

"No," I said. "I mean…"

He raised his eyebrows. "Bridget."

"Okay, I would have."

"I know, and it would have destroyed everything that was left of her," he said. "So I forced your hand."

"Kale, I don't understand," I murmured. I felt sick as I looked him over. That had been my single hope for months, the only thing that kept me going. He knew that, and he'd manipulated me? For what, a sick joke? "I trusted you."

"I told you I'd always watch out for you," he said. "I never said I'd always be truthful. You convinced yourself her death was your fault and—"

"It was."

"It *wasn't*. I don't know how to convince you of that," he insisted. "And even if it had been, you've punished yourself long enough."

"If it wasn't my fault, then why did I see her when I only see wrongful deaths?" *Saw*, I realized. Now I'd laid down a welcome mat for all of them.

"When you flatlined, she waited for you. And when they brought you back, she wanted to stay here to watch over you, so she made a deal," he explained. "Basically, she gave up her seat on the flight. Once that happened, she had to wait for you to set her free."

"But—"

"And you weren't setting her free," he said. "After a year you were holding on tighter than ever. So I told you about this secretive ritual that *had* to be on your birthday."

"But I sent her off on the day she died," I whispered.

"That day made as much sense as anything else," he said. "I knew I had to force your hand somehow. You wouldn't have believed me if it was just any day. And I knew you'd choose to let her go over making her suffer longer."

"So you played me."

"Yep."

Even with the ghostly door wide open, I still couldn't slap him. But I tried my best, my hand passing harmlessly through his insubstantial chest like cold water. Too bad. "You're an asshole, you know that? I can't believe you lied to me."

"For your own good," he said. "You'll get over it."

"You're definitely not an angel," I said.

"Duh. I've been telling you that all along," he replied. With an irritatingly calm smile, he lifted the crown and put it back on my head. "You earned this."

"I didn't," I said, reaching up to take it away. His cold hand passed through mine. My arm tingled, cool and electric, as he leaned in close. His blue-lagoon eyes were inches from mine.

"You did," he said. "I tested you again and again. I tried to talk you out of helping Emily, tried to stop you from opening the door, even tried to get you to forget it all. And you kept doing it anyway."

"So I failed?"

"You passed," he said. "Now I can do this. Think of it as a promotion."

He put out his hand, and Valerie's necklace slithered out from under my shirt. The dragonfly floated up and settled into his gleaming palm. The silver loop floated up and over my head, landing in his hand. He closed his eyes. There was a flash of light and a sound like a plucked harp string. As it echoed, he let the dragonfly dangle from his fingers. Its green gemstone eyes glowed faintly as it swung like a pendulum. "If you ever need me, just call for me and I'll be there. Anytime, anywhere. And if you ever need a break, just put this on. It'll dampen your ability."

"So I could just—"

He knew me too well. "Not *forever*. You won't like what happens then. But you've earned it. Whatever you think you've done, you've earned your peace. The only person who can let you rest now is you."

"Kale…"

"Go ahead and ask."

"What are you?"

"I'm your Guardian, and I'll always look out for you," he said again. "Now come on, you're going to get rained on."

He had no sooner disappeared when the rain began to fall, and I just stared into the empty space where he had been. There was a new cluster of white flowers around Valerie's memorial. A sweet, flowery scent rose above the damp-earth scent of rain. It didn't smell like any flowers I had ever smelled, but like Valerie's perfume. Was it bad that it didn't even surprise me?

How did you go on after something like this? How did you get up and move on when everything you knew changed?

"Same as any other day," I said to myself, brushing grass off my butt as I stood. The first droplets of rain kissed my neck as I took one last look at the wooden cross. Thunder rolled in the distance, and I dashed to the car and plopped into the seat. I had just gotten the door shut when the bottom seemed to drop out of the sky. The windshield went gray with the downpour.

"What the heck were you doing?" Emily demanded. "You were totally just talking to thin air for like ten minutes."

Instead of getting embarrassed, I just smiled and said, "Emily, I have a story to tell you."

WHAT NOW?

If you enjoyed getting to know Bridget and the ghost gang, then please let your friends, family, and the whole world know by sharing on social media and leaving reviews on Amazon or Goodreads! Just a few minutes can help another reader find a story they may love. Thank you!

If you'd like to find out more about upcoming books, short stories, and giveaways, make sure you find me online! You can sign up for my mailing list by scanning this QR code. I promise to never abuse or give away your email.

Here are some of the places you can find me online!

Facebook: https://www.facebook.com/AuthorJessicaHawke/
Twitter: @JJHawke
Website: https://www.jessicahawke.com

Keep reading for a sneak peek at the upcoming sequel to Phantom Touch!

Phantom Traces

Chapter One

Thursday—8:19 p.m.

IT WAS ONLY FITTING that my little brother was an angel, an actual messenger of God, complete with sparkling white robe and a halo wrapped in dollar-store tinsel. If my mother had forced me to participate in the Christmas play instead of just using me as free labor for the costumes, I probably would have been a lowly shepherd. Or maybe an ass.

Definitely an ass.

I turned to tell my friend Sal as much. He laughed.

"Bridget, watch your language," Lena May said. "You can't say...a-s-s in church."

"What? They definitely said it in the Bible," I told her. And that made it even funnier.

Besides, it wasn't like anyone was going to hear us. We had the dusty balcony of the Parkland United Methodist Church all to ourselves. The red-upholstered cushions smelled like old books and mothballs, and the wooden benches creaked in protest every time I shifted my weight. Sal and Lena May didn't have that problem, what with them being ghosts and all. They also didn't seem to notice the puffs of dust that came up when I dropped my backpack on the pew. There were certain benefits to death, I supposed.

Piled in my lap was a heap of scratchy brown fabric that would eventually be a Wise Man's robe. Mom didn't trust me with her sewing machine, which was sort of a running theme these days. But she'd deemed me suitable for the task of sewing on the snaps and hooks that she didn't have the patience for.

"Bridget. Young ladies should not use such coarse language," Lena May said primly. She folded her hands neatly over her crossed legs. Her gray hair was neatly curled, and her best pearls lay on translucent skin. If I looked hard enough, I could see through her like a sheer curtain to the dark stained glass on the opposite wall.

There were certain advantages to speaking to the dearly departed. For one, Lena May had overheard Mom telling her friend Donna that what she really wanted for Christmas was a day at the spa. Consider it done. I'd used some of my birthday money from my dad to get her a gift certificate for a massage. If I was honest, I had to admit I had ulterior motives. I mean, I really did want to make her happy, but getting Mom a good Christmas gift would go a long way toward ending her reign of terror over my free time.

Then again, there were drawbacks to counting the dead among your bosom companions. For one, most teenage girls didn't have the ghost of a ninety-eight-year-old woman constantly criticizing their behavior, all of which was appalling by her standards. Since I'd first encountered Lena May, I'd given up on arguing about how things were nowadays, because she stopped all of my arguments dead with, "Well, just because that's how it's done doesn't mean it's being done right."

I mean, how could you argue with that?

Lena May leaned over, passing one translucent hand through my pile of fabric. She made a *tsk* sound. "You need to double that thread up before you sew on the hook. Like I showed you."

I fumbled the brown thread through the eye of needle and looped it. "Like this?"

"That's good," she said. "A young lady should know how to sew on a button at the very least. It's a good skill for when you get married and have to take care of a husband."

I wasn't touching that one with a ten foot pole.

Sal snorted a laugh. "That's right, Bridget. I can see it now. Housewife of the century."

"Shut up," I told him. Like I said, speaking to the dead had its drawbacks, most notably a never-ending commentary on my life.

Lena May ignored him as she watched me sew the first stitches onto the little wire hook. She gave me a little nod of approval, then turned her attention back to the choir rehearsal. "This is just lovely," Lena May told me. "They sound like angels. You know that's my—"

"Great-granddaughter, I know," I said gently. She only reminded me every time I saw her that the little redhead with the adorable pigtails on the third row of angels was her great-granddaughter. I didn't get irritated, though. The dead had their own particular kind of senility, so it wasn't Lena May's fault she was fixated on her family. She was so attached that she had literally held on beyond death.

The church was in a state of festive chaos, with big plastic storage tubs all over the pews and sparkling tinsel stretched out on the floor down the aisles. Ladders stood near each of the two half-decorated Christmas trees. Volunteers fastened lengths of spiky pine garland to the wooden bannisters around the altar. Mom knelt by teenage Mary's feet to pin up the hem of her robe while Mary took a selfie on a pink rhinestoned phone.

"Hark! I bring you glad tides and—" my brother shouted. I winced. He was good at a lot of things, but acting wasn't on that list.

"Glad tidings," the choir director corrected. Colin sighed. "Glad tidings, Colin."

I suppressed a smirk.

"Oh, look," Lena May said. She pointed to the Christmas tree on the right side of the church. "I sewed the dress for that angel. Goodness, it had to be forty years ago now." Her translucent features gleamed as she watched a woman in a Santa sweatshirt carefully unwrap the tissue paper from the figurine and place it on top of the tree. "They've put it up every year since."

I'd met Lena May a few weeks earlier, when Mom had insisted that I help her with the costumes for the annual Christmas play. Before then, I hadn't known a whip-stitch from a bullwhip, but she'd told me that she'd find something for me to do. Church wasn't really my thing, though I came along when Mom heavily insisted. She usually only put down her foot on Christmas and Easter, but that had changed recently.

I wasn't stupid. After what happened to my best friend, Emily, Mom didn't want to let me out of her sight. When Natalie Fullmer, a girl from my school, had disappeared a few months ago, most people thought she'd just run away yet again. They were wrong. Natalie's angry spirit had come to me to make sure I knew it, too. When Emily had disappeared soon after that, I'd known Natalie's killer had taken her. No one else took me seriously, so I'd taken matters into my own hands. Emily was alive, but Mom still had questions I couldn't—or *wouldn't*—answer for her.

Her response had been predictable, but completely unhelpful. Now she was keeping me on a tight leash. No, it didn't even qualify as a leash. Imagine when you didn't have a leash handy, so you just grabbed the dog's collar so he just kept choking himself every time he tried to take off. That was more like it.

So here I was, sewing snaps onto Wise Man robes with pointers from a woman who'd been dead for four years. As far as I could tell, she'd attended the church since it was built and simply hadn't gotten the memo that she was supposed to go elsewhere when she died. I hadn't figured out what she wanted. Most spirits lingered for a reason, and they usually weren't shy about letting you know what it was. But Lena May was different. I'd tried to ask her several times, and she'd just waved me off and changed the subject. It had even occurred to me that she might have just passed along without realizing it. When I'd broached the topic, she rolled her eyes and said, "Bridget, I'm dead, not senile. I know." I'd left it alone since then, which was probably just as well, considering I could barely get away from Mom long enough to handle any kind of ghost business for the last few weeks.

"What do you think of some nice earrings?" Sal asked suddenly. "She loves jewelry."

I frowned and turned to him. "Earrings?"

"For Veronica," he said. "Christmas? I was thinking diamonds."

"Right," I said. "I mean, I guess that would be nice."

He sighed, his golden features creasing in dismay. "You think it's stupid."

"Not stupid," I said. "I swear."

"Then what? You've shot down everything I've suggested."

I winced at his turn of phrase. Sal was a former police officer who'd been killed in the line of duty almost ten months ago. The neat bullet hole and accompanying trickle of blood still stained the faded blue of his uniform shirt. I'd met him on a trip to the police station while snooping around for information on Natalie's disappearance.

"It's just a little weird," I told him. "I mean, try to see it from her point of view. If you walked out your front door and found a random gift on your doorstep that happened to be the exact thing your dead boyfriend would have picked out, wouldn't that freak you out?"

Not to mention there was no way I could afford diamonds. Sal seemed to forget that he couldn't show up at the jewelry store with his credit card, so he was relying on my meager bank account. And they weren't about to give me his police discount.

"But I just wanted to—"

"Bridget? Who are you talking to?"

My stomach leaped into my throat, and I turned to see my mother standing at the top of the balcony stairs. "Uh, I was just talking to Emily on speakerphone," I said. *Please tell me you didn't hear the dead boyfriend part.*

"Why are you up here all by yourself?" Her hands were planted on her hips, which meant she was in full-on Disapproving Mom mode. A pincushion was strapped to her wrist, and she had a measuring tape strung around her neck. She still wore her bright pink scrubs from work.

Because it's exhausting to pretend I don't hear all these ghosts chattering around me. "I don't know."

Mom sighed. I caught the eye roll, though I'm sure she'd deny it if I called her on it. Apparently it was only rude when I did it. "Rehearsal is over soon. Did you finish?"

I held up the robe. "Close."

"Well, try to finish it up quickly. We're going home soon."

Get Phantom Traces in February 2016!

ACKNOWLEDGEMENTS

The daily business of writing may be solitary, but bringing a novel kicking and screaming into the world takes a community. While the cover only bears my name, the pages are marked by the fingerprints of dozens of creative people.

Thank you to my local writers' group, who are a bunch of coffee-fueled superheroes in disguise; special thanks to the usual suspects: Jimmy, Jeremy, Maria, Betsy, Val, and Beckie.

Thank you to Candie, who whipped this book into shape and gave it its name.

Thank you to Hildie and Kathy, who shared their tremendous professional experience.

Thank you to Kate who did early edits on this book.

Thank you to my best friend, Carmen, who has been, by turns, cheerleader, editor, therapist, and drill sergeant throughout this process. I could not ask for a better friend.

Thank you to Mom and Dad, who have said I would be a writer since the ripe old age of seven. As usual, you were right.

Finally, thank you, generous readers, for giving this book a chance. I hope you enjoyed reading it as much as I enjoyed writing it.

About the Author

Jessica Hawke's first stories were painstakingly scrawled on notebook paper in second grade. While the story of the Three Little Fish will never again see the light of day, her parents felt this was a sign, and as usual, they turned out to be right. She has written a number of paranormal and fantasy novels, including Phantom Touch and its upcoming sequels. She also writes for adults under a pen name.

51627861R00183

Made in the USA
Charleston, SC
29 January 2016